"*Splitsville* is a winner—well-written, with fully ac v. characters and a narrative thrust that keeps you turning the pages. William Bernhardt has not only written another expert legal thriller, but once again he has his fingers on the realities of the modern legal system, and his portrayal of a female lawyer struggling to succeed is honest and compelling."

— GARY BRAVER, BESTSELLING AUTHOR OF
TUNNEL VISION AND, WITH TESS GERRITSEN,
CHOOSE ME

"Bernhardt is the undisputed master of the courtroom drama."

— *LIBRARY JOURNAL*

"William Bernhardt is a born stylist, and his writing through the years has aged like a fine wine...."

— STEVE BERRY, BESTSELLING AUTHOR OF
THE KAISER'S WEB

"Once started, it is hard to let [*The Last Chance Lawyer*] go, since the characters are inviting, engaging, and complicated....You will enjoy it."

— *CHICAGO DAILY LAW BULLETIN*

"[*Court of Killers*] is a wonderful second book in the Daniel Pike series...[A] top-notch, suspenseful crime thriller with excellent character development..."

— TIMOTHY HOOVER, FICTION AND NONFICTION AUTHOR

"I could not put *Trial by Blood* down. The plot is riveting —with a surprise after the ending, when I thought it was all over....This book is special."

— NIKKI HANNA, AUTHOR OF *CAPTURE LIFE*

"*Twisted Justice* has the most mind-blowing twists of any thriller I've ever read. And everything works."

— RICK LUDWIG, AUTHOR OF *PELE'S FIRE*

"*Judge and Jury* is a fast-paced, well-crafted story that challenges each major character to adapt to escalating attacks that threaten the very existence of their unique law firm."

— RJ JOHNSON, AUTHOR OF *THE TWELVE STONES*

"*Final Verdict* is a must read with a brilliant main character and surprises and twists that keep you turning pages. One of the best novels I've read in a while."

— ALICIA DEAN, AWARD-WINNING AUTHOR OF *THE NORTHLAND CRIME CHRONICLES*

SPLITSVILLE

SPLITSVILLE

WILLIAM BERNHARDT

BABYLON BOOKS

For my mother, my sisters, and my daughters

When justice is done, it brings joy to the righteous but terror to evildoers.

— PROVERS 21:15

JOY TO THE RIGHTEOUS

CHAPTER ONE

His wife was the easiest to kill. His daughter was the hardest.

But they were all dead now, and soon to be buried in a mass grave beneath the terrace. One wife. Five children. Two dogs.

Darien stirred the wet concrete in the wheelbarrow. Once he finished disposing of the bodies, he would disappear and no one would ever know what happened to any of them. No one but him.

The remains would be discovered, eventually. Busybodies or relatives would break into the home. Someone might notice that part of the terrace had been resurfaced. In time, someone would start digging. But by then he would have a new life elsewhere, with a new name, a new path, and a very different calling.

His true destiny began today.

It didn't have to happen like this. She forced his hand. How much was a man expected to tolerate, and for how long? The perpetual whining. The endless self-martyrdom. The woman was so busy playing her own violin that she couldn't hear a word he said. He had tried to help her. Again and again. But she wouldn't listen. She always found some trivial fault to complain about. Ignoring all he did for her. For all of them. Resenting him when she should appreciate him. When she should worship him.

You are so charming, she said. Everyone thinks you're wonderful. They have no idea what you really are.

That part was true. They had no idea…and neither did she.

She rallied the children around her, using them as a shield and a ransom. She isolated him, distanced them from him. She would win the battle by winning the children, or so she thought. The offspring became the spoils of war.

She left him no choice.

She didn't think he was serious, not at first. But when he raised the shovel over her head, she realized how wrong she had been. He would never forget the expression on her face, the change wrought in an eyeblink when she understood how disastrously she had miscalculated.

Blood gushed from her head. With the second blow, hot red tendrils splashed across the terrace. Each swing of the shovel spread more splatters across the ceiling, his face, his hands. Black blood puddled on the barbeque.

Then he heard Abigail scream.

His second daughter, usually at her mother's side, was the first to see what he had done. Her voice was an earsplitting siren that shattered his already jangled nerves. Until then, he had options. He could've stopped it before the cancer spread to the children. But after that, he had no choice. The story would not end until all the plot threads were sewn together.

One by one the children ran out of the house, panicked, terrified. And one by one he knocked them down like targets in a shooting gallery. Grit. Bone. Blood. At one point, his hands were so slick he could barely grip the shovel. But he managed to finish the job.

Strangely, he did not feel sick afterward. He did not collapse.

He did not vomit. If anything, he felt elated, surging with the natural high produced by a job well done.

Now he could work in peace, stirring the concrete and digging the grave. Afterward, he would have to clean the whole area. That would be time-consuming—but he had all the time in the world. No one could see him. No visitors were expected. He worked all night long, sometimes humming to himself. He knew the first day of his new life had arrived.

A sailing expedition might be the thing to clear his head and, after that, a change of venue. Happily, he had always maintaned an escape hatch. Money. Transportation. Safe house. All waiting.

Once the grave was finished, he returned to the pile of bodies. His wife should enter first, with her sad minions piled on top. They could be attached to her apron strings for eternity and—

Wait. Something was different. Something had changed.

It took him several moments to realize what it was.

Someone was gone.

He rummaged through the pile, shoving bodies aside and taking a blood-stained inventory.

Two were missing. His oldest daughter and his youngest. The toddler. Annalise. The baby of the family.

Perhaps his job was incomplete. Perhaps he did not see as clearly as he thought.

They could not have been gone long. And where could they go on foot this early in the morning, injured and alone? He had purposefully bought a home far from prying neighbors. He had time.

He grabbed his shovel and started running.

ELIZABETH DIDN'T KNOW WHAT HAD HAPPENED OR WHAT SHE could do about it. All she knew was that somehow, miraculously, she was still alive. Like an abrupt burst of light in the darkness, her consciousness had returned. She felt stunned, disoriented. What was happening? Why had Father tried to kill her? She felt sticky with blood, and the stench surrounding her was intense, sickening. This, she realized, must be what death smells like.

Her mother and siblings lay beside her, bloody and still— except one. She saw her baby sister, Annalise, stir slightly. She was alive. But that would end if her father noticed. Somehow, Elizabeth had to get both of them out of here without him noticing.

She tried to be quiet. Father was busy shoveling and didn't seem aware of what was happening behind him. He was lost in his own private world. She would take advantage of that.

The night was pitch black, but maybe that was to her advantage. It would be hard for him to see them in this inky darkness. Or so she hoped.

Their estate was almost a mile from any other homes, but if she could get Annalise into the nearest neighborhood, surely someone would come to their rescue.

She had to move quickly. Once Annalise was fully conscious, she would probably not remain silent or still. She couldn't possibly comprehend what was happening. Annalise would be even more horrified than she was.

Quietly, she rose to her feet, scooped up her sister, and raced out of the backyard.

She ran track one year in grade school. She didn't last long because she wasn't very good, but she learned a few things. Don't look back. Point your toes straight ahead. She couldn't swing her arms because she was carrying a little girl who seemed to weigh nothing at first and seemed to weigh two tons now. Every part of her ached, but she ignored that and focused on the road, the destination. She was Annalise's only hope of survival.

She could imagine what she must look like. She could feel blood on her mouth, caked and smeared. The flat side of the shovel had struck her on the head, knocking her to the ground. How had she survived? She didn't know, but it didn't matter. She had a job to do.

She was not going down without a fight. She would fight for herself and her beautiful baby sister.

Tears flowed from her eyes with such intensity that they soaked the collar of her shirt. Waves of grief rippled through her. She saw what Father did to the others. Mother didn't have a face anymore. He almost decapitated her. And then he started on Abigail, and Chris, and Donny. Maybe he was tired by the time he got to her. Maybe he was too far removed from reality to notice that he hadn't killed her. Maybe—

She felt Annalise stir in her arms. "Lizzie?"

She *was* alive. And awake. "You're okay, sis. You're fine."

"Why…are you carrying me?"

It was hard to talk and run at the same time. "Can't explain now."

"Daddy…hit me."

"I know, honey. He hit all of us."

"Why?"

"I don't know. Something…isn't right." She tried to keep her voice flat, to mask the terror she felt.

"Where we going?"

"Someplace safe."

"Is Mommy dead?"

She bit her lip. "I don't know. We just need to get somewhere safe."

She saw the gates at the entrance to Forest Glen, just as the sun's corona crept over the horizon.

She could do this. She knew she could. She—

"Elizabeth! Come back this very minute!"

Her body seized up. It was him. He was not far behind them and closing fast.

She knew her track coach wouldn't approve, but she glanced over her shoulder.

He was swinging the shovel.

A shudder raced through her, like razor blades slicing her into pieces.

She knew she couldn't outrace him, not with Annalise in her arms. But if she could just make it to the first house, the one on the corner…

The house had a small open window on one side. Was someone awake? Did they like the night air? She couldn't be sure.

"Sister," she whispered, "I love you with all my heart."

"Lizzie…what…?"

Elizabeth ran up to the house and shoved Annalise through the window. She heard a crash as her sister landed somewhere on the other side.

"You idiot!" Father grabbed her hair and jerked her down to the ground. Pain electrified her head. He twisted her around at an excruciating angle, dropped the shovel, then grabbed her by the throat with his left hand, choking her.

His fingernails scraped her face. She tried to kick him, to grab his wrist, but she wasn't strong or quick enough. She felt his right thumb pressing against her eye.

Another wave of pain pulsed through her. It felt as if her eyeball was pressed against the back of her brain.

"Do you know what you've done?"

Yes, she thought, I know. I've made it impossible for you to eliminate my entire family. You can't get through that window and you can't ring the bell without starting a conversation you don't want to have.

Even as she felt her consciousness fading, she smiled. No

matter what happens next, there will always be a dangling thread. You will always be looking over your shoulder. You will always wonder if this is the day your past comes back to destroy you.

Her last thought was a happy one. My baby sister. Annalise. She'll be the one who delivers the justice you deserve.

CHAPTER TWO

Thirty-Two Years Later

KENZI STARED AT THE WOMAN ON THE WITNESS STAND, TRYING not to blink, gape, or otherwise betray her thoughts. Possibly everyone in the courtroom needed an extra moment to digest what the witness had just said.

"I'm sorry. I'm not sure we all got that. Could you please repeat your last statement?"

The witness appeared peeved. "I don't know how I could say it any more plainly. I got inseminated in the bathroom at Dick's Drive-In."

Kenzi glanced around the courtroom. Judge Cornwall, an African-American man in his mid-fifties, was nodding, obviously trying to maintain his judicial poker face. Even opposing counsel seemed to be struggling to remain composed.

Why could she never have a normal case?

Because in divorce court, nothing was ever normal...

"And...what brought you to this point?"

"My husband, Frank, that's what. He's useless in every

possible way. I wanted children and I wasn't going to get any with him."

Kenzi took a deep, cleansing breath. Family court was always an adventure here in Seattle—Rain City, Coffee Capital of the World—and she doubted it was different anywhere else. Like most of the lawyers in her firm, she specialized in matrimonial law—divorce, separations, child custody, and everything that went with them. She'd made a reputation for herself, achieved considerable financial success, and developed a significant social media following, all from the ashes of failed romance. Severing couples who didn't want to be together anymore suited her just fine. She didn't see why anyone should be stuck in a relationship that didn't work.

"You and your husband tried to get pregnant, I assume?"

"I tried. Frank wasn't trying. I'm not sure he's capable of trying."

"What…exactly did you try?"

"A sexy dress. Lots of beer. Ravel's *Bolero*. African tribal chants. Oysters. Fertility idols. A Wonder Woman costume. Nothing tripped his trigger."

"You must've had some…intimate relations prior to marriage."

"He faked interest for a while, but it's pretty darn clear at this point that he's…I'm not even sure what. A member of the LGBTQ community? Which is fine with me. Everyone should feel free to be who they truly are. But I don't understand why in this day and age someone would fake being straight when they're not."

"Has your husband acknowledged this?'

"No. Frank is so deep in the closet you'd need a telescope to find him."

"Did you try any…scientific approaches to fertility?"

"Yes. But he has a low sperm count and apparently what

little he has isn't worth much." She paused. "Which brought me to the bathroom at Dick's Drive-In."

The witness, Marcia Greenburg, was Kenzi's client, so she knew all this was coming. That didn't make it any less startling when she heard it spoken out loud. Marcia was from a prominent Seattle family and had an excellent job—but she chose her work better than she did her lovers. She couldn't believe Marcia's underperforming husband wanted exclusive custody of the child he played no role in creating. Divorce was hard enough without people playing stupid games for spite.

"I wanted a child of my own," Marcia continued. "Is that so much to ask? I considered asking a friend to…you know…be the sperm donor, but I was afraid that would lead to parenting battles down the line. Frozen sperm was an option but I didn't want a donor I knew little about. I considered everything, but at the end of the day…"

"Dick's Drive-In?"

"Exactly. Seemed like the best option."

Kenzi flipped back her black hair. She favored a side shave cut, buzzed on the left, flipped from the part to shoulder-length on the right. She couldn't wear blue jeans in the courtroom, but she wore black skinny pants that were basically jeans that didn't look like jeans, plus a chic gray blouse. Instead of the silly vests some of her female colleagues wore—which always made her think of Will Smith in *The Wild Wild West*—she rocked a black leather jacket, same shade as her hair. And sensible shoes. Always. She didn't need heels to be imposing.

"Can you describe the steps that led you to Dick's Drive-In?"

"Sure. I work for Amazon. There's this guy in the office I like. I mean, not in a sexual way, but he's cool with that. He offered to be my donor. He's smart, cute, gentle—perfect. So I agreed. He signed a contract relinquishing parental rights. He's married, but he and his wife decided not to have children, and I think he regrets that. He wanted this to be discreet, so we met at the Dick's Drive-In near the Space Needle. He brought me his sample in a coffee cup. I think he did the deed in the men's room. I knew that stuff was fragile and I was ovulating, so I took my turkey baster into the bathroom and got the job done right then and there." She paused. "And then I got a burger. I was famished. Went to my car and laid on my back with my feet in the air for about an hour. That's supposed to help."

"And the end result?"

"Nine months later, I got a beautiful baby boy."

"Did your husband approve of this?"

"I didn't even tell him about it till I was starting to show."

"What was his reaction?"

"Unhappy. He called it adultery, though I reminded him that I had never had sex with the father. He got all pissy and refused to have anything to do with the child."

"Then why would he seek custody?"

"To punish me. He doesn't like David and David doesn't like him. He'd be happier if he were rid of both of us. But some people can't appreciate a blessing when they get it. Like children on a playground, they act out of anger and malice—"

"Objection." Horace Jennings, counsel for the hubby, rose. "This has stopped being factual testimony and become personal invective."

"I disagree," Kenzi said. "The witness is entitled to explain what this marriage was really like."

Judge Cornwall looked as if he might speak but instead let out a ferocious sneeze. He glanced at his clerk.

Kenzi had been around long enough to interpret those signs. Judge Cornwall was new to the bench and still on training wheels. That fake sneeze was a cry for help.

His clerk gave him an ever-so-subtle nod.

"That objection will be sustained," the judge said. "Are we about done here?"

"Yes, your honor." No point in arguing with the clerk's

ruling. She knew who was running this courtroom. She made a mental note. Next time she came to court, bring that clerk some chocolates. It might be inappropriate to bring gifts to a judge, but buttering up a clerk was always fair game.

Kenzi helped her client out of the stand and escorted her back to the table.

Jennings called the husband, Frank Greenburg, to the stand. According to him, Marcia was a drunk, a tyrant, and a sexual reprobate. He chose not to have sex with her, or to have children with her, because he disapproved of her lifestyle choices.

Kenzi didn't care about any of that. She knew that in the modern divorce world, mudslinging and namecalling rarely garnered much attention from the court. Judges expected that nonsense and ignored it. Divorce cases were primarily about dividing assets, and since the split was fifty-fifty with few exceptions, these smear attacks were irrelevant.

Unless there were children involved.

When Kenzi had a chance to cross-examine, she wasted no time. "Mr. Greenburg, isn't it true that you met your wife through an online dating service?"

"Yeah. So?"

"Isn't it true that you posted a photograph that wasn't even you?"

"That's common."

"It's called catfishing. Using a fake identity to attract unsuspecting victims."

"That's absurd." Greenburg was slender, pale, nervous. Of course, most witnesses were a little nervous. Testifying was an unsettling experience. "A guy has to protect himself. You don't know who might be out there."

"That's for sure. You sent romantic texts to my client, didn't you? Even before you met her face-to-face."

"I liked her."

"Before you met her?"

"Yes. I could tell she was smart. Intelligent. Well-read. When we finally met in person, it was at a bookstore. She works at Amazon. She's a Kingdom fan. I thought she was perfect."

"And you almost immediately asked her for money."

"I did have a short-term financial problem..."

"You asked her for money three times in the first three months. You borrowed over twenty thousand dollars."

"I was building a business. For our future. By the time she made the last contribution, my business was launched and we were engaged."

"Did you marry out of love? Or because you needed her cash?"

"I find that question offensive. Everything she gave to me, she gave voluntarily." Sadly, Kenzi knew that was probably true. Online dating sites had become a treasure trove for scam artists. Sometimes they claimed there was a crisis or emergency situation. Sometimes they claimed they were in the military overseas —an excuse for why they couldn't meet in person. Kenzi had seen these cases arise again and again. According to the FTC, there were about 21,000 cases of these so-called romance scams each year, costing Americans over thirty-three million dollars annually.

"How much return did Marcia see on her investment?"

Greenburg's head lowered. "My business was...not the success I had hoped."

"Because it was a fraud from the get-go?"

"No. It just...didn't work out."

"I don't think you ever tried. I think it was a front. I think you banked the money somewhere secret. Or paid off preexisting debts."

"That's a flat-out lie."

"It doesn't matter." Though it gave her one more reason to intensely dislike the man. "You continued to take money from Marcia after you were married. And now you want out. Fine.

What offends me is this ridiculous effort to take custody of the child you played no part in bringing into the world. Are you after child support payments? Is that your game?"

"Marcia is dangerously unstable." His expression became grave. "David is not safe with her."

Of course, he would have to say that. Normally, Seattle courts—probably all courts—favored the mother in custody cases, and since he wasn't even a biological parent, he didn't have much chance of shutting her out. Unless he could prove it was not in the child's best interests to be left with his mother.

"She's got a nasty temper," he continued. "Loud. Violent. You haven't seen her when she's mad. There were times when I was in fear for my life. And for David's."

"Bull."

Jennings rose. "Objection, your honor. I don't believe that's a question."

Judge Cornwall nodded. Apparently he could handle this one on his own. "Less commentary, Ms. Rivera. More questioning."

Kenzi continued. "If Marcia was so violent, why didn't you call the police?"

"I was trying to hold the family together. I kept hoping Marcia would calm down and we could have a happy family life. But she never did."

"Marcia says you've never given David the time of day. This custody grab is just another scam."

"That's not true."

"So you genuinely care about David?"

"Absolutely."

"And you've been a big part of his eight years of life?"

"Definitely."

"What's his middle name?"

The pause was prolonged, and that suited Kenzi just fine.

"His…what now?"

"His middle name. What is it?"

Frank craned his neck. "Oh…jeez. Tip of my tongue..."

Jennings rose, obviously trying to bail his client out. "Your honor—what is this, *Jeopardy*? Trivia questions don't prove anything."

The judge squinted. "I'll allow it. The witness will respond."

"Middle name." Frank shifted his weight from one side to the other. "My memory isn't as good as it used to be. I can't remember."

"Does David like to play Pokemon Go?"

"Uh…yeah. He loves it."

"That's odd. Does he have a cellphone?"

"Well…no."

"Then how can he play Pokemon Go? It's a phone app."

"Uhh…maybe I'm thinking of something else…"

She was on a roll. Did she dare push it further?

Of course she did. "When's David's birthday?"

Frank shook his head. "It's…in the summer. We had a party a few months ago."

"Which you failed to attend."

"We spent time together after the party. We're very close."

"So close you can't remember his middle name or his birthday. Can you identify any of David's friends?"

"Does he have friends?"

"Who does he have lunch with at school?"

"I assume it varies…"

"Can you name any of his teachers?"

"They change so often…"

"Have you ever attended a parent-teacher conference?"

"I've been busy."

"Scamming people on social media?"

Jennings rose. "Your honor, that's uncalled for."

Kenzi addressed the judge. "What's uncalled for, your honor, is this pitiful, grasping attempt to take custody of a child he barely knows. Imagine what life would be like for David if this man got custody."

The judge pursed his lips. "There would be no more birthday parties, that's for certain."

"Your honor, I move to dismiss the petition for custody on grounds—"

The judge raised his hand. "You don't even have to say it, counsel. We'll divide the marital estate fairly. I think some deductions for the business loans the wife gave her husband might be in order. And there is no chance I'm turning this child over to someone who doesn't know his full name."

Jennings protested. "Your honor, we have other witnesses who—"

"I can't stop you from calling witnesses, counsel, but I warn you, I don't like people who waste my time."

"That's not fair. You don't know what the other witnesses might say." Jennings seemed distraught and desperate. "The truth is, the court is playing favorites."

"No, sir. The truth is, your opponent did her homework and came to court prepared. Your opponent saw the truth of the matter and revealed it, which is what officers of the court are supposed to do." He turned his head. "Anything more, Ms. Rivera?"

"Not at all, your honor. If we're done here, we're going to grab David and go celebrate." She winked. "At the nearest Dick's Drive-In."

CHAPTER THREE

AFTER THE CELEBRATION, KENZI HEADED DOWNTOWN, PARKED her Lexus, and walked toward her office building. She needed to post a livestream video to social media. She had promised her followers an update. As she walked, she extended her right arm and talked.

"Score another slam dunk for yours truly, KenziKlan," she said, grinning at the screen. She knew that the secret of a successful livestream was looking good and being relentlessly entertaining, so she made an effort to do both. "The do-nothing daddy took a drubbing. The judge was dazzled by my cross-ex prowess. Or who knows—maybe it was my stylish do and stunning wardrobe."

She tilted the phone lower so the camera could drink in her outfit. "Can you believe that alleged father? Let's make a rule right here and now. Call it Kenzi's Rule Number One. Any parents who don't know their kids' birthdays get tossed out of court on their butts. Hashtag KenziKlan. Hashtag RiveraLaw."

Since she'd started livestreaming daily and posting constantly, she'd seen her business almost triple. Everyone was on social media these days, and eventually, most of them needed a divorce lawyer. Some of her colleagues at the firm, Rivera & Perez, complimented her on this innovative and strategic use of cyberspace. What they didn't realize was that most of the credit should go to her very special social media manager...

"Enough about the case," she continued. "What do you think of the jacket? I cannot tell you how challenging it is to assemble an outfit that's stylin' but still courtroom-appropriate. Does the blouse work? Would solid black be better? And what do you think about the shoes?" She lowered the phone and raised her foot. "These are sneakers—in the true sense of the word. Sneaky sneakers. They look like dress shoes, but they're not. Rubber soles for the girl on the go. You may disagree with Kamala Harris' politics, but you gotta admit that when it comes to shoes, she's the bomb. Hashtag SensibleShoes."

She noticed that other downtown pedestrians were veering around her, trying to stay out of her way. She was glad they were paying attention. It was hard to stare at a screen and also watch where you were going.

The meter at the bottom of her screen told her how many people were viewing, and it was a significant increase from the previous day. She could also see that #KenziKlan was trending, rising rapidly up the list. Her media strategy was working.

"I'll be back tomorrow, KenziKlan, but remember—don't just wear clothes. Rock them. And wear sensible shoes."

She ended the stream and entered the lobby of the office building. The security guard knew her on sight and waved her past the turnstiles. A few minutes later she was on the four-teenth floor.

The offices of Rivera & Perez were as plush as they came. Her grandfather, then her father, wanted it that way. This was the top Seattle firm run by Latinx lawyers. It had to shine. And it did, even beyond the lobby. Gourmet snacks in the kitchen. On-site day care. Private planes at the top attorneys' disposal. They'd turned matrimonial law into an empire.

Around town, people called the firm "Splitsville," which some of the partners hated, but she loved. When people start referring to you by a one-word nickname—you've made the big time.

Personally, she thought they spent too much on the plush carpet and the Scully & Scully furniture, but she couldn't deny that it was a source of pride to know that she—that her family— was part of a top-drawer, obviously successful enterprise.

Though she would've drawn the line at the floor-to-ceiling glass office walls. Those might look cool on television, but who on earth wanted to be visible when you were trying to get work done?

"Morning, Sharon."

Her assistant glanced up from her desk. Sharon had worked with Kenzi for almost five years and in that time they had become both collaborators and friends. Sharon was African-American, a little heavier than she wanted to be, a little snarkier than she should be—and didn't care what anybody thought about it. She was great at her job, and that meant she could get away with more than most. "Hear you scored another success at the courthouse."

"True." Kenzi fanned herself with her hand. "But what else is new?"

Sharon touched her fingers to her lips, then puckered. "Chef's kiss. My pal in the clerk's office says your cross of the husband was devastating."

"I like to think I put on a good show."

"You know you do. You seduce the judges like a pro."

Was that a compliment? A pro *what*? "I prefer the word 'charm' rather than 'seduce.'"

"Was the KenziKlan pleased?"

"My numbers keep rising. I think I'm the most popular streaming lawyer."

"Certainly the most flamboyant."

"I got lots of positive comments from the Klan on my new outfit."

"Because they know they could never afford it. In my neighborhood, dressing like that would make you a target."

"But on the internet, it makes you a superstar." She grabbed a tower of pink message slips. "Any of this require my immediate attention?"

"No. But there are some potential clients of interest."

"Interesting because they have money?"

Sharon shrugged. "You got some techie type who doesn't want his wife getting any of the stock in his startup."

"Pass. I don't do men."

Sharon arched an eyebrow.

"I mean, I don't represent men. They can go to any lawyer in town and find an open door. Women, who too often don't control the purse strings, need someone who understands their special challenges. As you've heard me say many times before."

"Especially after your divorce. But this guy—"

"Plus it's tech. I'd have to do a lot of research to understand the business. I hate research."

"How well I know it. Since I'm the one who usually ends up stuck in the library."

"Put me in the courtroom, I'll charm—*charm*, not seduce—the pants off the judge. Put me in the library and I can feel my skin tone blotching." She rifled through the pink slips. "Tell me which message is the tech guy. So I can tear it up."

"I didn't bother writing it down."

"How well you know me."

"I know your professional passion. Or obsession."

"The word you're searching for is 'focus.' All good businesspeople have focus." She winked. "And impeccable taste." She started toward her office.

"Don't forget. Partner meeting in fifteen."

"How could I forget? I'm expecting big things."

"I still can't believe your father is stepping down."

"He's been managing partner for almost twenty years. Time to pass the torch."

"You're a shoo-in."

Kenzi surrounded her face with jazz hands. "Top billing attorney for three years running."

"That's why you make some of your colleagues nervous."

"Like my underachieving brother?"

"Among others. No one likes being shown up over and over again. And the thought of being led by a woman...well. Some are predicting disaster."

"Like the world run by men has been flawless. Testosterone-fueled decision-making has—"

Sharon stopped her with a wagging finger. "Girl, watch your tongue. If you're going to be managing partner, you need to be more circumspect."

"I'll take that under consideration."

"You so won't."

"But thanks for the advice, just the same."

———

TEN MINUTES LATER, KENZI WAS IN THE MAIN CONFERENCE room. She didn't arrive early because she had nothing better to do. She wanted to make sure she got the catbird chair to the right of her father, so she would be in the limelight when he anointed her. The passing of the torch could be executed without even standing. He could just slide right and she could slide left into the big chair at the far end of the table.

Two of her friends, also female divorce attorneys, sat beside her.

"Fingers crossed, sweetie," Christie said.

"You've got this in the bag," Marianne echoed.

"It's not over till it's over, ladies." A little modesty usually went down well. Didn't want people to think she'd gotten the big head.

"Who else could it be? You're obviously the most qualified. No one else comes close."

Another partner streamed through the door and gave her a big thumbs up. Even her younger brother, Gabriel, offered a clenched fist of solidarity. He was a nice guy but a fairly dreadful attorney. He'd yet to build a significant client list. More than once she'd had to bail him out, both in the office and in court. A nice guy, but nice wasn't always the dominant quality of successful attorneys.

Five minutes later, all the partners other than her father had arrived. The only one who did not appear enthused, Emma Ortiz, was also the only partner who was not a divorce lawyer. Kenzi's father had never wanted his firm involved with criminal law, which he thought tawdry and perpetuated the stereotype of the Latinx community as illegals and "bad hombres." But over time, so many of the firm's divorce cases touched on criminal matters that he recognized the need for someone familiar with that niche. Emma handled those cases but rarely left her office. Her frosty attitude and hermetic existence had given her a "weirdo" reputation.

At last, Kenzi's father strolled into the conference room, nodding, waving, taking the backslaps and high fives that came his way. She knew why he had chosen this conference room. It was the biggest but also the one he had personally decorated with artifacts and artwork from Mexico—what he liked to call the homeland, though his father had emigrated when he was two. Some people complained that it made the room look like a Day of the Dead parade, but she liked it. She was bored by the mundane conformity of most law firms. They did not all have to look alike. Just as every lawyer did not have to look alike.

Her father settled in his big chair and started the meeting.

"Thank you for coming, my colleagues. This is an important

day for me, and I hope it will be important for you as well. Together, we have made my father's firm into one of the largest and most successful in Seattle. We're in the Top Two every time someone issues a list. Personally, I think we're Number One." He let a sly smile creep across his face. "But there are some who would disagree."

Kenzi knew who he was thinking about—Crozier & Crozier, their biggest competition. Crozier had fewer lawyers but appeared to net more income, so the title of Most Successful Seattle Divorce Firm depended upon the measuring stick being used. All she knew for certain was that Crozier was gunning for them. The head of that firm, Lou Crozier, was a detestable conspiracy nut who frequently appeared on the other side of her cases. Uber-liberal Sharon wouldn't even take his messages.

"I've enjoyed my time in this chair," her father continued. "I never considered myself a boss. I saw myself as a shepherd. It was my task to continue the work my father started, to build and grow the firm that has employed us so long and so well. But the time has come for me to step aside. This is a partnership, not a dictatorship."

Many laughed, but Kenzi thought the remark was not entirely frivolous. Her father tended to rule with an autocratic hand, and she doubted that would end today. Sure, he might let someone else be managing partner, but he would remain on the Executive Board and act as a sort of Manager Emeritus, telling the new boss what to do.

Well, he could try. But she had a mind of her own and she wasn't going to lose it when she sat in the big chair.

"Enough of my rambling," her father said. "I don't want to become one of those old men who ramble on forever with stories that have no point. I have in fact chosen my successor, who I assume will be ratified at the next meeting of the Board of Directors. So without further ado, let me tell you what you've come to hear. The next managing partner for Rivera & Perez…"

Kenzi drew in her breath and pushed herself up.

"...will be my trusted and beloved son, Gabriel Rivera."

A silence filled the room. Kenzi froze. She slunk back into the chair, her face burning.

A moment later, the room burst into applause. Gabriel strode past her to the front of the room and shook hands with his father.

Kenzi slid halfway under the table and wondered whether, if she tried hard enough, she could hold her breath until she was dead.

CHAPTER FOUR

KENZI WATCHED THROUGH SLITTED EYES AS HER BROTHER TOOK the command chair.

"This is an honor, sir. A true honor."

His father gave him a square-jawed smile and a slap on the shoulder. "You deserved it, son."

Deserved it? Kenzi clenched her teeth. Gabriel hadn't made half the money for this firm that she had. A quick scan of the room told her that more people were watching her than the jackals onstage, looking for signs of her mortification. She would have to behave herself, hard as that might be.

"I won't let you down, sir."

"I know you won't, Gabe. Why don't you say a few words to the troops?"

Gabriel offered an 'aw-shucks' shrug but didn't have to be pushed hard. He launched into a State of the Firm address so polished she knew he must've practiced it for days. Which meant he knew what was going to happen. Even when he gave her that fist of solidarity.

"I don't see this as a new beginning," Gabriel said. His voice tended to be high, but he was deliberately lowering it, probably to sound more authoritative. "The smartest thing I could possibly do as your managing partner is continue the sound and profitable policies initiated by my father, the strategies that have made this firm the success it is today."

She wanted to gag. Is this why he got the job? Because he was a bigger suck-up? There was no other rational explanation for it.

"We know our competition is gunning for us. We must remain light on our feet and strong in our determination. I want everyone to redouble their recruiting efforts. Spend more time at the country club. Take your CEOs out to dinner. Work those showbiz and Big Tech connections. I want Rivera & Perez to be the first—in fact, the only—name that pops into people's minds when a top-dollar divorce surfaces. I want the world to think that if they don't have Rivera & Perez, they're putting their future in jeopardy. I want people to come to us, if for no other reason, because they're afraid that if they don't, their spouse will!"

Everyone laughed—everyone but Kenzi. A strained smile was the best she could muster. And that took some doing. She put her teeth on display, but her eyes weren't smiling. They were spitting daggers.

AFTER WORK, KENZI INVITED SHARON TO SHERMAN'S FERRY, an upscale bar near their office. She probably shouldn't call it a bar. They served food, or so she believed. She'd never tested the theory. She only allowed herself 600 calories in the evening, and she was likely to exceed that with vodka gimlets.

Sharon was the first to raise the delicate subject. "I must say, girlfriend, you're handling this like a pro."

"I'm really not," Kenzi replied. "Years of family court have made me unflappable."

"If I were in your shoes, I'd be crying salty tears all over myself."

Later. After she'd drunk herself into a stupor. "It's just a title. Doesn't even come with a salary hike."

"But you deserved it."

"Life isn't fair. Which is probably a good thing, because if life always worked out fairly, no one would need lawyers." She signaled the waiter for a refill.

The Ferry had the feel of an old-school British gentleman's club, with wood-paneled walls and mahogany tables. It was on the top floor of a skyscraper, and the panorama windows offered a gorgeous view of the Seattle skyline, particularly breathtaking as the sun set. She could see Pike Place Market, the Space Needle, even a trace of the Museum of Pop Culture. Inside, it was all Spode china and sterling silver tableware. Those little bowls that let you pinch your own salt. She loved those. She didn't use salt—it caused water retention. But she still loved the little bowls.

She thought coming to her favorite watering hole might elevate her spirits. So far, it wasn't working.

"Oh look, honey. It's your archenemy."

"I didn't know I had an archenemy. Outside of my family." Kenzi glanced over her shoulder. Lou Crozier. The five-hundred-pound gorilla at Crozier & Crozier. "What's he doing here?"

"Guess QAnon gave him the night off."

"He saw us. Should I wave?"

"I'll wave."

Kenzi grabbed Sharon's hand and slammed it down on the table. "What are you doing?"

"Waving."

"You were flipping him off."

"That's better than he deserves. I can't stand people who are wrapped up in all that 4chan crap. Probably a white supremacist."

"You don't know that."

"He retweeted a post that called the insurrectionists at the US Capitol 'American patriots.'"

"Nonetheless, I have to work with him. Frequently."

"I don't. And I never will."

"I have noticed that you put extra energy into your work when he's on the other side." Sharon had trained as a legal assistant, but with Kenzi, she had a much more all-encompassing position that amounted to doing whatever Kenzi needed done and then some. She was a legal assistant, file clerk, researcher, appointments manager, personal shopper, and occasionally, caterer, which was no small task given Kenzi's exacting dietary restrictions.

"That man is the spawn of Satan."

"There are many contenders for the title of Spawn of Satan," Kenzi replied. "Crozier's in the Top Ten, certainly. And now, my father. My brother. But they're not Number One."

"And who would—oh wait, I don't need to ask."

"No. You don't need to say it, either."

"Your ex."

"You just said it."

"Because we both know it's true. Heard anything about him lately?"

"I try not to."

"Still teaching at SPU?"

"Apparently sexual predation, child abandonment, violence, and alcoholism don't disqualify you from teaching math."

"If they knew the truth, they'd fire him in a New York minute."

Kenzi's ex had been her professor during her second year in college. Then she took a Work Study job with him. And then one fateful night, after far too many vodka gimlets...

Pregnant. And being a good Catholic girl, she married him. Stupidest mistake of her life. Her father was opposed to it, no big surprise.

She winced. Probably her most painful memory. How could she have been so blind?

That was when the rift between her and her father became the Royal Gorge. He still hadn't forgiven her for that mistake, years later, after she'd divorced the loser, retaken her maiden name, and become the most profitable member of his firm. He spoke to her politely—but something was missing. Something important. He kept her at a distance and it broke her heart. She'd been a major Daddy's girl growing up. Used to leave the family pew and sit with her father in the choir loft so they could take communion together. She'd been Daddy's favorite and she knew it. But now...

Sharon interrupted her reverie. "You know Gabriel won't last."

She brought her brain back to the present. "How do you mean?"

"That lightweight? He's a white feather in a hurricane. First time something bad happens, or one of the partners has a serious problem, he'll crumble."

"Maybe not. Maybe this will be the test that tempers the sword. Brings out his steel."

They both looked at one another, and a moment later, burst into laughter.

"Okay, maybe not. But my father must've had some reason for giving him the job."

"It's the Peter Principle, honey. Promote them to their highest level of incompetence."

"Is that a real thing?"

"For men? Yes."

Kenzi shook her head. "No. There's something more going on here. But I don't know what it is."

"How are you going to react if your little brother starts telling you what to do?"

"He wouldn't dare. He's afraid of me."

"I grok that."

"How my father could do this to me? *I'm trending!*"

"Does he even know what that means?"

"He knows I bring in more money than anyone else. Twice as much as my brother."

"Maybe that's why he did it. Promoting Gabriel might inspire him to step up his game. Your father knows he can count on you to make money for him."

Her head jerked up. "How does he know that?"

"It's not like you're going to leave the family firm."

Kenzi's eyes narrowed. "Maybe that's exactly what I should do."

"Wait a minute, honey. Don't you do anything rash."

"Why should I slave away for someone who doesn't appreciate me?"

"He does pay you pretty darn well."

"Not enough."

"Cry me a river. You live in the nicest apartment building in the city. You have a personal trainer."

"That's not a big—"

"You drive a Lexus. I drive a Prius."

"I get your point. But I still think I'm underappreciated."

"Then talk to the man. Daddies and daughters are supposed to chat every now and again."

"I will. I'll march into his office tomorrow morning and demand answers."

"And if you don't get the answers you want?"

"Then I'll go out on my own. Start my own firm."

"You don't want to do that."

"I could. I have enough clients and contacts."

"Sure, you could. But you don't want the administrative

hassles. You want to start dealing with payroll? Insurance? Workers Comp?"

"You can do all that."

"I already do more than I can keep up with. I'm working nights and weekends."

"Then you're used to overtime."

"This is a mistake, Kenzi."

"It's my mistake to make. I'll give Daddie Dearest an ultimatum. And if he doesn't give me what I want..." She started to sing, a bit too loudly. "'It's a new dawn, it's a new day, it's a new liiiiiife...'"

"Uh huh." Sharon clamped a hand over Kenzi's mouth. "I think you better take an Uber home."

CHAPTER FIVE

KENZI FUMBLED WITH HER KEYS FOR AT LEAST A MINUTE BEFORE she got the apartment door unlocked. She steeled herself, took several quick breaths, and closed her eyes.

Hold it together, she thought. Look normal, like nothing is bothering you and you haven't been inhaling vodka. No need to bring your work home. Or to look like you were drinking your sorrows away.

She took one step into the dark apartment…

Music was playing. On vinyl, if she wasn't mistaken. Was that actually Frank Sinatra?

Tentative step forward. More short quick breaths. One foot in front of the other—

"Wow. How much have you had to drink?"

She froze. Seemed she had company.

"You can stop acting like you're sneaking out of jail. Did you think I wouldn't hear you come in?"

"I was…trying not to disturb you."

"Seriously? You were making more noise than a rooster."

"Well, I…" Oh, what's the use? She flopped down on the living room sofa. "I've had a rough day."

Sharon had exaggerated when she called this the nicest apartment building in the city…but it was nice. The security was excellent. She liked having a doorman who knew her on sight—though nights like this, she wished she could creep in more anonymously. The apartment walls were freshly painted in a modern style that had a name she couldn't recall at the moment. The carpet was clean and the view outside the bay windows revealed nighttime Seattle at its best.

Hailie rolled up beside her. "I heard about the meeting."

"Heard? Like people are talking about the Rivera & Perez partners' meeting?"

"Online, yes. The SeaTacLaw Reddit stream was talking about it five minutes after it happened."

She pressed her hand against her forehead. "What did they say?"

"You got passed over for Uncle Gabriel. True?"

"True."

"You practically accepted the award before Granddad said Gabriel's name and looked crushed when it didn't go to you."

She slouched lower down the sofa. "True."

"And you're planning to bail on Rivera & Perez and start your own firm."

"What?" She sat up straight. "How could anyone possibly know that?"

"Maybe they just assume?"

"That I would ditch my daddy's firm?"

"Have you said this to anyone?"

"Only Sharon."

"She wouldn't post. Did you say it loud enough that anyone else could hear?"

She thought for a moment.

Crozier. Damn it all, Crozier. Was he eavesdropping? That was exactly the kind of slimy stunt she would expect from him.

"It's possible I spoke too loudly."

"After the second vodka gimlet? Mom, I've talked to you about that."

"Am I about to be scolded by my fourteen-year-old daughter?"

"Yes." Hailee flipped the lights on and spun her wheelchair around so she could look her mother in the eyes. Her dark hair cascaded down both sides of her head. Big glasses framed her eyes. A half-finished Balzac novel rested in her lap. "Mom, I'm your social media manager, remember?"

"True…"

"I can't turn you into a high-profile influencer if you're running around acting like a petulant sore loser. Or stumbling around drunk."

"No one saw me…"

"Grow up, Mom. Everyone in this city has a cellphone with a camera. You can't do anything anywhere anytime without being spotted. And possibly recorded."

She didn't bother arguing. It was embarrassing to admit that your teen daughter was smarter than you. But when it came to the internet—and many other matters—she was.

Hailee suffered from a chronic illness called ME—myalgic encephalomyelitis. Some people called it Chronic Fatigue Syndrome, but she hated that label. It made the victims sound like sluggards when they should be described as fighters battling a serious physical condition.

It surfaced when Hailee was five. They thought she had the flu at first, but it never went away. She felt giddy when she rose out of bed, glands swelled up in her neck, and she ached from head to toe. Then it got worse. Ever since, Hailee's activities had been severely limited. She could walk, but for no more than a few minutes at a time. The wheelchair was much easier. She'd learned to pace herself, not to overdo. After several disasters, she'd started homeschooling which, given Kenzi's schedule, basically meant Hailee was educating herself. Fortunately, this little autodidact was a better teacher than her mother could ever be. Hailee was already better read than ninety-nine percent of the people on earth and knowledgeable about a wide range of subjects. She talked about going to medical school. Kenzi didn't know whether that was realistic, but she admired the girl's spirit.

Kenzi had hoped her father might be more useful when the ME diagnosis was delivered, but he played an "I told you so" card and used it as more evidence that she should have listened to him and not married the man who bailed about ten seconds after Hailee was diagnosed.

"I have more pressing concerns at the moment than social media."

Hailee laughed. "Now you sound like an old person."

Old? She wasn't old.

"I've told you this before, Mom. You let your social media presence slip and no one will be listening when you need them. Posts equal likes. Likes equal influence. Influence equals referrals. Referrals equal clients. Clients equal money."

"We're doing okay."

"But you could do so much more. There's a real opportunity out there. Influencers are raking in big bucks for endorsements, building prominent profiles in fashion, sports, makeup, cooking. Even roller skating. Or poetry! But so far, there's no dominant attorney influencer. LegalEagle on YouTube has a decent following, but you could be bigger. You could be the one who changes everything. You could convert your influence into awesome power. You could dominate the world."

"Are you a social media manager or a supervillain?"

"You need a change of pace," Hailee said. "Let's do something fun this weekend."

"Movie? Restaurant?"

"Nah. Let's be adventurous. How about we take the ferry to Bainbridge Island? Go to that coffee place you love."

"It would be simpler to go to Pike Place Market and visit the world's first-ever Starbucks."

"Who wants simple? Let's motor. Inhale the sea air. Feel the mountain chill."

Kenzi couldn't help but smile. Here was her daughter, who suffered from a debilitating illness, talking about adventuring. "That sounds wonderful. But I should probably work."

"Mom, you're the highest-billing attorney in the firm and you still got passed over. Screw them. If Uncle Gabe wants to be the managing partner, fine. Let him work weekends."

"You know what? You're right. I don't have any major cases pending. I should be able to escape." It would be a wonderful change of pace, and it would allow Hailee to get a little exercise, which was important. ME was a black hole for its victims. First it took your physical health, then your mental health, then your friendships, then any sense of independence that might remain. Many people with ME got worse, not better. Some ended up completely bedridden, unable to take a step. Some developed intolerance to light or sound. Some ended up being fed through a tube because they weren't able to swallow.

That was why she'd agreed to make Hailee her social media manager. In addition to school, Hailee had a job. Something to keep her active and give her a chance to shine, to be treated with respect. She would not let Hailee's sparkling spirit disappear into the folds of this illness.

"Saturday or Sunday?"

"Not sure. I'll check my calendar."

"Playlist?"

Kenzi shrugged. "You know more about music than I do. Just don't make it...ancient."

"What's that supposed to mean?"

"Hailee, you're currently playing Frank Sinatra. On vinyl."

"He's the Chairman of the Board! And vinyl is cool."

"Well, use those cool computer skills of yours and see if you can find some music by someone who's still alive."

"What, like Coldplay?"

"Stop. I'm not that old." She pushed herself off the sofa. "Let me shower. Then we'll talk more. You should scan the internet. See if anyone is talking about me. See if the bad news has hit the KenziKlan."

"It will. Do you want me to take offensive action?"

"What did you have in mind?"

"Nothing much. Maybe a massive Twitterstorm targeting Uncle Gabe."

"I can't believe you would even suggest that."

"He stole your job."

"My father gave him my job."

"If you're serious about starting your own firm, I could visit GoDaddy and start reserving domain names."

"Riveralaw.com is already taken."

"How about, KenziRiveraLaw.com? That isn't taken. I checked."

Kenzi paused. It did have a certain ring to it.

But not yet. "I'm going to talk to your grandfather before I make any decisions."

"And if he doesn't give you an answer you like?" Hailee wheeled her chair around, blocking her mother's path. "What then?"

Kenzi stepped around her and headed toward the bathroom. "RiveraDivorce.com? Nah. Sounds too negative. How about: KenziKlanSuperstarLawyer.com? That has a nice ring to it."

CHAPTER SIX

KENZI STRODE INTO THE OFFICE WITH HER HEAD HELD HIGH. SHE knew people would be watching her, so she made a point of acting as if nothing had happened. No embarrassment. No shame. She was still the most profitable attorney in this firm. She and her father were about to have a reckoning.

After she left the elevator but before she entered the office, she pulled her phone out of her shoulder bag and started a livestream. "Greetings, KenziKlan. Quick shoutout before I get to work, because as regulars know, photos and videos are not permitted inside. Some of you may have heard yesterday's big news. Suffice to say, I'm not taking it lying down. I'm going to march into the big boss' office, tell him what I think, and take no prisoners. It's the KenziKlan way."

She winked into the camera phone. "Details later. Keep the faith. And let me know what you think of these new earrings. Aren't they the bomb?"

She shut off the phone and headed inside. A few minutes later she was at Sharon's desk. She spotted the spindle with a tall stack of phone messages. And ignored it. "I'm going to do it, Sharon. Just like you said. I'm going to march into my father's office and tell him exactly what I think about all this. I'm going to demand an explanation. I'm going to—"

"You have a client waiting."

"—read him the—wait, what?"

"Client. Or potential client. In your office."

"Someone I know?"

"Newbie."

"I prefer to vet my clients before I meet them face-to-face. I won't take just anyone. And I've got to see my father about—"

"I know all that. But I thought you might want to make an exception this time."

Kenzi frowned. She was losing her train of thought, not to mention the anger that had fueled her entire morning. "Why would I want to do that?"

"For starters, you shouldn't be turning away work if you're planning to start your own firm."

"Does she look like she comes from money?"

"Frankly, no. She's a scientist."

"Oh, then she must be loaded."

"Her husband filed on her yesterday. Wants everything, though he hasn't worked in years."

"Deadbeat. But—"

"And he wants exclusive custody of their daughter."

Again? She'd just thwarted one husband's revenge-custody scheme. "He's out of work and he wants custody?"

Sharon nodded silently.

Kenzi glanced at her watch. She knew at some point her father would start taking meetings and it would be harder to get his attention. But she might have a few moments…

"Fine. I'll talk to her."

Sharon handed over a file. "Here's everything I've dug up so far."

Kenzi thumbed through the paperwork. "I can't believe this loser wants sole custody."

"Me neither," Sharon said, picking up the phone. "I mean, not every cult is evil."

Kenzi froze. *"Cult?"*

THE WOMAN SITTING AT THE ROUND TABLE APPEARED TO BE IN her late thirties, a little older than Kenzi. She did not look the part of a stereotypical female scientist—no thick eyeglasses, no white coat. She didn't wear much makeup and her haircut was unfortunate, but Kenzi had seen worse.

She rose when Kenzi entered. "Hello. I'm Maya Breville."

"Nice to meet you. Please sit." Kenzi had this table moved into her office years ago. She hated peering at clients over a desk. It seemed like a hierarchal, male power play. *I'm the Big Cheese in this room because I'm sitting behind the desk.* She preferred to talk to people like equals. "I'm Kenzi Rivera."

"Oh, I know." The woman laughed a little. "I'm in the KenziKlan."

A scientist followed her on social media? Not bad...

"I love your tweets. And your livestreams. You always make me laugh. These days I appreciate the chuckles. Wherever I can find them."

Okay, now she officially loved this woman. "How can I help you? I understand your husband has filed for divorce. And he wants custody of your daughter."

"Yes. Brittany. She's six. We're extremely close. I would do anything for that beautiful girl. She would be devastated if Michael got custody."

"Maybe we should take it from the top." Kenzi laid her phone on the table and started the recorder. She preferred that to taking notes. Every time she touched a legal pad she felt a thousand years old. "Okay if I record?"

"Sure. Michael and I married about ten years ago. I work as a research scientist at a lab just outside of town. I have a Ph.D. in chemistry, but my work is far more wide-ranging."

"And your husband?"

"Was a scientist. But Michael has never been able to hold down a job. He has a hard time…getting along with others. He's abrasive. Temperamental. Angry."

"Violent?"

"Sometimes."

"Has he ever hit you?"

Her eyes lowered. "Yes."

She could see how much this shamed Maya. She was an intelligent woman, probably someone who thought "It could never happen to me." Until it did. "I'm sorry to hear that."

"If it makes you feel any better—I hit him back once."

"Good for you."

"Only made him madder. I was afraid he might take it out on Brittany. So I stopped. But he didn't. He took it out on me later that night. In bed."

Kenzi leaned forward. "Has he ever hit Brittany?"

"No. I mean, not that I know of. And I think she would tell me."

"Good. But if Brittany is in any danger, I want a restraining order."

"Of course. I've thought about leaving Michael, but I know how hard divorce is on children. I was hoping to avoid that if possible."

"Where are you living now?"

"We have a little house in the suburbs."

"Is Michael still there?"

"Two nights ago, right after he told me he was filing, he left and didn't return. The next day I was served. I don't know where he is now."

"If he comes near you or your daughter, call me immediately."

"Understood." Maya seemed to relax a bit. She had probably been worried sick.

"It's going to be all right. I promise. Before you know it, this will be an unpleasant memory in your rear-view mirror."

"I hope so."

"What's his beef? Sounds to me like you're the one who should be filing."

Maya hesitated. "He…objects to some of my friends."

"Work friends? Girl posse?"

"My…church friends."

Kenzi's Spidey-sense was tingling. "My assistant said something about a cult."

"It's not a cult!" Maya's voice soared. "It's my religion. People are so prejudiced. If your religion isn't one of the Big Three, then it's a cult."

"So your husband objected to your religion."

"And more. It's also a female empowerment group."

"I'm all for female empowerment. What's the group called?"

Maya drew in her breath. "Hexitel."

Kenzi had heard of Hexitel. Anyone active on social media, or who kept up with the news, had heard of Hexitel. Several high-profile members had recently fled the group, accusing it of being a mind-control cult, or a money-sucking pyramid scheme, or worse. People compared it to Scientology at best and NXIVM at worst. Stories had blanketed social media and TV news shows. She thought she'd read someone was making a Netflix docuseries about it. "Your husband objected to your involvement with Hexitel?"

"He objected to some of its principles. Hexitel focuses on executive training. Making women feel confident enough to deal with the toxic males who inhabit the professional world."

"Your husband must've felt threatened. Executive training is not remotely controversial."

"But some of Hexitel's…programs for building confidence might be."

"Can you give me some examples?"

"Most of the training is classroom work. Lectures and exercises designed to help people recognize their flaws and eliminate them. No different from what self-help coaches do. But we also have some rituals and…ceremonies that are more unusual. And of course, anytime you do anything outside the mainstream, critics come swarming."

Kenzi was getting an uncomfortable feeling about this. "Give me some examples of these ceremonies."

"They're mostly about actualization. Hexitel takes you on a journey from subservience to self-awareness. You earn your way to where you want to be. We're paired with a senior member who becomes sort of a sensei. We work for them and perform small services to show our devotion. In time, we progress and become the master."

"Excuse me. *Master?*"

"That's what we call our group leaders. It's just a title."

"It implies dominance. Slavery, even."

"It's no different than calling someone a captain. Or a boss." She sounded defensive. "We just happen to say 'master.' As in 'schoolmaster.'"

The uneasy feeling spread. "Have you taken your daughter to any of these ceremonies?"

"Of course not."

Thank goodness. "Anything dangerous in the ceremonies?"

Maya craned her neck. "We did this thing where we put out a match with our fingertips. Like in *Lawrence of Arabia*, you remember? To see how long we can handle the pain."

"That's…masochistic."

"The point is to realize how strong we are. To unleash our inner strength. No one ever did it long enough to cause permanent damage."

"Anything else?"

Maya hesitated. "I do have tattoos."

"Hexitel tattoos?"

"We all get them. I have a stylish H and X on my left shoulder blade. That's sort of the Hexitel logo. And every masterclass—that what we call each small group led by a master —has its own symbol." She stretched out her arm. Just below the wrist, the tat was visible. Three concentric semi-circles with something that looked like the tip of a red knife at the center.

"That looks like a murder weapon."

"It's a symbol of empowerment. We don't let anyone push us around."

"You stab them in the heart with a bloody dagger."

"It's just a symbol. In Hexitel, we believe all women are born with innate power."

"So do I, but I don't need a tat to remind me."

"We believe that by participating in these studies and rituals, we come to a better understanding of ourselves, our society, our world, and our universe. We believe it's a path to joining with a cosmic consciousness. We hope to attain oneness. That's our ultimate goal."

"Did your daily life change because of your membership?"

"Not that Michael would know about."

"Did you give Hexitel money?"

"Some. But it's my money. If I want to donate to my church, shouldn't I be able to do so?"

"He'll say you diminished the marital estate."

"How is this different from Christians tithing? Or donating money to a political campaign? Michael has joined a church, too."

"I'll make those arguments at the proper time. But I feel like I'm missing something. If you didn't preach your gospel to Brittany and you didn't take her to the ceremonies, what is it your husband objects to? And why does he think he should have custody?"

Maya laid her hands on the table, as if bracing herself. She slowly drew in several deep breaths. "I think what really bothered him most...was when I took a wife."

CHAPTER SEVEN

THE SENTINEL STRETCHED OUT IN A CAR PARKED IN THE LOT opposite the offices of Rivera & Perez. Not an ideal vantage point. But it would suffice.

These people were so oblivious. So distant, so removed from the world and what it was meant to be.

The current wardrobe had been selected to blend. Jeans. Sweater. Ball cap. A ski mask would be better, but that would attract attention. There could be many reasons for sitting in a car. But those explanations became somewhat suspect when you were dressed like a cat thief.

Three nights ago, the Sentinel had waited outside Maya's house. The commotion inside was audible, even from a distant vantage point. They were fighting. No surprise there. Must be hard to pretend you wore the pants in the family when your wife made the money. And it must be hard to pretend you're number one in someone else's life when they've joined a cult.

How much of the bellowing had their daughter heard? It was past little Brittany's bedtime, but who could sleep through this ruckus? The poor girl was probably hiding under the covers, quaking in her booties. No child should have to endure this.

The Sentinel cared about that girl, naturally, and hated knowing she must be suffering. When the time came—that suffering would be alleviated.

As if the yelling weren't bad enough, someone started throwing things. And it wasn't pillows. Sounded more like dishes, or vases, or something that made a satisfying smashing noise.

And then Michael filed for divorce. No doubt Hexitel would be mentioned, although that wasn't what bothered Michael most. Maya was buying a lawyer to help her get out of problems she'd created. All so predictable.

It was impossible not to feel for Maya. She was so unhappy. But those feelings had to be ignored. There were far more important matters at play. Work to do. Much to accomplish. These people and their petty mortal concerns could not be permitted to interfere. Certainly not some lawyer.

How much would Maya say about Hexitel? *It's a cult, but it's harmless.* Sure, all cults are harmless, until someone gets nailed to a tree. Or the congregation drinks cyanide Kool-Aid.

Or something even more sinister happens.

Perhaps this surveillance should be intensified. It might not be a dangerous situation yet. But it could become one. Quickly.

Or perhaps it wouldn't come to that. Better to wait and see how this story unfolded. Maya had become an obstacle, and that would get worse before it got better.

Violence was never the ideal choice. But sometimes, it was inevitable. The most extreme sanction was always an option.

The Sentinel was watching.

CHAPTER EIGHT

KENZI LOOKED AT HER POTENTIAL CLIENT WORDLESSLY, IN PART because she was stunned, but mostly because she couldn't think of anything intelligent to say. "Your *wife?*"

"You heard correctly."

"You have a husband and a wife."

"In a way…"

Kenzi tucked in her chin. "Okay, talk fast. This is obviously relevant to any divorce settlement. If you've committed adultery, or worse, bigamy—"

"It's nothing like that." Maya looked uncomfortable. Her face reddened.

"You said you had a wife."

"Not a wife-wife. Not a legal wife."

"An illegal wife?"

"A spiritual wife."

Kenzi tried to process this in the most positive way possible. "A wife to…help you on your journey to…cosmic nirvana."

"In a way, yes. It's something we do in Hexitel and it's not wrong or immoral. It's about spiritual awakening. Maybe we should use a different term but it's supposed to indicate the importance of the position. The level of commitment. All our members are women, remember."

"But I still don't—"

"There are no husbands, no sexual predators. When you take a wife, it's not about sexual bonding. It's more like choosing your shaman. Your spirit partner. The person you know will always be there for you."

"And yours is…"

"Candy Trussell. She's a wonderful woman. She's made my life so much better than it was before. I don't think I could've made it through these past few months without her."

Candy? Did her name have to be Candy? "Has your wife met your daughter?"

Maya squirmed. "They have met. Candy came over one night to get a book I wanted her to read. She ended up staying for dinner."

Kenzi pressed her fingers against her forehead. She instinctively wanted to prevent a child from being torn away from her mother. But Maya's story seemed inconsistent and this Hexitel stuff was just…weird. "This is bound to come up in the divorce."

"We did nothing wrong."

"You gave Michael's attorney dirt to throw around the courtroom. They'll say you exposed your daughter to a dangerous cult and aberrant practices."

"I would never do anything to harm my daughter."

"I believe you. But your husband's attorney will do his best to make you look vile. And incidents like this give him ammunition."

"I'm an American. Aren't I entitled to freedom of religion?"

"Yes. But it's my job to identify potential problem areas. And to be blunt—you've got a lot of them."

"Let Michael take all my money. I've got a good job. I can build back. But don't let him take my daughter. He's mean and violent and vindictive. Living with him would destroy Brittany."

Kenzi closed her eyes and focused. That was what it all came down to. Her client might be a whack job in a freaky cult, but at the end of the day, she was still the better parent. Michael was a menace. Maya might have made some mistakes, but she loved her daughter with all her heart.

Just as Kenzi's mother had loved her.

She still remembered the day when she was twelve and learned her parents were splitting up. Neither bothered to tell her beforehand. She found out by reading documents her father left on his desk. Her mother moved out. Kenzi felt as if her entire world was falling apart, and for a while, it did. Her grades tumbled. She stopped seeing her friends. She didn't want to do anything but hole up in her room and try to forget. But painful though that was, it was nothing compared to what she endured after the custody battle began…

And two months after that ordeal ended, she lost her mother forever.

Despite the obvious problems, she would take this case—for the daughter's sake. And she would do everything possible to avoid an ugly custody battle.

"May I ask you something, Maya?"

"Of course. Anything."

"You're a scientist. You've been trained to propose hypotheses and reach conclusions based upon evidence. How could you be drawn in by…some whackadoodle cult?"

Maya's back stiffened. "Science does not hold all the answers. Not everything can be reduced to ones and zeroes. We have souls."

"I'm just…surprised."

"Would you be equally surprised if I told you I was a Christian?"

Kenzi didn't answer.

"And yet, Christians believe all kinds of things that science tells us are impossible. Virgin births. Miracles. People returning from the dead. No one hassles Christians—because they're in the majority. But any time a new theology or faith comes along, it's a cult."

She supposed there was some truth to that, but it wouldn't make this case any easier. "If you still want me to represent you, I'll enter an appearance. And the first thing I'll do is arrange a settlement meeting. It will be best for all parties if we can resolve this amicably rather than drawing it out for years and spending tens of thousands of dollars on legal fees."

"Sounds good to me."

"Most divorce attorneys in this town are reasonable and don't exacerbate cases with motions practice or discovery just to run up billable hours. We should be able to work something out. But I will warn you. Settlement means compromise. No one gets everything they want. If you've been the breadwinner, you're going to have to give Michael some money."

"But I'll keep Brittany."

"His play for custody is probably just a scare tactic. You're her mother. Courts aren't going to take a child from her mother absent extraordinary circumstances. Your situation is far from typical, but I haven't heard anything that rises to that level. You'll probably have to give Michael reasonable, possibly supervised, visitation rights."

"As long as I'm the custodial parent, I'm happy."

"Good. Expect to lose half of everything you've gained since the marriage, but any gifts, bequests, or trusts are yours and yours alone. Since your husband has a college degree and is employable, there's no reason he should receive alimony, except perhaps in the short term. I can't make any guarantees, but most judges in this county favor the American rule."

"Meaning?"

"Meaning litigants pay their own legal fees. He'll cry poverty and maybe the judge will do something short-term, but in the long run, it's in your husband's interest to wrap this up as quickly as possible."

"He's angry. He wants to punish me."

"Well, we can't always get what we want, can we?"

"And the cost?"

"I charge a flat fee, not an hourly rate. Billing by the hour just makes people distrust lawyers. A flat fee encourages everyone to resolve disputes. If I can wrap this up expeditiously, I do all right. But even if it drags out for five years, it won't cost you more than the flat fee."

"Sounds fair. Should I write you a check?"

"Leave it with my assistant. I'll file the papers and call opposing counsel to schedule—" She opened the folder Sharon had given her and saw the name atop the signature block on the last page of the Petition.

Maya's husband was represented by Lou Crozier.

The lawyer Sharon called "the Spawn of Satan."

Was it too late to double her fee?

CHAPTER NINE

KENZI WALKED HER NEW CLIENT BACK TO THE LOBBY, TRYING TO assure her everything would work out. She found a young girl sitting in one of the overstuffed chairs in the waiting area, peering at a business magazine that couldn't possibly interest her.

"Is this Brittany?" Kenzi asked.

Maya nodded. "I wasn't sure if you'd want to talk to her."

The young girl looked up from the magazine. She was slim, a bit small for her age. Curly blonde locks. Gravity Falls T-shirt. As soon as she spotted her mother, she ran forward and wrapped her arms around her legs.

Several moments later, Brittany noticed she was not alone. "Are you the lady who's gonna help my mommy?"

Kenzi crouched down so she could look Brittany straight in the eye. "I am. You don't need to worry."

"Are you helping my daddy too?"

She glanced at Maya. "No. Someone else is helping your daddy."

"Where is he?"

"I don't know."

"He left home and he hasn't been back."

"You'll see him soon."

Brittany frowned. "Did Daddy leave because of me?"

Maya leaned in. "Oh, sweetheart, no."

"Is he mad because I asked for a puppy?"

"No!" They both said simultaneously.

Kenzi felt a deep knife-cut to her heart. She totally understood where Brittany was coming from. "It has nothing to do with you, Brittany. Sometimes grownups have problems, that's all."

"Is Daddy going to take me away from Mommy?" Her eyes widened. "'Cause Mommy knows how to make jelly sandwiches and where to get me after school and what kind of ice cream I like best."

"No," Kenzi said firmly. "Absolutely not."

"You promise?"

"I promise. No one will take you away from your mother."

"Nothing bad is going to happen to anyone," Maya said. "Daddy and Mommy may live in separate places, but nothing else will change."

Brittany smiled a little. "That's good. Maddie doesn't like a lot of moving around."

Maddie?

Maya pointed toward the chair.

A large doll, almost as big as Brittany. A soft cuddly blonde doll that looked very much like the girl.

"Tell Maddie not to worry," Kenzi said. "I'll do my best to get all the problems settled as quickly as possible."

"Maddie wants to be a scientist when she grows up."

"Does she? Like your mother. Very ambitious."

Brittany looked down. "But sometimes…she's not sure she's smart enough."

Kenzi placed her hands on Brittany's shoulders. "Listen to

me, Brittany. Maddie is smart enough. She can be anything she wants to be. Girls get the job done. And I will get this job done."

Kenzi informed Sharon that she'd accepted the case and asked her to start drafting the Petition and assembling the preliminary documents. Despite Crozier being on the other side, she could see Sharon was pleased.

But she hadn't forgotten her Number One task for the day.

She marched to her father's office—and had to wait almost half an hour before she could get in. She'd delayed too long, and his assistant Marjorie acted more like his Chief of Staff. Access to the Main Man was severely restricted, even for his daughter. Kenzi had always felt Marjorie disapproved of her. Maybe it was just paranoia. But probably not.

She heard a buzz, then Marjorie looked up. "You may go in now."

She wondered if she should kiss Marjorie's ring. "Thanks so much."

She entered the office. Her father had his own velvet pile carpet, much more luxurious than what the rest of Rivera & Perez sported. Two walls were adorned with a burnished red wallpaper and his worktable displayed two authentic Lioveras sculptures. The walls bore no diplomas but several works of art by minor Latinx painters, including one behind his desk highlighted by a small overhead spotlight. This was by far the best-decorated office in the firm, but her father could afford it, and it was important to him. She knew how much he thought appearances mattered. He wanted visitors to know he was successful—and rich.

He smiled amiably. "How's Daddy's little girl?"

"I've been better."

"Looks like you're doing great to me." He gestured toward a chair on the other side of his desk. "Sit. Take a load off."

She did, thinking of the irony. In her office, she sat on a level plane with visitors, even ones she didn't know. In his office, his daughter got the subservient chair on the opposite side of his hierarchal throne.

Alejandro Rivera was just past sixty but he didn't look it. Partly because he maintained a strict daily Peloton routine. Partly because of his spa visits, frequent facials, regular Botox injections, and a little hair dye. He looked distinguished, but not old.

"Thank you for seeing me."

"Stop. You're my daughter. I'm always happy to visit with you." It wasn't true, but it was nice that he would say it. "As long as you don't have your cellphone in hand."

"I don't stream inside the office."

"Thank the sainted mother for that. Isn't it time you gave that up? You're a partner in a major law firm. It seems beneath you."

Only because you're old, she wanted to say, but didn't. "Dad, social media is how people market today. My online publicity has brought this firm many new clients."

"I still think you'd be better off putting the phone away and spending more time at celebrity galas. Tech-startup open houses. Country club balls. That would bring in the kind of clients we want on our list."

"And who would that be?"

"Blue chip clients. Movers and shakers. Titans of industry."

"Dad…we're a divorce firm."

"And fifty percent of all American marriages end in divorce. So we can pick and choose."

"And you want me to pick rich people."

"Larger estates lead to larger legal fees. Speaking of which—are you still offering clients flat fees?"

"According to our bylaws, every attorney is free to set their own billing schedules."

"Don't quote the bylaws to me," he snapped. "I wrote those bylaws. I asked you a question."

"Yes, I'm still offering people flat fees."

"Honey, you've seen the studies. When attorneys bill by the hour, they make more money."

"And also engender more resentment from their clients."

"Not if you handle it correctly. You need to work so hard they feel grateful to you. Feel like they got a bargain because you did so much to help them."

"Flat fees are fairer and no one gets mad afterward. No sticker shock. Clients pay exactly what they knew they were going to pay. It would be better for the reputation of lawyers if we all went back to flat fees."

He waved his hand in the air. "And while we're at it, why don't we go back to wearing suspenders and practicing out of our living rooms?"

She tried not to be irritated. More irritated than she already was. He always thought he knew more about everything than anyone else. "This isn't what I—"

"And what's this about a cult?"

How did he hear about that? "Are you talking about my new client?"

"Marjorie says she's some kind of cult crazy."

Kenzi felt her back stiffen. "She's a chemist. A serious scientist with a young daughter. Her husband is trying to get custody."

Her father leaned back in his chair, folding his hands behind his head. "Marjorie says she even has cult tattoos."

"How would she—"

"I gather they're visible on her wrist. Marjorie keeps her eyes open."

She'd like to take Marjorie's eyes and...but that was for

another time. "Tattoos are common these days, Dad. Almost everyone my age has them."

"Would you stop treating me like I'm 212? I'm aware that some people have decorative tattoos. Like you, for instance."

Ouch. How did he find out—

"But most people don't have cult emblems burned into their skin. Marjorie googled it. Your client is or was in Hexitel."

"I know that."

"So I assume you declined the case."

Long painful pause. "No."

He slapped his hand across his forehead. "You're kidding me. You said yes to some Manson groupie?"

"She is not—" Kenzi drew in her breath. He was baiting her. She knew that. He was also trying to distract her, divert her, because he knew damn well what she came here to talk about. "She considers Hexitel her religion."

"I don't care if she considers it her grandmother. I don't want her on our client list."

"Look, it's a simple case. I'll offer the husband a fair settlement and he'll go away. He's mad now, but I can't imagine he really wants to raise a young child by himself. I can probably wrap it up in a single settlement meeting."

"Which is exactly the wrong way to practice law. Haven't I taught you anything? Have you sent discovery requests? This man may have skeletons in the closet you know nothing about. What about a motion for attorneys fees? Or a motion to disqualify opposing counsel?"

"You know those would fail."

"A lawyer is obligated to try everything that might benefit his client."

"A lawyer is not obligated to run up fees chasing ghosts. That's the Old School way of practicing and it's done a lot of damage to lawyer reputations. I won't work that way."

He shook his head slowly. "And that leads us, squarely and directly, to what you actually came in here to talk about."

Son of a bitch. He'd seen her coming and outflanked her before she'd even begun to fight. "You're saying you passed me over because I won't inflate fees?"

"You're not setting the right example. Your self-righteousness interferes with your duty."

"My clients adore me."

"This is a business, not a lovefest. Do you know how many people this firm employs?"

"Not exactly…"

"More than two hundred. That's a lot of people depending upon you not to be arrogant, but to be a responsible businessperson who helps them pay their mortgage and keep the lights on."

"Still sounds like you passed me over because I won't bill bogus hours."

Her father closed his eyes, as if he were meditating in his chair. A few moments later, he'd composed himself. "You are my daughter. I love you dearly. And I did not pass you over. Frankly, I don't know why you ever thought you were in contention. Your brother was the obvious choice for the position."

"Everyone in this firm thought I was going to be the next managing partner."

"Are you sure about that? Or are *you* the one who assumed you were going to be the next managing partner? Because your ego blinded you to the realities most people could see more clearly."

"I'm the top biller in the firm. And I have been for years." She couldn't resist. "Despite charging my clients a flat fee."

"But you're an island. Gabriel is a continent."

"What the hell does that mean?"

"You're a self-contained unit, having precious little to do

with anyone else. Other lawyers like you, but they don't really know you."

"You're saying I didn't get the position because I have poor social skills? I have twenty-thousand Twitter followers!"

"That has nothing to do with real people, much less co-workers. You're a lone wolf. And a loose cannon. Gabe is a leader."

Her stomach was beginning to roil. She didn't know how much more of this she could stand. "Gabe is an idiot!"

"Honey…"

"His billables are poor. His client list is short. The only reason he has clients at all is because you toss him work and don't think I don't know it."

"There's nothing wrong with that."

"How come you never sent any work my way?"

"Because you don't need it. But if you're pretending I've never done anything for you, sweetheart…grow up. I've always taken care of my family."

"Including Mom?"

He sighed heavily. "That's another big difference. You take after your mother. Gabriel takes after me."

Kenzi felt as if she were about to explode. "You did this to punish me."

"No. I did what I believe to be best for the firm. Gabriel will use this. He'll take his heightened status and make the most of it. It will be good for him and it will be good for the firm."

"So you gave him the job to boost his confidence?"

"In part. He has a family to support."

"I have a family to support!" she screamed.

"It's not the same. He's a man. He's the head of a household. He's my natural heir. People expect to see him on top."

"That is so sexist."

"Maybe, but it's true."

"You always liked him best."

Another deep sigh. "I have certainly done better with my sons than my daughters. That much is certain."

"Gabe is an idiot. And you know it."

Her father tossed his head to one side. "Is he as smart as you? Probably not. Does that mean he's disqualified from running this firm? Absolutely not. People like him. He's prominent in the Bar Association. This firm is important to him. He needs this."

"And I don't?"

His left eyebrow rose. "You have your KenziKlan."

Kenzi shot to her feet. "This is without question the most infuriating conversation I've had in my entire life. I'm outta here."

"Would you at least think about what I said? It might do you some good."

"I will not bow down and become your obedient little girl."

"All I want is what's best for you."

"Which would be what? Marry someone and bake cookies, while you and the men do all the hard work?"

"I didn't say—"

"Here's what you need to understand, Daddie Dearest. I will not take this lying down. If you don't do right by me—I'll go somewhere I'm better appreciated. I'll start my own firm and take all your clients wiht me."

"Kenzi...calm down."

"I'll fight you. One way or the other. Because that's who I am. And you're right—I did get that from my mother. We don't let men push us around."

She slammed her fist on his desk. "This isn't over. You just wait and see."

KENZI STORMED OUT OF THE OFFICE. HER HEAD SWAM WITH SO many simultaneous thoughts she couldn't think straight. She needed an adult slushie (codename for frozen margarita) and a good night's sleep. Tomorrow morning, she'd start laying groundwork for her new firm—her own firm. Let the Good Old Boys have this rickety joint. It was about to become a dinosaur. Her firm would be mean and lean and built for the twenty-first century, not the Victorian Era.

She stopped by Sharon's desk. "Girlfriend, we need a drink. How about a stop at the Ferry and I'll tell you—"

Sharon cut her off, shoving a phone message into her hands. "Your new client called."

"Maya? Why?"

"After she left here, she took Brittany to school, ran a few quick errands, and when she returned—her daughter wasn't there."

CHAPTER TEN

Kenzi blinked several times, trying to clear her head. Plunged from one crisis to the next. She could barely keep track of it all.

"Did her husband—"

"Yes. Michael says he took Brittany for her own safety. And get this—his lawyer got an emergency ex parte protective order. To shield Brittany from her own mother."

Crozier. Bastard. "What possible grounds could he have for an emergency order?"

Sharon handed her a copy. "He says Maya has endangered Brittany's life. By trying to indoctrinate her into a dangerous cult. Exposing her to immoral and sexually deviant behavior. And he specifically mentions Maya's wife."

Kenzi lit into the principal of Bakerfield Country Day School.

"I can't believe you don't have better security protocols. You've placed a young child in serious danger."

"We do have protocols. Nothing untoward is ever allowed—"

"My client's child was abducted!"

The principal, Dr. Laurel Thomas, was obviously striving to remain calm. "No. She was picked up by her father. Unusual, true, but he showed his ID and the child recognized him. He was on the pickup list signed by both parents."

Kenzi took a moment to gain perspective. Principal Thomas was about twenty years older, heavier, and seated behind a desk. She was clearly accustomed to dealing with difficult parents and probably had several lawyer encounters under her belt, too. Aggression and incrimination weren't going to get Kenzi anywhere.

She tried another tack. "Brittany's father has a history of aggression. Of hitting his wife, to be blunt."

"I knew nothing about that. And even if I had, I can't withhold a child from a parent based on rumors. I could do it if I had a court order. But you haven't brought me one. Not before and not now."

"Did he say where they were going?"

"I wasn't present, but the teacher on pickup duty said they were going home."

"He's not there." He'd taken Brittany somewhere else. Someplace Maya couldn't find them. "This is an extremely serious situation. The child is in grave danger. It's basically a kidnapping."

"Didn't you say the father has a court order?"

"An ex parte emergency order. Which I will get quashed the second the judge returns to his office."

Principal Thomas held out her hands, palms up. "I'm sorry, but we have not done anything improper. And there's nothing I can do to help you at this point."

Kenzi glanced at her phone. Maya had called about a thousand times, hoping for information about Brittany. "If you see that man again, like if he brings her back to school tomorrow, I want you to call me."

"I can do that. But..."

She didn't have to complete the sentence. Kenzi knew what it would be.

They both thought it was extremely unlikely that would happen. Michael had taken his daughter for a reason. And he wasn't going to give Maya a chance to get her back.

FIRST THING NEXT MORNING, KENZI MANAGED TO GET JUDGE Benetti on a Zoom call. He was gray-haired, sixtyish, and tended to be cranky even when someone wasn't interrupting his breakfast. She was careful to dial it down and act appreciative.

"First of all, Ms. Rivera, where is opposing counsel?"

"I haven't been able to get a call back from my disgust—er, distinguished opponent."

"So this is an ex parte meeting. I can't do that."

"You did it when you granted my client's husband a custody order."

"They said it was an emergency situation. That the child was in danger. And they had evidence to prove it."

"Like what?"

Judge Benetti rifled through the papers on his desk. "Like apparently your client is in a cult."

"It's a church. That's her religion. Are we stealing children from their mothers when we don't like their religion?"

"They say it's a cult with dangerous and immoral practices. And your client was trying to indoctrinate her daughter."

"That's completely bogus."

The judge's eyelids fluttered. "I have set this matter down for a full hearing next week. At that time, you can make your arguments and present whatever evidence you have. But I will warn you—don't make light of this cult business. We just got past NXIVM. No way I'm going to let a child be exposed to the next generation of craziness."

"Hexitel is completely different. And the father is the dangerous one. Violent. He—"

On her laptop screen, Kenzi could see the judge raise his hand. "No more, Ms. Rivera. If you have evidence, present it at the hearing. I can't do anything based on hearsay. You know that very well."

"I have to alert the court of any potential danger—"

"If there's so much danger, why wasn't your client the one who came to court for a protective order?"

Damn. "I hadn't had time." Because she prioritized yelling at her father. Like that did a lot of good. "Your honor, I would not say this if it weren't true. Her father is a far greater danger to the child than her mother's religion."

"Then you may make that argument at the hearing."

"And until then?"

"Let's hope for the best. I'll see you in court."

The Zoom connection went black.

Kenzi pounded on her desk in frustration. But she knew that wouldn't help. She was going to have to deal with this. Immediately. Everything else had to go on the back burner. This case was Priority One. Maya would freak when she heard she wouldn't see Brittany for a week, so Kenzi would set up a settlement meeting before they even got to the hearing.

And that meant she had a lot of work to do.

CHAPTER ELEVEN

KENZI ARRIVED AT HER OFFICE FEELING OVERWHELMED, LIKE SHE barely had her head on straight. She'd spent the last several days trying unsuccessfully to locate Brittany and to make sure she was safe. So far she'd accomplished nothing. Crozier wouldn't tell her a thing except that the child was unharmed—and everything else was confidential. Michael had legal possession of the child. Maya said Brittany had used her father's phone and texted her once. The girl was traumatized and terrified—but there was nothing they could do about it.

Kenzi had managed to schedule a settlement conference and she hoped they could make progress. Maybe even resolve the entire case. At the very least, lay some ground rules and establish a visitation schedule so Maya could see her daughter.

Sharon didn't wait to be asked. She pointed down the corridor when Kenzi approached her desk. "In there."

"Already?"

"Yeah. The Spawn of Satan rises early."

She suppressed a grin. "You probably need to stop saying that. At least when he's around."

"Appropriate though, isn't it? The Spawn of Satan reps the babynapper."

"Stop. I have to focus."

"Did you bring your bulletproof vest?"

"Left it at home. But Hailee put a wooden stake in my satchel." She glanced into the reception area. "Who's the guy with the beard? Dressed like a Old Testament prophet."

"He's going for Jesus, actually."

"Whaaaat?"

"That's Michael's spiritual advisor."

"The childnapper is religious?" She paused. "I guess Maya did mention that he'd joined a church."

"I think it's an outbound Bible camp or something. People getting in tune with nature. Organic crops and hydroponic farming. And prayer."

"And he wants to criticize Maya about Hexitel?"

"Michael's group is Christian and, so far as I know, it doesn't assign wives to its members. Or have masters and slaves."

"What's with the costume? Is he putting on a show? Look how holy I am?"

"I don't know. Michael dragged the guy in here, supposedly for moral support."

"Michael needs moral education, not moral support."

She figured she'd probably regret it, but she couldn't resist pumping the man for more information. She approached. "Hi. I'm Kenzi Rivera."

The man stood. He was wearing what looked like a burlap robe and sandals. In Seattle. Where it rains one hundred and fifty-six days a year. His craggy, bearded face was reserved but freidnly. "I'm Adrien Messie."

"I understand you're Michael's...counselor."

"He's been going through a rough patch. We all need the support of others at times like these. I believe our flock has brought him much comfort."

"So this is an actual true-to-life church? What denomination?"

"We're not affiliated with any large organization. I don't see the need for it. We have a small settlement outside Seattle. Michael has only recently joined us."

"Did he bring his daughter with him?'

Messie stroked his beard. "I'm…not at liberty…"

Of course not. "Is this a Christian church?"

"Very much so. We believe in living simply, as Jesus did, apart from the temptations of urban life."

"You certainly seem to dress…simply."

"If it was good enough for the prophets, it's good enough for me. Michael tells me you're…more concerned about clothing."

Her reputation preceded her. "I like to look good."

"Goodness comes from within. Dressing simply might lead to simplifying your life. Allowing you to focus on matters of greater import."

What would the KenziKlan think if she started appearing in burlap? "I'm a lawyer. I have to dress professionally."

"Do you like working? I know some women do, and they should be afforded that opportunity, but I've found that many of the women in my flock are happier leading…simpler lives."

"Changing diapers and baking casseroles?"

He smiled. "Every woman has to find her own peace. Often that comes from the home."

"I have a home and a daughter. Neither brings me much peace. Is your church in a small town? Rural area?"

"Yes."

"And your followers live with you? Like a commune?"

"We live together as a community. Worship together." He smiled. "And work the farm. For our own sustenance. Not for profit."

Out the corner of her eye, she spotted Maya entering. "I would love to learn more—"

"I have another matter I need to attend to, and I can see you're busy." He bowed slightly. "Perhaps we can talk another time. Peace be with you." He left the lobby.

Kenzi approached Maya. "How are you doing?"

"How do you think? My daughter's been kidnapped and I can't even talk to her."

"Crozier assured me Brittany is safe."

"I want to see her."

"I know. And—"

"I'm not sure I can be in the same room with Michael without wringing his neck."

Kenzi raised a finger. "No fighting. No arguing. We came here to resolve conflict. One stray remark could torpedo the entire process."

"I'll try. But if Michael starts lying—"

"Try harder."

Maya asked for five minutes to make a phone call. Kenzi entered the conference room and found Lou Crozier at the far end of the table surrounded by legal pads and documents. How could he have so much paperwork on a case that was only a few days old? She suspected most of it was bogus. Set decoration designed to make him look busy and important.

"No client?" she asked.

"Stepped into the men's room." Crozier was about the same age as her father and definitely of that generation of lawyers. He wore a close-cropped beard, probably to compensate for the hair he did not have on the top of his head. "Long time no see. How are you, Kenzi?"

"Ready to kick butt and bend steel with my bare hands."

"I'm hoping that won't be necessary."

"Don't be so sure. I can't stand kidnappers."

Crozier drew in a weary breath. "There's a huge difference between a kidnapper and a concerned parent who legally removes a child from a dangerously unstable parent with connections to a deviant and probably criminal cult."

"Save the speeches for the judge. Your client is the violent one."

"Look, the clients aren't here yet, so we don't have to put on a show. Why don't we just talk like normal people? How are you holding up?"

Her face twisted. "What do you mean?"

"I heard about your...disappointment."

Damnation. Word travelled fast in the Seattle legal world. Or was her previous guess correct—he overheard her talking at the Ferry.

"That must have been a crushing blow," he continued. "Bad enough to be passed over when you've worked your butt off. But to be passed over by your own father?" He whistled. "That's gotta sting."

"I never expected the job, for your information." Was she really lying to Crozier? Why? But she couldn't seem to stop. "Gabe will do a fine job."

He gave her a long look. "Kenzi...I've been in court opposite Gabe. More than once. Nice polite man. But...kind of a bumbler. You lawyer circles around him."

"I'll take that as a compliment. And ignore the rest."

"I'm trying to be sympathetic. I haven't always gotten everything I wanted in life, either. I suppose no one does. But this is a gross injustice. And most people, when they feel they've been treated badly, start looking for alternatives."

The more time she spent with this man, the more she disliked him. Had he guessed she was planning to open her own shop?

"You know...we could definitely make room for a gal with your talents at Crozier & Crozier."

Ignoring the sexist "gal" part for the moment, was this

odious man actually offering her a job? "Are you saying what I think you're saying?"

"I'm offering you a position with our firm. A partnership position. One that makes you a ton of money and puts you in line to run the joint a few years down the road. Like, before you turn forty. When I step down."

She hardly knew what to say. Her firm's biggest competitor was headhunting her? Was he trying to soften her up so she'd be generous when they negotiated the settlement? Or was he doing this because he knew how much it would disturb her father? He might perceive that as the ultimate blow—having a Rivera work for Crozier & Crozier.

"I'm not sure I'd be a good fit in your firm. I'm pretty liberal."

"I don't give a damn about your politics."

"You say that, but I've heard you're way far right. Like, QAnon-Proud Boys-Oath Keepers-conspiracy theories far right."

"What the mainstream media call conspiracy theories, others call truth the mainstream refuses to print. Because it doesn't fit with the far left antifa plan to turn America into a socialist state. We use the dark web and encrypted messaging apps because we've been silenced everywhere else."

Sharon was right about this guy. "I'm afraid I don't agree—"

"You don't have to agree. My law firm is my business, not my megaphone. Our goal is to make money. Politicking is a spare-time activity."

"Still, it makes me…uncomfortable. Especially after the January 6 insurrection at the US Capitol."

"That was a misguided demonstration that got out of hand. A few extremists damaged the cause. Most of the people present that day only came to protest peacefully. Including me."

Her eyes fairly bulged. "You were there?"

"And I'm proud of it. I did nothing illegal. I didn't enter the Capitol building. But here's something relevant to our discussion. I consider myself the Attorney for the Damned. In fact, I have it on a plaque on my desk. You know what that means?"

"You handle cases no one else will take?"

"No. I don't care about that Last Chance Lawyer crap. I'm talking about people who've been vilified by the press and consequently can't get a fair shake. Can't speak their mind. As lawyers, we have a duty to help people in that impossible situation. That's the oath I made when I became a lawyer. And it's a promise I made to God."

"You're religious."

"Of course."

"Same church as your client?"

"Oh, hell no. I have no idea what those people are doing out in the woods. But my faith is my cornerstone. It made me the man I am today."

She decided not to comment.

"I couldn't make you managing partner on the first day," Crozier continued, "but I could definitely put you on track. Unlike your father, I have no children in my firm. No designated heir. And when I make a promise, I keep it. I won't walk this back."

"Hard to believe you'd give up the reins."

He shook his head. "I have a higher calling."

"Is this a...God thing?"

"There's a prophecy. You can find it on YouTube. I'll show you, if you like."

"Maybe you can bottom line it for me."

He nodded. "I expect to be appointed Chief Justice of the United States. In a very few years."

Okay, didn't see that one coming. "You know, John Roberts is relatively young..."

"He's tainted. Surely you know he was pals with Jeffrey Epstein. It's just a matter of time."

"That sounds rather far-fetched."

"You don't have to agree. Or even understand. I'm offering you a job. You pick your own clients. You bill them however you like. And you don't have to subscribe to my beliefs. All you have to do is make money and take good care of my firm."

"I—I hardly know what to say—" His politics appalled her—but then, she didn't agree with anything her father said either. The offer did have a certain appeal. And it would give her father a much-needed lesson in Kenzi-appreciation.

"You don't have to say anything now," Crozier added. "Just think about it. Mull it over. Give me a call when you're ready."

"I will." She swallowed. "Um…thank you."

"No problem. Now let's get down to business."

CHAPTER TWELVE

A FEW MINUTES LATER, BOTH CLIENTS ENTERED THE CONFERENCE room. Michael was better looking than she expected—tall, with curly hair and a thick moustache that worked for him. He might still be a useless loafer, but he didn't look the part.

Kenzi and Crozier launched into the negotiations. They followed the usual pattern. First, they attempted to identify the marital property, what was undisputed, what the other party could take without contest. After that, each lawyer would confer with their client in private. Then they could start making offers.

If they got that far.

"Here's how I see it," Kenzi began, speaking to Crozier. "Your client has a college degree. He can support himself, so he's not going to get alimony. He'll get a share of the proceeds from the sale of the house. We'll offer you fifty-thousand dollars, which is way too much, but worth it to get this resolved efficiently and to minimize the stress on the family. But this part is non-negotiable—Brittany must be returned to her mother immediately. We'll agree to some level of reasonable supervised visitation.

But no more kidnappings. No parent takes Brittany without the knowledge of the other."

"What if she's busy when Michael needs to contact her?" Crozier asked. "Say, at a cult meeting? Or on a date with her wife."

Kenzi felt her fingers stiffen. Just a few moments ago, Crozier had been trying to persuade her to join his firm. But as soon as the clients entered the room, he reverted to his usual Spawn of Satan persona.

Correction: Attorney for the Damned. Because who could be more damned than someone who abducted his own daughter and kept her imprisoned, separated from her mother for days.

"I'm afraid I disagree with everything you've said," Crozier said. "The parties had an arrangement. Maya worked while Michael tended the home and child. No one would have any trouble giving alimony to a housewife and I don't see why it should be any different for a househusband."

"Welcome to the twenty-first century. Alimony barely exists anymore. Your client is employable. Time for him to get off his butt and go to work."

"And who will care for the child? Brittany is accustomed to having a full-time parent at home."

"Brittany is accustomed to being at school all day. Your client didn't even pick her up after school. Except when he wanted to kidnap her."

"Ms. Rivera. That inflammatory language is not helpful."

He was right, of course. Name-calling never advanced a settlement. But she was having a hard time containing herself. Michael may have chosen sloth. But he had options.

"I don't want to make things more difficult than they already are," Kenzi replied. "But the inappropriate removal of the child from school, disallowing contact with her mother, coupled with your sneaky legal maneuverings, have created a serious trust problem."

"I agree that there's a trust problem. How can we trust a mother who's enslaved to a dangerous and bizarre sex cult?"

Sex cult? "Here in America, we enjoy freedom of religion."

"Don't try to buffalo me. Hexitel isn't a religion. I'm a man of faith. My client is a man of faith. We know what religion looks like. And it isn't women taking extramarital wives or tattooing themselves."

"And branding themselves," Michael added quietly.

Kenzi rolled her eyes. "A tattoo isn't a brand."

"No," Michael murmured. "The brand is in a more…intimate location."

Kenzi whipped her head around to look at Maya. Who wasn't denying it.

"There's nothing threatening about my religion," Maya said evenly. "But there's definitely something threatening about a violent man who can't control his temper. He has physically struck me. More than once. Every second Brittany is with him, she's in danger."

"That's total bull," Michael said.

"Is it?" Maya rolled up her left sleeve. "How do you think I got this bruise?"

Michael looked away. "Probably from a cult hazing ritual."

Maya's eyes flashed. "As you very well know, you gave me this bruise when you punched me in the arm, followed by two blows to my ribcage. You threw dishes and vases and broke a mirror. You threw a tantrum because I used the wrong towel to wipe off my bathroom mirror."

"I put that towel on my body. Why would I want it smeared across your mirror?"

"You're right. It's a capital offense. So it's okay to beat your wife."

"Okay, this isn't productive," Kenzi said, stretching her arms across the table between the combatants. "We know the parties have disputes. But that shouldn't extend to the daughter. Keeping a young girl away from her mother is cruel."

"I'm only trying to protect her," Michael said.

"Her mother would die before she would hurt that girl."

Crozier shook his head, slowly and sadly. "I don't know that. I do know this. That cult, like virtually every cult, thrives on coercive control. Manipulating people in various ways—emotional, economic, and physical. The end result is always the same. Domination. If the cult controls the mother, how long before it controls the daughter? And what happens to poor Brittany then?"

Kenzi spoke slowly, emphasizing each word. "Maya would never harm her daughter."

"If she's under the control of a charismatic cult leader…or a wife, she might not consider it harm. In her delusional state of mind, she might think she's doing the child a favor. Providing religious education. Discipline. The same way parents rationalize corporal punishment."

"Which the cult also favors," Michael murmured.

"Furthermore," Crozier continued, "your client will have to compensate the marital estate for every penny she's given the cult. Michael believes she's given this group more than a hundred thousand dollars, and apparently the contributions increase each year as she ascends to a higher level in the cult pyramid scheme."

"You can't prove that."

"Yet. Which I fear is why we will have to conduct discovery on financial matters and more. Extensive and likely expensive discovery. Unless we can reach some kind of agreement today."

Kenzi took a calming breath. Ignore the threat. Eyes on the prize. "Let my client see her daughter. Let them spend the afternoon together. That would de-escalate the situation. Then we can move forward more productively."

Michael made a scoffing noise, but Crozier ignored him. "I would actually consider that. But I have one condition."

"Which is?"

"Your client has to renounce the cult. Cut all ties with Hexitel. Agree in writing to have nothing whatsoever to do with them in the future."

"You can't require someone to give up their religion."

"And you can't expect me to put a child in the hands of someone who's trying to indoctrinate her into a sadistic sex cult."

Kenzi and Crozier glared at one another for a long moment. They appeared to be at a complete impasse. And she wasn't sure what to do about it. "That's your final offer? Because if it is, we're not getting anywhere today."

"I'm sorry. But that's our line in the sand."

Crozier didn't want to settle. He wanted to drag this out and bill time for a year. "Hexitel is not a...sadistic sex cult."

"You know this? Have you investigated them?"

No. But she would. As soon as possible. "I know Maya would never endanger her child."

"A woman under the coercive control of a cult does not know her own mind and cannot make clear-headed decisions. Did you know your client calls the leader of her Hexitel group 'Master?' Did you know she does subservient chores for her master? That she gives her 'collateral' in the form of sexually explicit photos?"

"That's a lie." She hoped.

"My client assures me that it is true," Crozier continued "And standard practice in Hexitel." He started packing his files. "It's apparent at this point that we have many unresolved issues of fact. I can't see settlement discussions being productive at this time."

"At least let Maya see her daughter."

"She isn't here," Crozier said, stacking his legal pads. "And frankly, I wouldn't agree to that even if she were. I believe you need to do your homework, Ms. Rivera. You do not fully appreciate the threat presented by Hexitel to your client and her daughter. These people have no scruples. They crave money and power. Go home and read *Helter Skelter*. Bone up on the Symbionese Liberation Army."

"Can I find that on your QAnon page?"

"No," he said, "you can find it on a page labeled, Things Every Responsible Mother Should Know. And Avoid." He rose. "These people want to destroy the moral fabric of this country. The Storm is coming, take my word for it. You and the rest of the mainstream can ignore or underestimate it. But I cannot."

"At least let them talk on the phone!"

Crozier ignored her.

"Please!" Maya's voice was more a shriek than a plea. "Let me talk to my girl."

"I don't believe that's in the best interests of the child."

"You don't know anything about it!" Maya screamed. "You don't know Michael. He gave you money, but you don't know him. You don't know what he's capable of."

Crozier looked away, his face a mask. "Ms. Rivera, I would ask you to keep your client under control. We can't possibly do business in this sort of environment."

"You didn't come to do business," Kenzi said, lips tight. "You came to conduct emotional blackmail. You're using a little girl as a pawn."

Crozier guided Michael toward the door. "Perhaps when you've conducted even the most basic research, you'll be able to speak with more professionalism and authority. Until that occurs, you're wasting our time. This meeting is terminated."

CHAPTER THIRTEEN

KENZI SPENT THE NEXT HOUR WITH MAYA, TRYING TO COMFORT her. Nothing she said had much impact. If anything, Maya seemed hostile toward her.

She got it. Maya was taking the hostility she felt toward Michael and his bullyboy lawyer and targeting the nearest available person. But the truth was—Kenzi hadn't handled that settlement well. She made the mistake of thinking everyone shared her desire to resolve disputes with minimal trauma to clients, but Crozier wanted to magnify the disputes for profit. And she didn't know nearly enough about the background facts. She'd hoped a speedy settlement might obviate the need. She was wrong.

She had to do better at the temporary custody hearing next week. And that meant she needed to know as much about this religion...cult...whatever it was as Crozier did. Or more. 'Cult' was a powerful and frightening word. She had to be able to assure the court there was no child endangerment. And if she couldn't, Maya would have to sever ties with Hexitel. But she'd address that issue after she knew more about it.

"I know words aren't much comfort now," Kenzi said, "but we have no reason to believe Brittany isn't safe."

"She's with that man!"

"Crozier has read him the riot act. He won't do anything violent or even...controversial now. This is his testing period. Crozier has probably given him a long to-do list, actions designed to make him look like the model parent."

"He's the worst possible parent!"

"I know. And I know you want to be with her. And you will be. But in the meantime, nothing is going to happen to her."

"Says the woman who promised Brittany her daddy wouldn't take her away from her mommy."

Kenzi's eyelids closed. She had said that, hadn't she? Another stupid mistake. "I should've been the one getting the emergency protective order. I didn't see the need back then. But I can—" She choked back the word 'promise.' She didn't need to make any more of those. "I can assure you that when the custody hearing rolls around next week, I will come to court with my bazookas armed and ready."

A FEW HOURS LATER, KENZI ARRIVED AT HEXITEL'S DOWNTOWN Seattle office—what its website called "the Gathering Place." The website made the organization look completely legitimate, all about education and female empowerment. The website was also actively recruiting new members. She considered calling to make an appointment, posing as a potential new member, then decided against it. If she showed up unexpectedly, she might learn more.

The office was located in the heart of the financial and tech districts. Several billion dollars probably walked past its doors every day. The front door was unlocked, but no one sat at the receptionist station. That wasn't a complete surprise, since it was after six, but it left her with a dilemma. Should she wait outside politely and hope someone appeared? Or should she plunge inside and see what she could learn from people who weren't expecting a visitor?

She didn't have to think about that one very long...

As Kenzi entered the main corridor, she heard low-pitched sounds coming from a suite at the far left. Moaning? Humming? The door was closed, but there was definitely something going on inside.

She looked both ways up and down the hallway.

No one was watching.

She slowly and quietly pushed the door open a crack. And peered inside.

The room was about the size of a grade-school classroom, but the overhead lights were off. The room was lit by candles. On the opposite wall, she spotted a tapestry bearing a dagger symbol similar to Maya's tattoo. There were eleven people in the room, all women, two at the front on a raised dais, and nine others kneeling before them. They appeared to be wearing robes and chanting something low and indiscernible. She scanned the faces. It was difficult to be certain in this low lighting, but she didn't think Maya was in this group. Thank God.

Her heartbeat quickened. This was beyond weird. Granted, all religions had rites and ceremonies that might look odd to outsiders. In the Catholic church she attended as a child, people wore robes and took communion and talked about transubstantiation, wine and wafers becoming the blood and bones of Christ. Virgin births. Ascension. Annunciation.

But this still seemed weird.

One of the women at the front of the room spoke, but Kenzi couldn't follow a word of it. She wondered if it might be in another language. Or completely invented gibberish.

Someone must've understood, though, because the kneeling

women rose and the woman on the far end of the line stepped onto the dais.

And bent over.

The woman who appeared to be running the ceremony reached for a large wooden paddle.

Kenzi's lips parted. Michael had referred to corporal punishment, but surely…

The leader lifted the woman's robe and paddled her bottom. Repeatedly.

The woman swinging the paddle didn't pull her punches. The recipient didn't cry out, though it was obvious from her recoiling and twisted facial expression that she was feeling the impact.

But, Kenzi supposed, this was like putting out a flame with your fingertips. You felt the pain but didn't let it show. And this was supposed to demonstrate your…

She couldn't even think of a theoretical explanation for this. Schools had moved past corporal punishment, but people were still doing it—voluntarily—in Hexitel. Was this part of the master-servant relationship Maya had described? Was this how they demonstrated their subservience?

Or was this, as Crozier suggested, how Hexitel achieved coercive control?

It seemed like the spanking went on forever, though it was probably only ten or twelve swats. Enough to leave some bruises and broken blood vessels, Kenzi suspected. When it ended, the woman rose, as if nothing untoward had happened. And said the last thing Kenzi expected.

"Thank you, Master. If it pleases you, I will happily take more."

Okay, now this was turning into a twisted variant of the "May I have another, sir" scene from *Animal House*.

The woman bent over and endured five more swats.

When it ended the second time, the recipient rose more

slowly, stiffly. She was hurting, no doubt about it. Kenzi could almost feel her agony. Was she being punished for some Hexitel crime? Had she committed a heinous offense against the powers-that-be?

Apparently not, because Kenzi watched every single one of the robed women get swatted hard, one after another, until all nine had run the gauntlet. If nothing else, she admired their resilience and self-control. Not one cried out. Not one complained.

Afterward, they chanted more incomprehensible mumbling sounds, and then the ceremony appeared to end. The supplicants removed their robes. To Kenzi's astonishment, they all appeared ecstatic. Even joyous. Hugs were shared by all—including the woman who swung the paddle. Tears streamed from many eyes. They looked as if they thought they had achieved something wonderful.

This could suggest that Hexitel's self-actualization goals were succeeding, that these women were discovering their inner strength.

Or it could suggest that Hexitel had brainwashed them with coercive control. What else might an investigation reveal? More mind games? Ponzi schemes? Extortion? All of the above?

Kenzi had an obligation to represent her client. But if this group turned out to be too twisted, or she detected any potential harm to Brittany, she would have to give this representation a serious second thought. And she hated to do that.

Especially since she had given Maya her promise. And it would mean admitting her father was right.

CHAPTER FOURTEEN

KENZI QUIETLY CLOSED THE DOOR AND SLIPPED INTO THE FRONT lobby. She took a chair and waited patiently. She would act as if she had been sitting outside since she arrived. And hope they believed it.

A group of three women emerged first. They noticed her but didn't say anything. More followed and did the same.

Then the leader, the woman who had swung the paddle, emerged. She was older than the rest, maybe mid-fifties. With hair slightly graying and a beauty shop bun, she looked like a remnant of another era.

She stopped in front of Kenzi. "May I help you?"

Kenzi rose, smiled, and introduced herself. "I'm representing one of your members in her divorce. I was hoping I could talk to someone in authority."

"About what?"

"About Hexitel. I'm afraid my client's ex-husband is planning to use her membership in your organization against her. He's trying to take away her little girl."

"You're talking about Maya Breville."

"Yes. You know her?"

"Of course. And her situation is unfortunate, but—"

"We expect this to be a high-profile case. There will probably be a lot of publicity."

The woman's face soured. "These are not office hours. If you could come back at another—"

"Please. I'm already here. And I'm going to be in meetings for the rest of the week. This may be my only chance. If I go to court unprepared, the results could be disastrous. For everyone."

The woman rolled her tongue around in her mouth. She obviously didn't like this, and it wasn't just because she was anxious to go home.

But she acquiesced. "Very well. Follow me to my office. Let's not make this take any longer than necessary."

Kenzi followed her, promising to be brief.

After all, she didn't want to end up on the receiving end of this woman's paddle.

⸺

"HEXITEL IS A MULTI-LEVEL EXECUTIVE-TRAINING ORGANIZATION offering personal and professional development programs in a wide range of areas. For the most part, we provide small-group seminars and large-group awareness lectures."

Patricia Clare spoke with a crisp and slightly East Coast upper-crust accent. She positioned herself behind her desk, which forced others to gaze upon her enormous Wall of Ego— more framed awards, certificates, and photos with the rich and famous than Kenzi had ever seen assembled in one place before.

"Are you the founder of Hexitel?" Kenzi asked.

"Oh no. Our founder was Randie Salvador. Our first and only male Hexitel member. He saw the way women were mistreated, especially in the business world, and he wanted to do something about it. So he started this group."

"But he's no longer associated with Hexitel?"

"No." Her lips twitched. "He dropped out."

"I think I read somewhere that he disappeared."

Clare smiled. "I prefer to think he ascended. If anyone ever deserved to rise to a higher plane of existence, it would be Randie."

"Did you know him personally?"

"No, I was recruited to replace him after he left. But I know his work. He was an incredible human being. Such insight. Such vision. I believe he ultimately thought an organization for women should be run by women. And I can't disagree."

Kenzi slid into the chair opposite Clare's desk. "You call Hexitel an executive-training organization. But my client calls it a religion. And some, as I'm sure you know, call it a cult."

"That would be people who don't know what they're talking about. But in today's world, there are far too many people like that, aren't there? People who think cynicism masquerading as insight makes them seem wise. And so we have a populace that denies science and embraces gossip."

"To be fair, you do have some practices that seem a bit…cult-like."

"Only to the uninitiated."

"I'm told you require members to pay increasingly large sums of money to remain involved. I'm told there are master-servant relationships. I'm told you conduct…secret ceremonial rites. And the devotion of your members does suggest a religious fervor, don't you think?"

"Education, religion, cult. What's the difference? And so long as people benefit and no one is hurt…who cares? Labels are unimportant. Jesus was a great teacher. It was only after his death that others turned his teachings into a religion—which was originally a small cult—yes, cult—within the Jewish faith. It's simply a matter of perspective. The majority always applies ugly labels to those who choose a different path. Do you see what I mean?"

What Kenzi saw best was that Clare had dodged her question. "Maya showed me her tattoo."

Clare shrugged. "I have several tattoos. Many people in various organizations get tattoos. Fraternity members. People working on the same film crew. Today, it's like having a secret handshake. We don't require tattoos, but if people want to do it, I'm not going to stop them. What's the harm?"

"They're permanent, and some say disfiguring."

"A typical example of people trying to create drama where none exists. Are you sure you're not a journalist?"

"As an attorney, I have to be prepared for anything the other side might sling at us in the courtroom. These allegations against Hexitel are certain to arise."

"I suppose." Clare looked down wearily. "I wish people could be less...judgmental. More open to new ideas. It is the great conundrum. Everyone agrees this is a harsh, bitter world, and yet we resist anyone who tries to change it."

She supposed there was some truth in that. "I'm particularly concerned about what Maya told me about certain...exercises in domination. Anything that could be deemed coercive control."

Clare raised an eyebrow. Did she suspect Kenzi had seen their little ceremony? "We do nothing illegal. We do nothing without the consent of the participants."

"But consent can be coerced."

"And who's the judge of that? If I urge you not to eat the chocolate cake when you're dieting, have I exercised coercive control? Should I be arrested? We're only trying to help women better themselves. And we've had many dramatic success stories."

Kenzi drew some papers out of her satchel. She didn't really need them but thought Clare might open up more if she appeared to be churning through paperwork. "Maya has mentioned something about putting out a match with her fingertips."

Clare nodded. "A great exercise in self-control. We never let anyone take it far enough to do any serious damage to themselves."

"Any other exercises that could cause harm, even temporarily?"

"A few. But that's such a small portion of our work. Occasionally you need something dramatic to grab people's attention. To stir their emotions. Most of our work is traditional executive training. Out intensives are renowned all across the country. In the basic-training sessions, participants are immersed in instruction for two weeks, fourteen hours a day, with few breaks. It changes them. In a good way."

"What does that cost?"

"What does it matter? If it heals the damage that's been done to their soul, any price is cheap."

Well, not any price, Kenzi thought, and she couldn't help but notice that the woman had once again dodged her question.

"We help our members probe their deepest childhood memories. Often that's the source of the trauma that holds them back. We urge them to confront it, wrestle with it honestly, and overcome it. So they can move forward and become better people."

"You know these programs have been criticized. People call them mind control. You make people weak, hungry, sleep-deprived—and they're easy to manipulate."

"Why must we always assume the worst possible motivations? Imagine Christ trying to spread his message of universal love and peace, only to encounter cynics saying, 'Well, your followers are all poor uneducated fishermen. They're weak and hungry and thus easy to manipulate.'"

"I get your point. But I have to explore anything Maya's husband could use to take her daughter away permanently."

"Maya's a strong woman. She'll survive."

"You know Maya well?"

"Of course. Because of the spiritual nature of some of our teachings, we don't get many scientists. She's smart, well-spoken, educated. A great asset."

"For recruitment?"

"For strengthening our base. I expect she will rise to the master level in a short period of time."

Did that mean she got to swing the paddle? "I'm concerned that the judge may see red flags when he hears about Hexitel."

"Is he an anesthetist?"

Kenzi blinked. "Is he...what?"

"An anesthetist. That's what we call those who try to suppress our word. To impede our work."

"Your enemies."

"Not necessarily. Some people are just ignorant. Some have personal motivations, like members of the press. Others are jealous or fearful. And some object to our mission of promoting the advancement of women, so they try to dull people's minds. Put them to sleep. With lies."

"How do you deal with that?"

"When the anesthetists hit us, we hit back hard. And fast."

"No messing around."

"Of course not. I was a high-ranking Nazi in a past life."

Kenzi stared at her. Was she joking? "That reminds me of another accusation I've had to confront. Maya's husband claims she's been branded."

"If anything of that nature has occurred, it was done without my knowledge or consent."

Sounded like a canned response she'd given before. "Why would anyone do that?"

"Some see it as similar to tattooing. But demonstrating an even deeper commitment."

"He suggested she'd been branded in an intimate location."

"To demonstrate trust. Allowing someone to mark you where you're most vulnerable."

A shiver raced up Kenzi's spine. This conversation was creeping her out. "What would the brand look like?"

"I don't know. Again, this has nothing to do with Hexitel. Perhaps it's something Maya worked out with her wife."

There it was again. "Can you explain this wife business to me?"

"People are partnered shortly after they join the organization. Once they indicate true commitment. It's a spiritual relationship. People tend to do better when they have a partner, someone they can talk to. Confide in. Like the buddy system."

"And you call them wives?"

"Can you think of a better word? It's an all-female organization, remember."

"It could lead to confusion."

Clare shrugged. "We live in a world where most conventional marriages lead to divorce and wives are habitually mistreated and oppressed. I would suggest that the Hexitel definition of what it means to be a wife is far healthier than the one utilized in the outside world."

As a divorce attorney, she wasn't about to argue. "May I speak to Maya's wife? I believe her name is Candy."

"Not for me to say. Up to her."

"I need to be able to assure the court this organization bears no threat or danger to Brittany."

"I've never seen Brittany and Hexitel has never said anything about how the child should be raised or treated. We focus on professional skills, not parenting. We're spreading an important message at a critical time. Women are starting to wake up, but this #MeToo and #Time'sUp business is barely nudging the percentage of women in the workplace—or what they earn. We want to train women to fight. We want to train women to win."

"Sounds like you're building a political power base."

Clare barely smiled. "We're building an army."

CHAPTER FIFTEEN

KENZI GOT HOME LATE, BUT SHE STILL BELIEVED IT WAS important to fix dinner, even if she suspected Hailee could survive just fine on Sun Chips and Sparkling Ice. Though Kenzi was hardly a gourmet chef, she was competent in the kitchen. She preferred fresh ingredients, but thought dinner should never take longer than half an hour to prepare, which sometimes limited her options. Tonight it would be sweet potato salad in pita pockets, with a little garlic aioli and cucumber side salad.

Hailee wheeled up to the kitchen table when dinner was ready. She looked healthy and happy and gave her mother no grief about coming home late. Kenzi let her savor two bites before she launched into the mandatory mother-daughter convo. "You left your record player on."

Hailee smiled while chewing. "I know. Isn't it great?"

Kenzi attempted a weak smile. "Sounds kind of...old."

"Mom—it's Sam Cooke."

"I know. My grandmother used to listen to this."

"He was a genius."

"You know, just because you like vinyl doesn't mean you

have to listen to old stuff. What are your friends listening to? Phoebe Bridgers? Billie Eilish?"

Hailee pulled a face. "Here today, gone tomorrow. I prefer the classics."

"Where did you get these old records, anyway?"

"From Papa."

Meaning Kenzi's father. One way or the other, he was determined to sabotage Kenzi's entire life.

"By the way, Mom, your pitas are the bomb."

"Just something I whipped up fast. Done your homework?"

"Yup." Hailee set down her fork. "Okay, is that enough family chatter? Can we talk business now?"

Her daughter never failed to surprise her. "I did want to speak to you about something."

"Good. You go first."

"Have you heard of a group called Hexitel?"

"How could I not? They recruit on the internet."

"They do?"

"They're on the prowl. All over Twitter. And Instagram."

"They want teenagers?"

"Yeah. I think it's like smoking. If you hook people when they're young, they can't give it up. Hexitel says they're an educational group offering a wide range of college preparatory and professional seminars."

"Tell me you didn't attend any of those."

"Well…actually, I kinda did."

Kenzi almost rose out of her chair. "Why am I just now hearing about this?"

"It was no big deal. I was curious, and they offered an online session I could watch for free from my laptop, so why not? They don't tell you it's Hexitel upfront. They wait until it starts getting good. They say they use rational inquiry to facilitate your personal and professional advancement. Sounds promising, right? And then they want you to pay for a more detailed intensive. You get access to their exclusive manual that apparently contains all the secret knowledge you need to succeed in life. And they pair you with other people learning the same stuff."

"But you didn't sign up for it, right?" Kenzi leaned across the table. *"Right?"*

"What do you take me for? I already have friends. I don't need any assigned to me."

Kenzi exhaled and settled back into her chair. It was a great source of comfort to her that, despite all the obstacles her daughter had been dealt, she did have friends, and social contacts and clubs and most importantly a positive attitude and practical outlook on life. In fact, she probably exceeded her mother in those categories. "I can't believe they're going after kids."

Hailee shrugged. "Some of my friends could use a little personal development."

"Not this kind." Kenzi wiped her mouth with a napkin and described what she'd witnessed at the Hexitel office.

Hailee's eyes almost popped out of her skull. "They let someone spank them? In front of other people?"

"Without complaint or comment. And acted as if they liked it."

"Wow. Oh wow." Hailee bounced up and down in her wheelchair. "That is so radical."

"At least it wasn't a man doing the swatting."

"That does not make it okay, Mom."

"I know. But still." She hesitated before she proceeded. "You're my pop culture expert. Does this make Hexitel a cult?"

"I don't know. But it makes them spooky as hell. Don't go there again alone, ok, Mom?"

"Agreed." Unnecessary, but she was touched by her daughter's concern. "What did you want to talk about?"

"Actually, it's related. It's about your new client."

"Honey, I'm not allowed to discuss confidential matters…"

"Who wants you to? Like I want to hear about stupid old people divorcing each other and wrecking their lives. This is about my work as your social media manager."

Well, Kenzi thought, that does make her part of the legal team. Sort of. "What about it?"

"I don't know if you've noticed, but the KenziKlan is shrinking."

"I did my livestream today."

"Not from the spanky salon, I hope."

"Earlier. Why is the Klan shrinking?"

"To be blunt—Maya Breville."

"How could anyone on the internet know about Maya?"

"Come on, Mom, you can't keep secrets from the internet. Not these days." Hailee pulled out her phone and scrolled through screens. "There's a whole subreddit about Hexitel. Mostly posts from former members who 'escaped.' They know Maya and they know she's deep into it. Did you know your client has a wife?"

Kenzi's eyelids fluttered wearily. "Yes. I need to track that woman down and talk to her."

"Nobody online thinks your client has any business raising a child. In fact, they don't think she should be allowed anywhere near a child."

Of course, only losers and troublemakers would be posting gossip to online bulletin boards. "How much do they actually know? Hexitel may have a bad rap, and there may be some bad actors, but that doesn't make it a cult."

"Mom, you just witnessed a mass spanking. That's a short step from drinking the Kool-Aid."

"And this is affecting the KenziKlan?"

"I'm afraid so. Word is out that you're helping Maya get access to the child who, according to these posts, was put in the exclusive custody of her father by a judge for the child's own safety. Is that true?"

She tossed her head back and forth. "In a...vague sort of way."

"Look at the posts yourself. Some people in the KenziKlan feel disappointed. Even betrayed. You're supposed to be an advocate for women's rights."

"I'm representing the woman in this divorce."

"People are more concerned about the female child than the female cult member. Look at these numbers." She reversed her phone so Kenzi could see the screen. "It's not tragic yet, but your numbers are dropping. As your social media manager, I have to be concerned."

"Okay, manager, tell me what to do about it."

"Simple. Dump the client. Replace her with an Instagram influencer."

"I can't do that."

"Then settle the case. As quickly as possible."

"Tried that. Didn't work."

"Mom, you're not making this easier."

All at once, Kenzi slumped forward, head falling into the palm of her hand. "I don't know what to do."

"Better figure it out fast. You're going to need the KenziKlan and the free publicity they provide when you launch your new firm."

"I know, I know."

Hailee hesitated a moment. "I'm worried about you."

"Don't. I'll be fine. This is just business."

"That's not what I mean." Hailee rolled away from the table, then scooted closer to her mother. "Hexitel is the subject of several investigations. And yet, they leave their doors unlocked? While performing a corporal punishment ceremony? With no one posted outside?"

"What are you saying? That they knew I was coming? That they wanted me to see what I saw?"

A deep ridge creased Hailee's forehead. "I don't know. But there's more going on with these people than you realize. They're dangerous." Hailee drew in her breath. "And I think they've made you a target."

CHAPTER SIXTEEN

"Seriously? That's the best appointment you could get? Six-thirty in the morning on a cold rainy beach?"

Sharon cackled on the other end of the phone, though Kenzi couldn't see the humor. "You think I should accept?"

"Honey, I think you should drop this case like a hot potato."

"You and Hailee."

"Love that girl. She has good sense. Better than you sometimes."

"I can't quit now and you know it."

"There's always a way to dump an undesirable client. Would you like me to prepare a memo?"

"No." Withdrawing at a critical juncture might be unethical, plus it would give her father too much pleasure. "Just set up the meeting. I'll make it work."

"You got it, girl. I'll have some hot cocoa waiting for you back at the office."

KENZI WAS AN EARLY RISER, A HABIT FORMED YEARS BEFORE WHILE being raised by her workaholic father who rose at sunrise so he could run three miles before breakfast. She skipped the running, unless it was on a treadmill, but she still rose early. She didn't think it made her virtuous. It was just how her body worked. Even if she didn't get out of bed she wouldn't sleep any longer, so she started her day around 6:00, just as the sun crept over the horizon.

That said, she normally didn't attempt speaking to anyone other than her coffee cup until at least seven. Even Hailee knew better than to plan a big face-to-face chat early in the morning. The fact that Mom was awake did not necessarily make her a morning person.

Except today. Because this was her only chance to meet Candy Trussell, Maya's so-called wife, bright and early at Discovery Park. Candy seemed edgy about the whole situation, so Kenzi took what was offered. Which was why she was on the beach ridiculously early clutching a Venti Pike Place. Living near the birthplace of Starbucks should have some benefits.

Discovery Park was, in Kenzi's opinion, the best of Seattle's beaches—over five hundred acres on a bluff extending from the Magnolia neighborhood, and every inch of it gorgeous. You could see both the Cascade and Olympic Mountain skylines. Some parts of the Park had grasslands and even forests, but her meeting was supposed to take place on the north beach not far from the famous West Point Lighthouse.

After a few minutes of searching, she found a woman sitting in the sand, legs crossed. She had willowy blonde hair and a face that exemplified calm. Kenzi almost hated to disturb her. "Excuse me. Are you Candy Trussell?"

The woman's eyes slowly opened. "I assume you're the lawyer. Katie or Kathy or something."

"Kenzi. I appreciate you agreeing to talk to me."

"Maya thought it was important. Normally I won't talk

about Hexitel to anyone. It never goes anywhere positive, you know? I don't need that kind of negativity in my life."

"I understand. This is a beautiful place. Do you come here to meditate?"

"Yes." Slight hesitation. "This is where I meet my coven."

Oh my. This case just kept getting better and better.

"How can I help you?" Candy asked.

"Maya's husband is trying to use her involvement with Hexitel in the divorce. To gain exclusive custody of Brittany."

"About what I would expect. Michael has so much negative energy he could create an alternate universe. A very bad one."

"There are a couple of specific problems, and one of them I'm sorry to say relates to you. You and your relationship with Maya. How would you describe that relationship?"

Candy shrugged. "She's my wife."

There it was. "Can you explain what you mean by that?"

"I mean what I said."

"But you obviously aren't legally married to her. She's married to Michael."

"That's not a marriage. That's a legal obligation. The law has taken what's supposed to be a spiritual commitment and turned it into dollars and cents. Of course, that's what the government does anytime they get involved in people's lives."

"So…you and Maya…"

"We're both straight. At least, as far as I know."

"She doesn't call you 'Master'? She doesn't do chores for you?"

"We're equals in the organization. She has a Hexitel master, but it isn't me."

"And no sex?"

"Hexitel is not about fornicating."

"What is it about?"

"Sex magic."

Didn't she just say… "Can you explain?"

Candy rose, brushing the sand off her stretch pants. "Why don't we cut to the chase? You heard me mention my coven, though you had the grace to let it go, at least for the moment. Yes, I am a witch."

"Like...Sabrina?"

"Except real. And I don't cast spells. Except in the way that all women do. That's one of the primary lessons Hexitel teaches. That's why the group is restricted to women."

"Hexitel practices witchcraft?"

Candy punched Kenzi in the shoulder amiably. "That's what puts the 'Hex' in 'Hexitel.'"

"Is Maya a witch, too?"

"In a way. We came to Hexitel from very different places. She's a scientist. I'm Wiccan. Worlds apart. Would you like to stroll by the beach?"

Why not? A scenic view could only improve her mental state while absorbing incredibly bad facts certain to damage her client in court. And she did love the touch of sea spray. "So you're not a scientist like Maya?"

They strolled along the beach. "A Wiccan scientist? No. When I joined Hexitel, I was working as an exotic dancer."

"Oh. I'm sorry."

"Don't be. I loved it. I'm not ashamed of my body. I don't think any woman should be. I lead yoga classes at a local gym now, which is much the same thing. Banishing dysmorphia and being proud of how you look. Before, I felt an emptiness. A feeling that I wasn't in control. Because I wasn't—till I learned to harness my sex magic."

Splendid. "Tell me more about that. If you don't mind."

"As long as it's to help Maya, and not for your next tweet. Sex magic is about harnessing the energy inherent in all women and implementing it with a specific intention to produce a specific outcome."

"I thought sexual energy was for...you know...sex."

"Energy can be put to many purposes. You can channel it into self-gratification. Orgasmic manifestation. Or you can put it to more productive purposes. It's up to the individual. All magical practices are about what we want to do with what we have."

"And what do you want to do?"

"I want to be the best person I can possibly be. Hexitel is about self-actualization. You must've learned that by now."

"I have certainly heard that. Many times. But I also keep hearing about spanking and branding and...other activities that do not immediately suggest self-actualization."

"You need to unlock your brain. Break away from dated mindsets. Those old-school ways of thinking have produced the screwed-up world we live in today. We need new ideas. Fresh approaches. What you call branding is just a small incision with a cauterizing pen. But it demonstrates commitment. A turning point. A departure. A new beginning. Spanking is harmless, but it demonstrates a willingness to submit to a new way of thinking. Let me ask you a question. Are you religious?"

Back to that again. "I was raised Catholic."

"Okay, so you think our spanking is weird, while you celebrate the Passion of the Christ, which is basically the step-by-step torture and murder of a human being."

"I'm sure you can criticize—"

"I'm not criticizing. My point is that, despite its odd rituals and constant focus on the state-ordered execution of an itinerant teacher, billions of people have drawn comfort from your religion."

"Hexitel has been accused of mind control."

"Aren't most people influenced by their religion?"

"And there's a significant price tag—"

"Do you tithe to your church? Do they pass the collection plate?"

"Sure, but—"

"I'm sorry, but to me it looks like the old club criticizing the new, even though they aren't that different. I grew up in a Christian home, too. Toxic Christianity. Really did me some damage. You don't need the details, but it was rough. I thought I was filled with sin and headed for hell. I was in my mid-twenties before I stopped seeing a noose of eternal damnation dangling around my neck. I had to learn to survive without the support of an invisible messiah who never shows up and never does anything tangible."

Kenzi made a note. Do not put this woman on the witness stand...

"As an adult, I've tried to spread the word about the potential harms of raising children in organized religions. I'm all for spirituality, but nothing that's going to permanently damage the child's soul. Conversion therapy. Anti-LGBTQ programming. Racial bigotry—in a religion that supposedly worships a Jewish teacher."

"My daughter showed me some of your online posts."

"Not on Instagram. And you know why? Because I got kicked off Instagram. They closed my account. They said I was engaging in hate speech. Because I spoke out against organized religion. My message is about love and self-empowerment, while established churches preach racism and homophobia. And I'm the hater. This world is so messed up it makes me want to scream."

"Were you posting sexual content?"

"Probably. People are such Puritans. They want to think they're so holy. I'm proud of my body and I'm not afraid to show that, in words and photos. But the Christian dogma preaches that we should be ashamed of our bodies and pretend that sex doesn't exist, except in marriage, and even then we don't talk about it. In my coven and in Hexitel, we teach people to take pride in themselves, to embrace sexual healing, to understand that this is a gift and it should be used to improve the quality of life on Earth."

"But just to be clear, you and Maya are not and have never been sex partners."

"We've never even kissed, and yet she feels much closer to me than she does to her husband. We have something better. A higher, more fulfilling relationship. A joining of minds. Of spirits. She's my home. I feel safe with her." Candy sighed. "That's something your courtroom is never going to understand."

Probably right about that. "You have a tattoo, don't you?"

"Of course." She held up her arm. It appeared to be a mirror image of Maya's wrist tat. "We each bear half the image. When we're together, we're whole."

"And the brand?"

"Upper left thigh, if you must know. A cross surrounded by a circle."

"And an HX on your left shoulder?"

"Of course."

"Are the other members of your coven in Hexitel?"

"Many are, but not all."

"So you're also a pagan."

"You are really into the labels, aren't you?"

"I'm just trying to identify possible landmines in my client's case. Before they explode." She gazed at a seagull passing overhead. Beautiful. But she also knew gulls were scavengers. What appeared lovely on the exterior was often ugly on the inside. "I guess that's all I need to know for now. Thank you for your time. If necessary, would you be willing to testify on Maya's behalf?"

"Do you think that would be helpful?"

"I'm not sure. But I'd like to know I have you in reserve."

"If you think I can help Maya, I'll be there."

"I appreciate that."

Candy stopped walking. "Have you considered taking a Hexitel intensive?"

"Not really…"

"You'd benefit. You have a lot of sexual energy. But I think you're still searching for your corner of the sky."

"I have been thinking about making some…changes…"

"You'd be a fantastic exotic dancer."

"That's not what I had in mind."

"Well, you have to plot your own journey. Unlock your magic." She touched Kenzi on the shoulder. "I could help if you like."

Kenzi took a small step backward. "Are you offering to spank me?"

A sly smile crossed Candy's face. "It might start there. And who knows where it might lead?"

CHAPTER SEVENTEEN

THE SENTINEL STARED AT THE DOWNTOWN OFFICE BUILDING. Maya was visiting her lawyer. Again. Cause for concern? Perhaps. And yet, everything was proceeding according to plan. If plan was the right word.

Maya's house was quiet these days. Almost empty. Michael had split, taking Brittany with him. Kicking and screaming, but she went. Of course, the Sentinel knew where they were and had toyed with releasing that information to Maya. Or her new lawyer. Would make little difference in the end, but it would definitely stir up trouble. That alone made it desirable. Stir the pot. Generate energy. Keep the game going. Enjoy it while it lasted.

They were all going to die anyway.

Maya had come home late last night. Why? She'd never been good at keeping secrets and, ironically, this split had made her more transparent just when she needed to become less so.

Did she suspect? Did she have any idea? That she was being monitored, watched at all hours of the day? And so much more...

No. She'd stayed late at work, that was all. They had that

new Defense Department contract, but it was probably more a matter of working late because she had nowhere to go. You're not supposed to have an empty nest when your child is in grade school. It was tearing her apart. Coming home to the empty house was like coming home to a cemetery.

She would not be the first to feel that way.

These surveillance efforts had to be stepped up, even if there was little true cause for concern.

Thus far.

Michael had hired a woman in his church group to keep an eye on Brittany during the day, not that it was making the experience any better for the poor girl. She spent most of her time crying for her mother and telling her father to leave her alone.

Not a daddy's girl, to put it bluntly. Only in America could you find a court system that gave custody to a parent the child detested. How easily the law could be manipulated. Hire a good lawyer, let him scare the judge with insubstantial specters, and *poof!* Custody granted. To a deadbeat father with a long history of combustive violence.

Despite what must have been enormous temptation, Maya stood by her little cult. Religion. Professional empowerment group. Which label was most accurate? It was hard to stifle a laugh. Only the Sentinel knew what this group was. And how much power it could wield.

And yet, there Maya was, clinging to what little she had left, a white-coat research job and an expensive support group currently being investigated by the attorneys general in three states. She was nothing if not loyal. Loyal to a fault, one might say. Loyal to the point that she had put herself and her child in danger. The Sentinel assumed that, after she lost custody, she would drop off the face of the earth.

That was the plan, anyway.

One way or the other, Maya had to be eliminated. Preferably without eliminating her child, but nonetheless, it had to be done. Let her take the blame for everything, before, now, and in the future. That seemed the simplest path.

Maya would have a target on her back. As would all the people she worked with. And that internet-hound lawyer she hired. They all were in danger. The greatest danger, of course, was the fact that they didn't realize they were in danger.

The bullet that does the most damage is the one you never hear coming.

CHAPTER EIGHTEEN

KENZI LIVESTREAMED AS SHE CROSSED FROM THE PARKING GARAGE to the ground floor of the Rivera & Perez office building. She didn't have much to say, but Hailee had emphasized the importance of regular updates. Given what Hailee told her about her plunging following, she needed to do some damage control, quickly.

"Here I am, KenziKlan, sporting my bright blue Prada coat and matching scarf, ready to wage war on the entrenched white male forces that would tear a young child from her mother without so much as a preliminary investigation or allowing the mother to speak in her own defense. That's not how we're supposed to do things here in America. Maybe in a Communist country, but not here."

She barreled through a typical Seattle morning, misty and gray, talking as she walked. "Now listen up. I hear some of you are disappointed that I'm representing a woman who's in Hexitel. I know the trolls have been posting all kinds of information about that group, some of it patently false. Friends, don't be part of the problem. Be part of the solution. Don't believe everything you read in your news feed. Demand truth."

She took a deep breath and made a right turn at the corner. "I'm not saying Hexitel is perfect, but then, I don't understand the appeal of the so-called self-help industry. I think if you need help—help yourself. Pull yourself up and get to work. But don't dis the mother because you don't care for her religion. I can tell you two things for certain, and to me, they are the only two things that matter. Hexitel is not posing any danger to my client's child. And my client loves her daughter. You want to be outraged about something? Be outraged about a husband with a history of violence lawyering his way into custody."

Almost there. She needed to wrap it up.

"We have to stick together, KenziKlan. I've always been committed to helping women in need and that commitment will not waver. No mother should lose her child unless she's a proven menace—emphasis on the word *proven*. That's why we have courts. That's why we have lawyers, too."

She ended the stream and passed through the revolving doors into her office building.

Did saying all that in a livestream meam she believed it?

She hoped so. Because if she couldn't convince herself, how could she ever convince a judge?

"GIRL, ARE YOU PLAYING WITH ME? SHE REALLY SAID, 'UNLOCK your sexual energy?'"

"She said it."

"And—'orgasmic manifestation?'"

"You think I could make that up?"

Sharon waved her hand in the air, mock-fanning herself. "How did you keep a straight face?"

Kenzi smiled. "It took some effort."

"I don't know how you do it sometimes." Sharon placed some paperwork on the edge of her desk, then pushed the overloaded message spindle closer. "As you can see, there have been a few calls."

"People wanting me to handle their divorces?"

"No. People bitchin' and moanin' about the way you're handling Maya's divorce."

"How does everyone know what I'm doing?"

"One word. Internet."

"Yes, but how? Stuff doesn't go viral spontaneously. Someone has to start the fire. I've worked hard to build the KenziKlan. But I've never managed to ignite a wildfire like this." Her forehead creased. "And look how well I dress. It's not fair."

"I did notice the coat. Prada?"

"Good eye. Scarf too. I was going to wear a headband, but I was afraid it might be too much for the judge."

"Good call. Want me to toss these phone messages?"

"No. I'll try to talk some sense into them. If I have time. I'm meeting Maya and—"

"Before you do that." Sharon tapped a particular message. "You've been summoned by Daddie Dearest."

"Just the two of us?"

"Not sure. I saw our distinguished new managing partner enter your father's office earlier."

"They're ganging up on me."

"Theoretically, young Gabriel is now the boss. Maybe he's going to act like it. Or at least watch to see how it's done."

"I'll show him how it's done," Kenzi muttered. "Hold my calls."

She marched toward her father's office—and almost trampled someone in the process.

Papers flew into the air and tumbled to the floor. "Oh, I'm sorry."

Her apology was met with a glare. It was Emma Ortiz, the token criminal lawyer on the bottom floor. Hadn't seen her since the fateful partners meeting.

Emma looked put out, as if Kenzi had crashed into her deliberately. "Maybe try looking where you're going?"

"That could go two ways. What are you doing up here? I thought you never left your office."

"I'd rather never leave my office. But people keep insisting that I solve their problems." She paused. "Or steamroller me on their oblivious path to the next livestream."

"I've got a meeting with the managing partner."

Emma almost smiled. "Daddy calling you to the woodshed?"

"It's nothing like that."

"Gonna bend you over his knee and swat your backside?"

Ugh. Kenzi skittered past her without comment. Right now, spanking jokes didn't seem remotely humorous.

WHEN SHE ARRIVED, SHE FOUND BOTH FATHER AND BROTHER waiting for her, Dad in his overstuffed chair and Gabe standing at his side like a dutiful lieutenant. She felt as if she were walking into an ambush.

She wasn't far wrong.

Her father minced no words. "Explain yourself, Kenzi."

Something about his tone—or maybe it was words-plus-tone—set her teeth on edge. "I don't know what you mean."

"I instructed you to drop the Breville case. That was a directive, not a request. And you haven't done it."

"What do you know about the case?"

Gabe replied. "Exactly what everyone in the entire legal community knows about it."

He tossed down a copy of the weekly *Seattle Law Times*. She was several feet away but still close enough to read the headline just below the fold:

RIVERA REPS CULT LEADER.

Uh-oh.

Her father drummed his fingers. "Care to comment?"

"I never—"

"And don't give me your usual insolent defiance. I want real answers."

Kenzi leaned against the chair on the opposite side of the desk but refused to sit in it. She did not want to be comfortable, and she did not want to be placed in a subservient position. "In the first place, that headline is totally wrong. Hexitel is not a cult and Maya is not the leader."

"Stop nitpicking. Are you appearing on her behalf this afternoon?"

"Sounds like you already know that I am."

Her father threw himself back into his chair. "It's like you haven't heard a word I've said."

Oh, I heard them. I just didn't give a damn. "I can't drop out now. I have interviews scheduled this morning, then I'm picking up my client for the hearing."

"Are you at least going to win the motion?"

"You want me to help the cult leader?"

"I don't want you to be in the courtroom. But if you're going to be there, I damn well expect you to win. People will be watching. And reporting. The Rivera reputation is on the line."

"It will be a tough battle. But chances are—"

"Don't give me that odds-making crap. I'm not an insurance adjuster. Are we going to win?"

"It's...possible." She was never comfortable making predictions, and this case had already proven far less predictable than most.

"That's not good enough."

Gabe cleared his throat. "Our concern, Kenzi, is that an alliance with someone in a notorious cult could cause more desirable clients to go somewhere else. We have a reputation for catering to the finest families in Seattle. Tech giants. Corporate

CEOs. People who want the best and are willing to pay for it. We can't afford negative publicity."

"What makes you think this will generate negative publicity?"

Gabe pursed his lips. She could see this made him uncomfortable. It was just like when they were kids and their father would pit the two of them against one another. "Well, for one thing, I, unlike you, have actually read this article. And it's mostly negative. I've also seen what people are posting online."

Oh.

"Kenzi, you bear the family name. Whether you like it or not, you're an official representative of this firm. Your successes have helped us in the past. But your failures could do permanent damage. And this association isn't going to help us even if you win."

Her father nodded. "The optics are horrible."

Kenzi suspected that was the only hip phrase he knew, so he used it over and over again. "I'm more interested in substance than appearance."

"How noble. But sadly, when building a business reputation, appearances are everything. That's how you get the five-hundred-pound gorillas to write big checks."

She knew that was true. But she still didn't like being pushed around by two men. She wondered if her father would speak to Gabe this way. She would never know, because Gabe would never put himself in this situation. He was always Daddy's puppet.

"My first instinct was to send Gabe to the courtroom with you today."

Oh God. Anything but that.

"But then I thought, no, putting another Rivera in there would only magnify our involvement. But once the hearing is over, I want this client fired. If you can't do it, Gabe can."

"Let's see what happens at the hearing and—"

Her father cut her off, his voice rising to a near-bellow. "I don't give a damn what happens. After the hearing, you bring your client back to the office. I'll have the withdrawal forms prepared. Gabe will sit down with her and explain...something. We'll give her a good referral. She can be someone else's problem."

Kenzi felt a lump in her throat. "Dad...Maya is counting on me. Her daughter is counting on me."

"Stop being sentimental. This is a business, not a sorority function. You have to do what's right for the firm, not what makes you feel all warm and fuzzy inside. Successful businesses are not built by soft hearts."

"Daddy—"

"This representation ends today."

"Daddy—"

"The irony is, you thought you should be the managing partner."

That stopped her short. Gabe looked extremely uneasy.

"Let me tell you something, Kenzi. The managing partner can't be selfish or self-indulgent. People depend upon you. Employees. Their families. You can't be managing partner if you have no business sense."

"But Dad, if you'd just—"

"You heard me, Kenzi. That's the final word. I will not change my mind." He threw himself back again, head shaking. "Managing partner? If you don't get rid of this client—you won't be a partner at all!"

CHAPTER NINETEEN

KENZI CROSSED THE DRIVEWAY LEADING TO LOVELACE ORGANIC Research Enterprises (LORE) wondering where the lab was. Judging from appearances, she was approaching a hippie commune, or perhaps a macrobiotic farm. Why weren't they downtown like the other Seattle research firms? Did they need to be outside the bustle of the city to create this rustic home-spun ambiance?

The main building appeared to be a converted house, or perhaps farmhouse, with a red picket fence and a porch swing. She could see several other buildings behind it which she assumed were the actual labs, although they looked more like barns and stables—exactly what you might expect to see behind the farmhouse with the red picket fence.

She couldn't say she disliked it. LORE appeared to have replaced the austere antiseptic Star Trek hallways of the stereo-typical laboratory for something much more relaxed and accommodating. As she opened the front door, her nostrils were not inundated by the smell of ammonia. If she wasn't mistaken, she was inhaling incense. Did they have diffusers in the lobby? Was it built into the ventilation system?

A woman in her mid-forties awaited her. No white coat. Instead, the woman wore blue jeans and a flannel shirt. Of course, you could see that anywhere in Seattle. Maybe grunge was alive and well in the scientific community.

The woman did, however, hold a clipboard. At last. Some semblance of normalcy.

"I'm Maggie Price. Managing Director for LORE. You must be Kenzi."

"I am. Thank you for agreeing to meet me. Is Maya here?"

"She's inside her lab."

"Do you two work together?"

"Not exactly. I oversee all the projects."

"So you're Maya's boss."

"Basically. I'm in vaccine development. Maya works on defense contracts these days."

She didn't recall Maya mentioning that. "She makes weapons?"

"In a way. Most of the applied weapons work is subcontracted to a larger firm in downtown Seattle. Maya's done a lot of work on chemical accelerants that could be deployed in weapons, though. Or a million other ways, some of which might actually benefit mankind."

It was hard to miss the cynical note. "You don't approve?"

Maggie shrugged. "I know what an independent lab has to do to stay alive. There's no point in complaining. Someone has to pay the piper."

"Vaccine work must keep you busy these days."

"And how. This was a quiet little niche when I came to LORE. After the coronavirus outbreak, it became the most active sector of the firm. You know, Moderna used some of our work to develop its vaccine. In record time."

"I did not know that."

"We keep it on the downlow. Let others take the credit. Your partners remember that. Leads to more work in the long run."

Maggie glanced at her clipboard. "I understand you and Maya have a court date."

"Yes, but we have plenty of time. I was hoping to look around."

"That's why I'm here. I seem to have become the lab's Walmart greeter and tour guide. Follow me."

Kenzi could see evidence of a workplace—stacks of paper, laptops, and copiers. But they hadn't erected cubicle walls or put in fluorescent lighting. For the most part, the farmhouse still looked like a farmhouse.

"We have three research buildings," Maggie explained as they walked outside and crossed to the first of them. "But we've tried to maintain a consistent appearance. Our founder felt it was important that this did not become another sterile lab. It's like everyone wants to imitate *2001: A Space Odyssey*. Why? I wouldn't want to work in a place like that. Why not create a friendlier workplace, a more humane workplace, something people can look forward to seeing every day?"

"I give you points for innovative thinking."

"That's the difference between a business built by a man and a business built by a woman. Men worry about impressing people. They design offices to placate their inner insecurities. Women think about quality of life. They design offices to nurture the human beings who work there."

"I assume LORE was named after Ada Lovelace."

Maggie smiled. "Props to you. Most people think it's the name of our founder. I've even heard men snigger and suggest the lab was named for some porn actress. Yes, this firm was dedicated to the great Countess Augusta Ada King, Lord Byron's only child, brilliant in her own right, possibly the first programmer for Babbage's theoretical computer and absolutely the first to realize that computers had potential uses beyond calculating. But of course, since she was a woman, her achievements were ignored by history."

"Until now."

"Exactly. It's #MeToo time for historical figures, too."

Maggie opened the door and, true to her word, revealed a friendly, homespun lab. While Kenzi could tell it was a workplace and people were working, it reminded her more of a family hotel room than a lab. Lots of wood. Paintings on the walls. Excellent lighting. And the same incense she detected the first moment she entered the main building.

Maggie slowly strolled through the lab, occasionally waving at people and pointing out various stations. "This is where we do our energy-related research. As you probably know, that's booming. Entire countries have pledged to reduce or eliminate fossil fuels. President Biden has said he'll spend trillions developing solar and wind power. GM and others have promised to distance themselves from automobiles with dangerous emissions. But for that to work, we need to make serious technological innovations. Work out the kinks in solar power. Create electric cars that go farther and last longer without recharging. We're only a small part of this major lifestyle change, but we like to think we're doing our bit."

"If you're helping protect our planet, I'd say you're doing a great service, for this generation and the next. We all need to do what we can to fight climate change."

"Climate change. Right." Maggie made a scoffing sound.

"You...don't believe in climate change?"

"Depends on what you mean. The climate is changing. That's obvious. But historical records indicate that this is natural. The planet goes through cycles. There's no reason to believe humans have altered or even influenced this."

The scientist was a science-denier? "I thought there was no serious dispute about climate change in the scientific community."

"People are just afraid to speak up. They've been silenced by the mainstream media."

She might expect something like this from Crozier…but from a scientist? "I take it you don't work in this area."

"Heavens no. I'd rather be working with stem cells any day of the week."

Wait a minute. If she worked with stem cells, her opinions weren't coming from the religious right. "May I ask where you got your ideas about climate change?"

"It wasn't Fox News, if that's what you're going for. Look, I'm a trained skeptic. All scientists should be. I don't believe something, much less advocate action, until I've seen convincing and incontrovertible evidence. And so far, that hasn't happened."

Kenzi decided to let it go. Surprising, but probably not relevant to Maya's case. And she needed to make friends, not enemies.

They passed out of the first building and entered the second. The décor was essentially the same, but there were more people working here and the atmosphere seemed more intense.

"This is my building," Maggie said. "Like I told you, vaccine research has become our busiest and most profitable line of work. We're toiling around the clock to protect humanity from the looming viral threats that could potentially decimate the population. I'm proud to be part of this effort to prevent threats —real threats—from taking untold lives. The coronavirus vaccines were developed more quickly than any in human history. That's a result of many minds working together, scientists all over the world joining hands to achieve beneficial results."

A few minutes later, they entered the third and final building. Kenzi expected to find Maya here, but didn't see her. Maggie took her to Maya's station, but it was unoccupied.

"She's around," a woman sitting to the right explained. "Stepped out for a moment. I'm sure she'll be back soon."

Kenzi nodded. "Any idea where she went? We have an appointment."

"No. Sorry. I don't keep track of her movements. By the way, I'm Zelda. Zelda Blake."

"Nice to meet you. Kenzi Rivera."

"This is the end of the tour," Maggie said. "If you need something, let me know. Otherwise, I should get back to my office."

"Of course. Thanks for showing me around."

Maggie disappeared through the back door. Kenzi turned back to Zelda. "Do you work with Maya?"

"We work in the same area. We don't have any projects together. I'm actually new to this."

"New to LORE?"

"No. I used to be in the immunology department."

"Like Maggie. She apparently loves it."

"She would."

Kenzi's eyes narrowed. "Sounds like you didn't love it. Do you mind if I ask why? I'm representing Maya in her divorce and the more I know about her the better."

Zelda seemed hesitant to speak.

"I don't blame you for being reticent," Kenzi added. "But I'd rather hear about potential problems from you than hear it for the first time in court."

Zelda paused another moment, then spoke. "I had serious reservations about the vaccine projects. Especially when they went forward with stem cell work."

"Isn't that an essential part of modern immunology? I read that some of the early coronavirus vaccines couldn't have been created without it."

"True. But those were lab-grown stem cells, not embryonic stem cells. Not actual fetal tissue. Though to me, it's just as bad. We're not meant to create life, and that's what scientists are doing when they grow living tissue. But when the world is running scared, it loses its moral compass. I think using stem cells of any kind is immoral. I mean, we might as well start doling out abortions. It would amount to the same thing."

Didn't seem like the same thing to Kenzi. "Are you religious?"

"Devoted Baptist. Turned my life over to Jesus Christ years ago. You?"

"I was raised Catholic."

"Oh."

There was something about the sound of that monosyllable that Kenzi severely disliked.

"The Pope disapproves of stem cell research, right? And you have to believe whatever he tells you to believe?"

"I wouldn't put it quite like that..." Kenzi knew better than to start comparing religions. No cheese down that mousehole. "But I'm surprised to hear how strong your religion is. Maggie just told me scientists only believe what's supported by evidence. No one is ever going to prove the existence of a religious deity."

"That's where faith comes in."

"Does that work in the lab?"

Zelda smiled. "I'm not going to ask the Defense Department to pony up for a faith-based weapon. But my faith sustains me and gives me strength. Evidence would weaken that. It would make faith irrelevant." She turned her eyes downward. "I don't mean to preach, but I believe I should witness whenever I have the opportunity. I've suffered from depression my entire life. Sometimes I've had...dark thoughts. At one point, I was at the end of my rope. Jesus brought me back from that. He's the only reason I can get up in the morning."

"Then I'm glad you found the faith you needed. And I know how controversial stem-cell research is. I'm surprised you're the only one who objected to using it."

"I'm not. We've had many complaints. Even threatening letters." Zelda rifled through her desk till she found what she sought. "This is a photocopy of a letter we received from something called Christians for the Sanctity of Human Life."

Kenzi took the letter and quickly scanned it. "Seems to be threatening you with the wrath of God. Literally." She noted some of the key passages. "Sinners will burn in eternal torment." "We must purge sin with the fires of righteousness." The name beneath the signature block was Bonita H.N. Hall.

"May I keep this?"

"Sure. I have it on my hard drive."

"Has Maya seen it?"

"I assume so. Why?"

Kenzi hesitated. "I get the idea that you don't like Maya very much."

Zelda looked away. "Look, if you're her friend, I don't want to say anything rude."

"I'm her lawyer. And I need to know everything. What's your problem with Maya?"

Zelda drew in her breath. "I take motherhood seriously. It's a holy appointment. And I can't approve of…Maya's approach to child raising."

This was the last thing Kenzi needed to hear when they were mere minutes away from an important custody hearing. "What is it you don't approve of?"

Zelda's voice dropped to a whisper. "You know she belongs to a cult."

"I know she's in Hexitel."

"Do you have any idea what they do?"

"I know Maya considers it her religion, so shouldn't we respect the choices her faith has made?"

Zelda pulled a face. "Surely you're not suggesting that cult is a legit religion. Her poor little girl will be a train wreck if she's raised around that crowd."

"Do you have any reason to suspect Maya has done anything…inappropriate with her daughter?"

"I have more than a suspicion." Zelda was still whispering. "I know she—"

"*Kenzi*! I didn't know you were here."

Kenzi jerked her head around.

Maya stood right behind her.

"Zelda was filling me in on all the lab gossip," Kenzi explained. "Seems like you've got a lively workplace."

Zelda scooted away, lips pressed tightly together.

Kenzi checked her watch. "We should leave now. I'll brief you in the car."

Maya led the way out of the building. Kenzi followed.

But as she did, she wondered what Zelda had been about to tell her. And worried.

CHAPTER TWENTY

KENZI DROVE HER LEXUS WHILE MAYA SAT IN THE PASSENGER seat.

"The judge will likely want to deal with at least three pending matters," Kenzi explained. "While he has us all together."

"Will I be able to see Brittany? That's all I care about."

"That is definitely not *all* you care about. But opposing counsel has agreed to have Brittany nearby."

"Then I'll get to see her?"

"Maya, I don't want to promise anything that is not in my control. I can guarantee that I will try my damnedest to get this emergency order rescinded. And I'll ask for a mother-daughter meeting in any case."

Maya pressed her hand against her forehead. Her face was wet. "I can't stand this. Who knows what he might do to get even with me? She's not safe."

"I know that. And very soon, the judge will know too."

"I remember the day Brittany was born," Maya said, gazing out the passenger-side window. "I promised her I would protect her. I would never let anything happen to her."

"And we won't. We—"

"She depends on me!"

"I know, Maya. I know. We'll make sure she's safe."

Kenzi tried to hold it together and drive. She wondered how she'd feel if Hailee's loser father suddenly appeared and tried to snatch their daughter. Not that he ever would. But the thought of Hailee in his hands would be enough to drive her over the edge.

"I never should have married him," Maya continued. "I knew it even when I did it. But I was a homely nerdy thing. Men never paid the slightest attention to me. I was so shy, I barely knew how to talk to anyone, especially boys. Science became my safe place because I couldn't deal with the real world. Science was dependable, predictable, logical. Like I thought I was. Till Brittany came along."

"And now she's your safe place."

"Yes." Maya pressed a hand against her chest, as if struggling to breathe. "We have to get her back."

Kenzi shifted the discussion to the hearing. "In the courtroom, you need to remain composed. You don't have to become a robot, but don't get excessively emotional, and above all else, don't get angry. You must appear calm and stable, a reliable parent."

"Michael is the one with a temper."

"And if I get a chance to draw that out, believe me, I will. But the judge will be watching you, trying to evaluate whether the other side's claims have any legitimacy. You have to be Mother of the Year."

"I can do that. If it gets my Brittany back."

"One slip and it will be all too easy for the judge to let what is sadly the status quo remain in place until we get to the divorce trial. Anything negative I should know in advance? Anything you haven't mentioned yet?"

Maya sighed heavily. "I was fired."

Kenzi nearly swerved into the next lane. "*What*? When did this happen?"

"Today. Just a few minutes ago."

And Maggie didn't even mention it during that entire guided tour. "Why were you fired?"

"The usual. Religious bigotry. Someone complained that I was acting weirdly and trying to recruit Hexitel members at work. Probably Zelda. She hates everyone who doesn't believe what she believes. But for some reason Maggie trusts her."

"Were you recruiting?"

"Absolutely not."

Kenzi clenched the steering wheel. "Maya, this is disastrous. If you're unemployed when the trial rolls around, your chances of getting custody drop dramatically. You need work."

"I know. I tried to tell Maggie that, but she wouldn't listen. Made me want to rip her eyes out."

"Please don't. That would not be helpful."

"I've already started looking, I'll have something before the trial starts. Promise."

"Is there any way we could turn this into a good thing? Like maybe you left LORE as a matter of principle?"

"What principle would that be?"

"I understand some religious organization has protested against your lab's work with stem cells. Maybe you also objected?"

"No, I don't have any problem with that. In fact, it was my idea. But I'll still get my girl back, right? *Right*?"

She hated to make promises, but if she didn't she feared Maya would completely crumble and the hearing would be a disaster.

She reached a hand across and patted Maya's shoulder. "We'll get Brittany back. One way or the other."

JUDGE BENETTI'S COURTROOM WAS ON THE SECOND FLOOR. IT was a small courtroom, but family court rarely attracted large crowds. The court clerk walked to her desk followed by the stenographer, which told Kenzi the judge would not be far behind.

Kenzi nodded at Crozier as she passed him.

"Given any more thought to what I said?" he asked.

About the case, or his job offer? She assumed the latter. "No. Been too busy."

"Don't wait forever."

"News flash. I have a court hearing coming up."

He grinned. "I don't think this will take long."

Judge Benetti entered the courtroom a few minutes later. His hair was gray and thin and he seemed lighter than when she'd seen him last. He moved deliberately, swishing his robe. He dumped a tall stack of paperwork on his bench. She got the impression he was in a grumpy mood. Which was unfortunate. Because this hearing was not likely to do anything to improve his temperament.

"Okay. *Breville v. Breville*. Action for Divorce. One child, custody in dispute. We appear to have three pending matters." He paused, scanning the paperwork. "A discovery dispute. Always love those. And a predictable request for attorney fees. And a challenge to the emergency protective order. We'll take up that one last, as it's likely to take the longest time to resolve. Do the parties plan to call witnesses?"

Both Kenzi and Crozier nodded.

"As I suspected. So that one comes last. May get kicked to the afternoon." He stacked his papers and bounced them against the bench till they made a perfectly squared bundle. "Let's start with the discovery. Mr. Crozier, I believe this is your motion."

Crozier rose. "Yes, your honor."

"Do you have any idea how much I despise discovery disputes?"

"Yes, sir. I have appeared before you on many occasions."

"Then I would think you'd know better."

"Your honor, in this case, I have no choice. This discovery relates to a serious threat to the child. I'm speaking about the mother's involvement with a dangerous cult."

"Oh yes, I remember. She's wrapped up in that…what's it called again?"

"Hexitel."

"What is that, like witchcraft or something?"

"They do have many supernatural beliefs and…outré rituals."

"Chickens? Do they sacrifice chickens?"

"Uh…not to my knowledge."

"Good." He swished his jaw around. "I love chickens. Couldn't abide anyone hurting a poor defenseless chicken."

Okay, now she was worried. Benetti not only looked older, but was acting way way older. She wasn't sure of his exact age but thought he was well past sixty. Was senility creeping in?

"What's the discovery you want?"

"All documents pertaining to the mother's involvement with the cult—"

Kenzi rose. "Your honor, I object to the repeated use of the word 'cult.' My client considers this her religion."

Judge Benetti peered at her as if he were having difficulty focusing. "She considers a cult her religion?"

"She doesn't consider it a cult. It *is* her religion. Is Catholicism a cult?"

"Of course not. I went to Catholic school when I was a lad. Do I look like a cultist?"

"No, sir. And neither does my client."

Crozier interrupted. "But there are reports that Hexitel may be involved in dangerous activities."

"And the Catholic church was behind the Spanish Inquisition. It's still a religion. We have the First Amendment in this country, your honor. No one can be punished because they subscribe to a religion."

The judge raised a finger. "That's not quite accurate. Everyone has the freedom to choose. But if those choices are hazardous, the child should be moved to a safer environment."

They appeared to be arguing the ultimate motion. She tried to pull it back to the discovery matter. "Your honor, this a fishing expedition. They're using this to harass my client and pry into her personal life."

"Unfortunately, that's what happens in divorce court. No way around it."

"May I add something?" Crozier asked. "Ms. Breville's personal life *should* be investigated. For the sake of the child. This cult is bad news, not only for the people in it but for their children. We have a right to pursue this line and to conduct discovery so the court can be fully and fairly apprised of any dangers."

"This isn't about the child," Kenzi said. "This is about their desire to sling mud."

"I can assure the court that is not so. I don't want to protract this or make it any uglier than it needs to be. In fact, we've already instigated a settlement hearing, though sadly it was not successful."

He instigated the settlement hearing? "Your honor, my client has never—"

The judge raised a hand, cutting her off. "I've heard enough. I always take a liberal approach to discovery and this will be no exception. Better to err on the side of doing too much than too little. This motion will be granted. Your client will provide the requested documents."

"But your honor—"

The judge looked cross. "Don't interrupt me, missy. Don't ever interrupt me."

"I'm sorry, but—"

"There is no but. Now be silent and listen. I've been charged with the safety of a minor. Believe me, there is nothing more unpleasant than having to choose between parents, knowing full well how harmful a bad choice could be. I want to know everything there is to know about this Hexitel outfit. I don't care what word we use to describe it. Many people think it's dangerous. And if that proves true, you may rest assured I will do everything imaginable to protect this child from those dangers. And the parent who brought those dangers to bear."

CHAPTER TWENTY-ONE

KENZI LOOKED SIDEWAYS AT HER CLIENT. MAYA LOOKED STRICKEN, and she could understand why. Technically, the judge had ruled on the discovery motion, but it sounded like he'd already made up his mind on the custody motion, and they hadn't even argued it yet.

"Very well," Judge Benetti said. "What's next?"

"That would be my motion." Crozier replied, an almost sheepish expression on his face. His voice dropped to barely more than a whisper. "I haven't been paid since this case began."

Judge Benetti's expression was somewhat akin to an "Aw, poor baby." "And you're telling me this for a reason, I assume."

"I've filed a motion for attorney fees."

Judge Benetti rustled through the papers on his desk, resembling nothing so much as a grandfather trying to locate his car keys. "I think I have that somewhere." His hands seized a thin document. He exclaimed in triumph. "Yes. So your client wants the little lady to pay his bills?"

"Yes, sir. She was the primary breadwinner for the family. By agreement. He looked after their child and he is still doing so. It's a fulltime job."

"If I may," Kenzi said, cutting in, "this arrangement was not so much by agreement as necessity. My client's husband has a college degree but he's had trouble holding a job. He's supposedly still looking."

"And what is this young man's field?"

She cleared her throat and tried to sound as non-judgmental as possible. "He's also a scientist, but he hasn't worked in years and has never held a job for long. He has a temper—"

"I'll ask counsel not to testify," Crozier said, drowning her out.

The judge squinted at Crozier. "So your out-of-work science boy can't find anything?"

"It's a tough market, your honor."

"Can he wait tables?"

"Not with a little girl at home."

The judge made a harrumphing sound. He obviously didn't like it but kept his thoughts to himself. "I favor the American rule. Everyone pays their own way."

Nonetheless, Kenzi knew some judges obliged lawyers the second they intimated that they hadn't been paid. Part of the old school attitude—in the legal world, we all stick together.

"In most cases," Crozier said, "I would support that. But here we have an extraordinary situation. A devoted househusband has been forced to file for divorce because he's concerned about the safety of his daughter. He couldn't wait till he found a job. He had to act immediately."

"He's only entitled to fees after he proves he cannot pay and the opposing party can," Kenzi replied. "He has done neither. It wouldn't matter if my client were Jack the Ripper. He doesn't get fees unless he proves need."

The judge turned to Crozier. "Are you prepared to present evidence on this point?"

Crozier squirmed, which was an answer in and of itself. "I

was hoping that wouldn't be necessary, your honor. We haven't completed discovery."

"Just to be clear," Kenzi said, "we oppose this motion. His client may have absconded with the child, but my client has always paid the bills. If the husband can afford to put the child up in an undisclosed location, he must have some money. Maybe we should file a claim for compensatory damages."

The judge nodded. "The little spitfire does have a point, Lou."

Wait. Was she the spitfire? She wanted to be flattered, but she was pretty certain the judge would never call anyone male a spitfire.

"Your honor," Crozier said, "I can assure you my client is struggling to make ends meet. He's been denied access to the household bank account—"

"There is no household bank account, your honor. There never was. The parties have always maintained separate accounts."

"Well, my client's cupboard is bare."

The judge's shoulders heaved. "I don't want that little girl to starve."

"I've seen no evidence of starvation," Kenzi said. "Or any deprivation whatsoever. If the girl needs a good meal, bring her to her mother. They can have a supervised lunch date. My client has always provided for that child and she will continue to do so in the future."

Crozier looked irritable. This wasn't turning out to be as easy as he'd anticipated. "What is it my esteemed colleague wants? Honestly, your honor, this is callousness of an unprecedented degree."

"So you say," Judge Benetti said, "but I still don't see any supporting evidence. It appears you are not prepared to meet your burden of proof at this time. Perhaps we should revisit the issue at the pretrial."

Crozier cleared his throat. "That's fine, your honor."

Kenzi almost smiled. Sure, that's fine and dandy. He didn't want to be paid anyway.

"And that leaves us with the custody matter," the judge continued. "I have read the briefs submitted by both parties."

"Your honor," Crozier said, "the mother belongs to a cult. End of story."

"It's not a cult," Kenzi insisted. "It's a religion. As I've explained. And there is no evidence that my client has endangered her daughter or done anything improper or illegal. Certainly nothing remotely close to the magnitude of offense necessary to remove a child from her mother."

"Sure," Crozier said. "And Charles Manson didn't commit any murders. Does that mean he wasn't dangerous?"

"This is hardly—"

"Osama bin Laden didn't fly any planes. I guess he wasn't dangerous either."

"Your honor—"

"The fact is, your honor, cults are dangerous. Whether you're the ringleader or the pawn, the potential for danger is immense. Cults thrive on coercive control, and no one has more power to coerce than a parent. Who knows what she might be planning? Cults are always looking for fresh blood. Hexitel actively recruits young people on the internet. They can't survive without new members. Young members."

Kenzi felt her blood rising but tried to keep it in check. When she got mad, she did not do her most persuasive arguing. "I am appalled that my opponent would stoop to comparisons of this nature. There is no evidence whatsoever that my client has ever done anything that might be harmful to—"

"Do we have to wait until the damage is done before we take action? Is the court aware that the cult has branded this woman?"

Kenzi felt woozy. "It's...more like a tattoo."

"A tattoo inflicted with a cauterizing pen. To an extremely intimate part of the anatomy."

The judge pursed his lips. "I knew some sailors who had tattoos. No mothers, though."

"Tattoos are colorful and ornamental," Crozier said. "This brand is a scar on the high upper thigh. The official logo of the Hexitel cult."

Kenzi felt herself floundering. "None of this suggests harm to the child."

"Is counsel delusional? If this woman will allow herself to be mutilated, what won't she do?"

"Your honor, my client would never harm her daughter. She would die before—"

"She might delude herself into believing cult involvement is to her daughter's benefit. And before you know it, the girl has been mutilated too."

The judge shook his head. "Still, to remove a child from the custody of her mother requires a showing of actual—"

"Did your honor realize this mother also has a wife?"

The courtroom fell silent for a protracted moment. "A...wife?"

"That's what they call their female partners. In the cult. They swear a vow, basically a wedding vow, pledging eternal faithfulness to another woman."

Kenzi tried to keep her voice steady. "It's a purely symbolic commitment. Kind of like the buddy system."

"They use the word 'wife.' And we all know what that entails. Your honor, err on the side of safety. The trial date will come soon enough. In the meantime, let's make sure this girl remains secure."

The judge appeared conflicted. "But—if the mother is the only parent currently employed—"

"Actually," Crozier snapped, "the mother is also unemployed. She just lost her job at LORE. Because of her cult involvement."

A deep ridge creased the judge's brow. He turned toward Kenzi. "Is that true?"

Damn, damn, damn. "It's more in the nature of a downsizing…"

"That's it, then." The judge reached for his gavel. "I see no reason to change the current arrangement."

Kenzi's heart sank. *No, no, no!*

"The emergency custody order will remain in place. The court finds that there are sufficient grounds for leaving the child with her father pending a full adjudication of all pending matters."

All at once, Maya rose to her feet, tears streaming. "Judge, I haven't seen my little girl in days! I don't know what Michael—what he—" She broke down, unable to say more.

Kenzi laid a hand on Maya's shoulder and gently guided her back to her seat. "I won't ask the court to change its ruling. But could my client at least have a…ten-minute visit? I understand Brittany is somewhere nearby."

The judge turned toward Crozier. "Is that acceptable?"

Crozier nodded. "Ten minutes. Supervised."

"You may do that in the conference room adjoining my chambers. Right now. Ten minutes, after which, the child will be returned to the custody of her father. I will see you all again at the pretrial."

He slammed down his gavel. "Court is adjourned."

CHAPTER TWENTY-TWO

KENZI TRIED TO STAY CALM, BUT IT WASN'T EASY. AS A DIVORCE attorney, she was accustomed to dealing with litigants who had strong feelings. But nothing like this. Never anything like this.

Both mother and daughter were swimming in tears. She wasn't sure who looked more traumatized and she supposed it didn't matter. This mother and daughter loved each other very much, had been separated against their will for a long time, and didn't want it to continue.

Kenzi had been charged with ending this torturous situation. And she'd failed.

Brittany wrapped her arms around her mother's neck, clinging as if dangling from a precipice. "Please don't make me go back with him. I want to be with you."

"I know, sweetie. I know." Maya's voice choked so much she could barely speak. She wiped her eyes and nose. "But the judge wants you to stay with your—your father." Her breath cut out. Kenzi could see how hard she was struggling. "At least for now."

"I don't like it with him. I hate that place. It's out in the woods and I don't have any of my stuff."

Where was that? She could hire a detective to find out, but

then what would she do? It wasn't as if she could barge in and grab the child. The judge had ruled.

"Maybe your father will let me bring over some of your things."

"He won't." Michael stood in the corner, arms crossed. Was he entirely unmoved by this? How was that possible? It had to irk him, seeing how fond they were of each other, seeing that his daughter considered time with him akin to captivity. "Make a list of what you need, Brittany. I'll go shopping."

"I don't want new stuff. I want *my* stuff! I want Maddie!"

"Maybe later. Not now."

So the impoverished unemployed dad was offering a shopping spree?

Maya glared at her husband. Her anger was barely contained, raging behind the eyeballs. "She needs more mommy time, Michael. It wouldn't hurt you. You could be there with me."

"The judge gave you ten minutes. And seven have expired. Don't waste the final three talking to me."

How could anyone be so callous? Even by divorce-court standards, this was extreme nastiness.

"You got lucky," Maya spat back. "If I hadn't lost my job, this wouldn't be happening."

"Don't kid yourself, Maya. Your problem isn't me or your job. It's that damn cult."

A frown crossed Brittany's face. "What's a cult?"

Maya pulled Brittany's head close to her chest. "Daddy doesn't like Mommy's friends."

"I don't like Daddy's friends," Brittany shot back. "They're creepy."

For the first time, Kenzi butted in. "What friends are you talking about?"

"This is none of your business," Michael growled.

She ignored him. "Who are these friends?"

Brittany clung to her mother. "Daddy took me to this place that has weird people coming over all the time. I don't like them. They keep asking me if I've been saved."

"Saved from what?"

Brittany shrugged. "I dunno. I just want them to leave me alone."

Maya whirled. "What's going on, Michael?"

His face hardened. "You have two minutes left."

Maya turned back to her daughter, hands on tiny shoulders. "Honey, I want you to listen to me. I need you to be my tough girl. I know you don't like this. I don't like it either. But it won't last forever. I swear it."

"I want to go home with you!"

"You will. But not today."

"Please!"

"And I want you to keep a close eye on your father. If he does anything…weird, or anything that makes you uncomfortable, or his friends do, tell me about it. First chance you get."

"I want to live with you!"

"That's what I want, too. You remember the story I read you at bedtime when you were littler? About the Kissing Hand? Well, I'm kissing your hand right now." She did. "That's Mommy's kiss, and it will stay with you wherever you go. And whatever happens."

"Time's up," Michael barked. "Thank God."

He reached for his daughter. She squirmed away.

He gritted his teeth. "You're making this harder than it needs to be."

"That would be you," Maya muttered. "Watch your back, Michael."

"What's that supposed to mean?"

"It means I will do anything—anything—to get my daughter out of your clutches."

"Right." He struggled with Brittany. She fought him every inch of the way. "There...is...no point in fighting!"

Brittany kicked him in the shins.

"You little—" He raised his hand—then froze.

Three pairs of eyes stared at him.

If only she'd been videoing this, Kenzi thought. But sadly, phone photography was forbidden in the courthouse.

"Just—come," he said, giving Brittany another sharp tug. The girl tumbled toward him.

"I'll see you again, honey," Maya cried. "Soon."

"*Mommy!*"

And then she was gone, vanished behind a closed door.

Maya's face could not have been wetter if she'd just stepped out of the shower. Kenzi strode over to her and, without even thinking about it, wrapped her arms around her.

Maya could barely speak. "He took my baby. He took my baby."

"I will get your daughter back," Kenzi said. "I don't know how. And I don't know how long it will take. But I will not rest until you're holding her in your arms."

CHAPTER TWENTY-THREE

Kenzi knew Asian takeout was the laziest way to put dinner on the table. On the other hand, she was exhausted, and the Pho from Little Saigon was one of the key reasons Seattle was known as an Asian food Mecca.

Hailee listened to a full account of Kenzi's day. LORE, Maggie, Zelda, Maya, the hearing. The ten-minute meeting with Brittany. If anything, Hailee was even more disgusted than she was. "What can't they just share custody?"

"They could. Michael doesn't want to."

"I remember you told me once that husbands are always assholes during divorces."

"Watch your language. And yes."

"Isn't that why we have judges?"

Kenzi sighed. "Judge Benetti is of an older generation. Very old. Crozier convinced him that Hexitel is a bunch of immoral pagan perverts."

"No, that's QAnon. Crozier's pals."

"He's making Hexitel sound almost as bad."

Hailee took a deep scoop from her Pho bowl. "To be fair,

they are weird. But not weird enough to take a little girl from her mommy."

"Let's talk about something else. Is my Twitter audience still in decline?"

"'Fraid so. Not dropping as dramatically as before, but there's still significant attrition. Someone on Reddit said Hexitel members are all witches."

"Actually, that may be true."

"Practicing witches. Brides of Satan. Someone posted on your Twitter stream that you were helping Satan seduce his next generation of sex slaves."

"What?"

"A perfectly logical conclusion to draw from you representing Maya in divorce court."

"I don't think you understand the meaning of the word 'logical.'"

"So people are posting hateful crap. Saying you should be banned from child custody cases."

"Maya might be better off if I were."

"Don't be silly. You're a great lawyer."

"You just say that because I'm your mother."

"No, I say that because you took a case no one else would touch. And Grandpa is giving you all kinds of grief about it." Hailee wheeled over and gave Kenzi a hug. "I'm proud of you."

"Thanks."

"But we've still got to do something about your numbers. Jeez, eighteen thousand followers? That's pathetic."

Her little media manager. Always on the job. "We can focus on that after I win this case."

"Is that even possible?"

"Of course it's possible. I just have to figure out how. I need to get Maya out of Hexitel and rehabilitate her rep. Focus on her parenting. The fact that she's supported Brittany for—"

Her phone buzzed. Maya. Probably thought of some more ugly things to say about her husband.

She glanced at Hailee. "I know I made a rule about taking phone calls during mother-daughter dinners…"

Hailee smiled. "Just answer it."

She did. "Maya, what's—"

"Kenzi, I need your help. Can you come now?"

The edge in Maya's voice conveyed extreme urgency. And there was so much background noise it was hard to understand her. Sounded like a siren, and several people speaking at once, and…some sort of crackling. "What's going on? Where are you?"

"I'm near my office. I mean, former office. LORE."

Why would she be at the lab after she was fired? "What's happening?"

"It's burning." She was obviously having trouble talking. Her voice sounded scratchy and she was coughing. "All four buildings are on fire."

Kenzi felt a hollow feeling in her gut. "I don't understand."

"Please come. I don't know what to do. The police have arrested me."

Kenzi's eyelids closed. This was not going to help the child custody battle or the divorce case. "They arrested *you*? What's the charge? Arson?"

A long silence elapsed before Maya replied. "No. Murder."

TERROR TO EVILDOERS

CHAPTER TWENTY-FOUR

As the Sentinel watched the flimsy buildings burn, it was impossible to suppress a smile.

They say Nero fiddled while Rome burned down. A dubious claim, since the violin had not yet been invented. But the point was, one did not have to suffer from schadenfreude to enjoy this illuminated tableau. Misery for others might be perfection for the one manipulating events behind the scenes.

The dominos were collapsing, one after another, tumbling toward an inevitable conclusion. The demise of the status quo. The end of the tyranny. And who would rise from the ashes?

The Sentinel. The leader of the new epoch.

Let the woman who endangered years of work take the blame. That would eliminate Maya, once and for all. She made it all too easy.

The girl would suffer, and that was unfortunate. But parenting was far from perfect. It was hard not to recall all the ugly things Father shouted, all those years ago. Loser. Quitter. Sinner. Seemed pathetic now. Father's ego was so large he couldn't see beyond his own success. Anyone who didn't follow in his footsteps was substandard. Ironically, he worked eighty hours a week and was never appreciated by anyone. Never loved. Died alone in a nursing home. Sure, he made a lot of money, but at the end of the run, no one cared. Was that success? Was that the highest and best endgame?

The Sentinel would be loved. All across the globe.

But one step at a time. Still many obstacles to eliminate.

Had fortune smiled? Yes. Didn't fortune always smile on the worthy?

Now it was simply a matter of capitalizing on current events. Striking while the iron was hot, to use one of Father's favorite cliches.

The Sentinel stayed far enough back to avoid attracting attention, but close enough that, with the aid of high-powered binoculars, everything could be seen. Everything could be watched. The fire department appeared to be gaining control over the blaze, though at this point little could be saved. Paper would be ashes. Experiments would be ruined. And bodies would be cinders.

At the far left, a new vehicle moved toward the embankment where police cars were sheltered. Who would be crazy enough to come here? No one would visit unless they had a good reason...

A petite dark-haired woman stepped out of a Lexus SUV.

It was the lawyer. Kenzi Rivera.

By God, she would not ruin—

Stop. Deep breath. Calm.

So what if the lawyer was here? Of course the lawyer was here. Her client had been arrested. It wasn't as if she could do anything. The bigshot divorce lawyer was hardly likely to descend into the grimy world of criminal law. She liked celebrities and the one percent, not real people. She liked profiteering off human misery, not defending criminals. This case was now officially too tacky for her aristocratic firm.

Rivera was talking to the arresting officer, agitated and

angry. The officer didn't appear much impressed. With an inferno blazing around them, this Latin loser must seem like the lowest item of interest. Perhaps she would be permitted to talk to her client. If not now, then at the jailhouse. Rivera would have to change out of her designer clothes before she went near that joint. For that matter, all this smoke wouldn't do her any favors. She would have to burn her clothes after tonight. Maybe invest in a long tub soak with a lot of bath bombs...

Was Rivera actually yelling at the officer? That took some chutzpah. And a strong set of vocal chords. Unlikely to accomplish much, though.

Still, this woman must be watched. Not underestimated. Not just when everything was falling into place.

Maya would spend the rest of her life behind bars. Perhaps her lawyer could join her.

Or a more permanent solution could be arranged.

Why not? The smile returned. It had happened before. And worked spectacularly well.

CHAPTER TWENTY-FIVE

OVER THE COURSE OF HER LEGAL CAREER, KENZI HAD ENDURED many unpleasant client conferences in many unpleasant venues. In her first year of practice, she'd represented an elderly woman who insisted Kenzi meet her at the beauty shop. Seriously? And there was the woman who insisted that Kenzi come to her ranch on Bainbridge Island and ride horses while she told the sad story of her ruined marriage. Still had saddle sores from that mistake. And what about the woman she had to talk down from the ledge of the Museum of Pop Culture because she believed Paul Allen was using telepathy to read her mind?

All memorable. But this conference had them all beat. She was trying to have an important meeting against the backdrop of a blazing inferno—noisy, hot, smoky, and intimidating—with police surrounding them, a client in tears, and the absolute certainty that the days ahead were going to be worse than she had imagined.

She felt as if she'd entered a scene from Dante's *Inferno*. Even though it was late and no stars were visible, the area was as bright as day, not because of the sun but because of the burning buildings. LORE in flames.

She covered her mouth with a scarf and tried to navigate the confusion. The officer in charge, Major James McConnell, had agreed to let Kenzi talk to her client. He warned them that the conversation would be brief, but at the moment, he was too busy dealing with the blaze to haul Maya back to the station. He seemed hostile from the start for no apparent reason—

And then she realized why he looked so familiar.

Kenzi had represented his ex-wife during their divorce. He, of course, had recognized her immediately.

And if she, given those circumstances, could persuade a cop to do anything for her, she was Lawyer of the Year.

Maya wrapped a black wooly blanket around herself. She didn't need it for warmth. They were all sweating from the heat and she didn't appear to be in shock. More in the nature of a security blanket, Kenzi suspected. She noticed Maya clung to it with both hands.

"We don't have much time," Kenzi said. "Tell me what happened."

"Not much…to tell." Maya struggled to speak, and it wasn't just because of the smoke. "I came to clear out my office. A few minutes after I left, the buildings were on fire. I watched, wondering if there was anything I could do."

"Did you call 911?"

"Eventually. They already knew. I walked to a convenience store on the far end of the front lawn. Across the street." She pointed. "Got some water, then returned. The police arrived shortly after that."

"They say you were hiding."

"I was sheltering. I didn't want to go up in flames. My car is here and it could be traced. What would be the point of hiding?"

Maya had thought it all out. Was that good or bad? "The police say your boss, Maggie Price, died in the fire. Apparently they found her corpse."

"Maggie tended to work late. She was usually the first one in and the last one out. Zelda works late sometimes, too."

"Why did the police arrest you?"

"I guess they think I set the fire."

"Yes, but why? The fact that you're in the vicinity might create suspicion. But they wouldn't charge you unless they had more."

Maya's shoulders heaved, then cratered. She had a hollow look in her eyes.

"What is it? Spill."

Maya looked up but didn't speak.

"Maya, I cannot help you unless you level with me."

Maya covered her mouth with the blanket, then spoke, barely audibly. "The police found chemicals in my car."

"What kind of chemicals? Incendiary?"

"They could be used to start a fire, yes."

Her legs felt wobbly. "Maya, if—"

"I didn't do it. I would never do that."

"Then why did you have—"

"I got fired, remember? I was told to clean out my office."

"You had chemicals in your office?"

"I…took home some of my experiments."

"Did Maggie know about this?"

"Of course not. She said all our work is owned by the company that pays our salary. Like we're work-for-hire, basically. Which I consider immensely insulting."

"Did you sign a contract?"

"Yes. I had no idea—"

"No one ever does." Kenzi's mind raced. Lawyers were supposed to simplify cases. This one got worse with every passing second. "So you stole your experiments."

"I've been working on some of those for months. One for more than a year. Do you think Maggie would continue them after I was gone? More likely she'd trash them to make space for my replacement's work."

"You still didn't have the right to take them. We could've initiated some kind of arbitration or...something."

"This seemed simpler. I'm sorry. It was a mistake. An error in judgment."

"Do you have any idea who set this fire?"

"I didn't see anyone."

"Who would have a motive?" She'd managed to excise the word "else" before she spoke.

"There's a religious group that's been harassing us."

"So I've heard. Anyone else?"

"You should see where Michael was tonight. See if he has an alibi."

"Why would he burn LORE down?"

"To frame me. To make sure he can keep Brittany forever. And if I go to prison, he'll get control of my money, too."

"I'll check it out. Anyone else?"

"Have you read some of the hateful things people have posted about me on the internet?"

Thanks to Hailee, she had. "I'll have my social media expert run a search and see if anyone online is bragging or taking credit for this."

"Sounds like a good idea."

She looked her client straight in the eyes. "Tell me the truth. Did you have anything to do with the fire? Was this some sort of...revenge plot that got out of hand?"

"I would never do anything like that. I'm not a violent person. Hexitel opposes violence of all types."

Major McConnell was giving her serious stink-eye. She suspected they didn't have much longer to talk. "Maya, I'm not going to minimize this—"

"I know I'm in trouble. I need help. Will you represent me?"

"You mean—on the criminal charges? I'm not a criminal lawyer."

"I don't care. A lawyer is a lawyer, right? I trust you."

"No, this is a murder charge. You need someone with expertise handling—"

"I don't want an expert. I want you."

"Maya—"

"Please!"

Kenzi bit down on her upper lip. "It's not that I don't want to help. I just think it would be a titanic mistake."

"I'm begging you. I—I don't think I can handle much more of this...constant...misery." Her voice cracked. "I know I can't handle it alone."

Kenzi peered into those eyes and felt her heart breaking. How would she feel if someone tried to take Hailee from her? How lost would she feel if she were charged with a murder she didn't commit?

"All right. I'll do it. Short term. Until we work something better out."

Maya wrapped her arms around Kenzi. "Thank you." She felt tears dripping onto her neck.

"But I'm going to consult an expert. Immediately. It would be complete malpractice if I handled this for a single minute without co-counsel."

"That's fine. Just—" Maya wiped her nose and eyes. "Thank you so much."

Major McConnell edged between them. "Sorry, but I have to end this. The firefighters have this blaze under control. I need to take your client back to the station and book her."

"Five more minutes. That's all—"

"I've already given you too much time. Most cops wouldn't let a lawyer anywhere near a suspect until they'd been booked."

"But still, if I could just—"

"You're not hearing me." He took Maya's blanket and slipped handcuffs around her wrists. "She's leaving now."

Kenzi followed the officer as he led Maya to his car. "I'll come by the jailhouse tomorrow afternoon and see if there's anything you need."

"Do you think this will impact the custody hearing?"

Was she serious? Bad enough she was in a group some people called a cult. Bad enough she'd lost her job. Now she was accused of setting fire to a scientific complex and killing someone in the process. What part of that did she think would help her get custody?

"I'll do my best to mitigate the damage. But right now, we have to make the murder charge our first priority. I'll ask for a continuance on the divorce case."

"I don't want a delay."

"We have no choice. Can you imagine how it will look if you come to a custody hearing with murder charges hanging over your head? If the marshals escort you into the courtroom in coveralls and chains? We have to get the criminal charges dismissed. Unless that happens...I'm sorry, but you have no chance of getting custody."

"But Brittany hates living with her father!"

Yes, Kenzi thought grimly. But she wouldn't be permitted to live with her mother in prison.

CHAPTER TWENTY-SIX

KENZI DID NOT OFTEN VISIT THE LOWEST FLOOR, THE subterranean depths, what she and her colleagues often called "the basement" of Rivera & Perez—but this morning, it was her first stop. Since this was primarily a divorce firm, and the divorce lawyers were all upstairs, the denizens of this floor were sometimes thought of as second-class citizens. A juvenile attitude, to be sure. But what else was new? Lawyers were the most cliquish people in the world, and the Basement Lawyers didn't sit at the same cafeteria table as the cool kids.

The office door was only slightly open, but she could see through the ubiquitous glass wall that the lawyer was in. She knocked quietly on the door. "Emma?"

The raven-haired lawyer was at her desk, hunched over a thick document, red pen in hand. Her short, layered hair wrapped around her oval face. "Come."

Kenzi stepped inside. The shades were drawn and the overhead light was off. The only illumination emanated from a candle, while an electronic diffuser filled the room with the scent of Tea Time. "Sorry to interrupt." Her eyes swept the room. "How can you work in here? It's so dark."

Emma sat back in her chair, lips pursed. "I like it this way. Is that a problem?"

"Your door was closed."

"The diffuser is pointless if the door is open. And I concentrate better without the constant hallway noise."

"Seems unfriendly."

"I'm okay with that." Kenzi noted that Emma was dressed almost entirely in black. If she were a decade younger, people would call her emo. "Did you come for a reason?"

"I haven't spoken to you in ages. Maybe I thought it was time for a girlgab."

"Uh huh."

"It's possible."

"It's possible that Bigfoot is on Mt. Rainier. But I doubt it."

Kenzi pulled out a chair and took a load off. "What's with the attitude? Have I done something to offend you?"

"No. You haven't done anything to me. Or with me. In forever."

"What about when we were on that...that committee together?"

Emma tucked in her chin. "That was in high school."

"And your point is?"

"Come to think of it, you mostly ignored me in high school, too."

"I was two years ahead of you. And busy."

"Busy being the flashy superstar. The pretty girl who attracted all the attention and got everything she wanted. I studied harder and made better grades. But you were the one the teachers adored. All flash, no substance."

"I'm sure some of the teachers loved you too."

"No. Never."

"But we worked well together. I remember. We were like—"

"Oil and vinegar?"

"I was going to say, partners-in-crime."

"And now, years later, even though I made much better grades in law school, wrote for the Law Review and graduated Order of the Coif, you have the flashy office near the boss and I'm in the basement."

"That's because you didn't want to handle divorce cases."

Emma sighed. "This is about your Hexitel case, isn't it?"

Kenzi hated to be so transparent. But it would be pointless to deny it. "Maya needs help. The divorce and custody fights were bad enough."

"But now she's facing criminal charges."

"How did you know?"

Emma swerved her desktop computer monitor around. "Because every online news engine carried the story. Some variation of: CULT MOMMY CHARGED IN FIERY MURDER. I suspected it was just a matter of time before you came to see me."

"Maya didn't do it."

"Of course not. None of your clients are ever guilty. Coincidentally, neither are mine."

"I don't need cynicism. I need assistance. Judge Benetti agreed to put the divorce on hold while we work out the criminal charges. He's probably secretly hoping she'll be convicted, which will make his decision on child custody much easier. But because of the dueling jurisdictions, he issued a memo requesting that the criminal case be fast-tracked."

"You can object to that."

"On what grounds? Slow down, because I have no idea what I'm doing?"

"Cop a plea. The DA doesn't want a high-profile case during an election year. Washington abolished the death penalty a few years ago. Offer ten years and settle."

"I don't think Maya did it."

"Shut up."

"No, seriously. She's innocent."

"Just happened to be at the scene of the crime with a car full of flammable chemicals?"

Seemed the DA was already building his case—with the press. "She was there to gather her belongings because she was fired."

"By the woman she murdered?"

"Someone else started the fire, Emma. She thinks it was her husband."

"That tracks. But I don't see a jury buying it unless you have a ton of evidence."

"Then help me. Divorce cases are bench trials. I've never appeared before a jury in my life. I have no idea how to convince jurors of anything."

"And you think I do?"

"I…thought you handled criminal matters for our clients."

"True. There are sometimes issues ancillary to the divorce that need to be resolved. But I hope you won't be shocked when I say we haven't had any murderers—until now. I don't think we've even had a serious non-drug-related felony."

"I'm sure you can handle this."

"But why would I want to?"

"Because that's why we keep you here."

Emma tapped her pen on the green desk blotter. "Who's 'we,' kemo sabe? Last I heard, you didn't get the managing-partner position you obviously expected."

"But I'm still a partner."

"So am I."

"Oh, technically…"

"What does that mean?"

"This is a divorce firm. And you're…"

"Not in the ruling class?"

"Not one of our top moneymakers. But it doesn't matter. I need help."

"Obviously. That's the only reason you're speaking to me."

"I need someone with experience in criminal law."

"You would be better off referring this to another firm. What about Berber & Smirnoff?"

"Maya wants me to handle it. *Please* help."

"Let me give you a brief education. Yes, I handle criminal matters for this firm. But that rarely involves actual courtroom appearances. Most times, my work is closer to what you might expect from a private investigator. And I don't mean the hard-boiled Raymond Chandler-type private dick either. I don't carry a gat and I don't call women 'ripe tomatoes.' I just dig up information."

"Like what?"

"Like a salacious detail that will encourage settlement. Amazing how reasonable husbands become when they think they might face criminal charges. And these days, evidence of sexual harassment is better than evidence of embezzlement. Spouses back down fast when they know their career could be destroyed by a few accusatory tweets."

"How do you obtain these salacious details?"

"Social engineering."

"I'm not following."

"That's the current trendy term. It means disguising your true identity and tricking people into giving you the information you want."

"That can't be legal."

"To the contrary, so long as I don't pretend to be a cop or a federal officer, there are few laws against lying. And no laws to protect the stupid from their own stupidity. So I pretend to be putting together a #MeToo documentary to get women to spill their stories about the boss sexually harassing them. I pretend to be an accountant to get the location of someone's offshore bank accounts."

"This sounds way too sleazy for Rivera & Perez."

Emma laughed out loud. "You have no idea."

"Meaning?"

"We didn't become the most prominent Latinx-controlled firm in Seattle with sunshine and lollipops."

Kenzi felt some serious irritation building. "So you're a glorified con artist. What do you do when you need documents to back up your claims?"

"More often than not—hacking."

"You mean on computers?"

"Haven't met a firewall yet that I couldn't get past, given enough time."

"Is that legal?"

Emma flipped her hair back. "Depends on the circumstances."

"Meaning no."

"Meaning, if you get the goods, cyberterrorism will be the least of your target's concerns."

"And you do this here? From this office?"

"I wish I could. But people are getting more protective of their files. The smarties leave sensitive information on stand-alone computers that have never been networked and thus can't be accessed through the internet."

"Then how—"

"By visiting their offices. Copying sensitive information."

"You mean, stealing sensitive information?"

"Pro tip. Remove the hard drive from the computer before you copy it. Computer logs and USB ports leave a trail."

"You break into people's offices and steal stuff?"

Emma smiled a bit. "There is a reason I usually wear black."

This conversation wasn't going at all as Kenzi expected. "Look, this is interesting, but what I need is a good criminal lawyer I can partner up with. I've never tried a criminal case."

"Neither have I. I've settled dozens of criminal cases. Before trial."

"I don't think Maya is going to plead out. No matter what they offer. So are you going to help me or not?"

"That is my role here. If you have a criminal matter, and you're too foolish to farm it out, I have to help. But let me warn you—I will advise, but I will not be lead counsel. I will not speak in court. I haven't made an oral argument since law school and I hated it then."

"But—"

"C'mon, Kenzi—you love being the center of attention. You're the internet superstar. And you're about to get more attention than you've ever had in your entire life. I'll tell you what to say. You say it."

"So you're Cyrano and I'm Christian?"

"Good analogy. Maybe you were paying attention in high school."

"Occasionally." She pulled out her phone and started making notes. "Okay, what happens first?"

"Arraignment. Don't sweat it. Just plead not guilty. You're not going to get bail. Many states have abolished money bail, but sadly, Washington judges can still charge people for freedom. Washington does not, however, require a grand jury to indict, which will speed the process along. The prosecution is required to present all exculpatory evidence to the defense. I'll consider what pretrial motions we might bring, but given that the case has been fast-tracked, you should focus on the trial. You must convince a jury of twelve that the prosecution did not meet its burden of proving your cult momma set fire to her workplace and killed her boss."

"How do I do that?"

"I have no idea. But I'll start investigating."

"Okay. Thanks." Kenzi realized her heart was palpitating. A murder trial? Never in a thousand years had she expected to be in charge of something like this. Divorce court was brutal, but at the end of the day it was mostly about custody and money.

This was about life and death. "I'm—really not sure I can do this."

"You'll be fine. With me propping you up."

"How can you be sure?"

"Things haven't changed that much since high school." Emma smiled. "You're the flash. I'm the substance."

CHAPTER TWENTY-SEVEN

KENZI STOPPED BY SHARON'S DESK BEFORE SHE RETURNED TO HER own office. She was not surprised to find she had messages waiting for her—but on this occasion, there were so many Sharon had been forced to break out a second spindle.

"Are any of these messages I want to return?" A wave of despair rushed over her as she glanced at the stack. Every passing moment convinced her she was in over her head.

"Probably not," Sharon replied, typing, texting, and talking simultaneously. "Most of them are from media agencies, so you're under no obligation to reply."

"I have no interest in making press statements."

"You may want to reconsider that, girlfriend. You lose the media war, you may lose the jury. The DA has already released a statement."

"The DA? The actual DA? Shel Harrington?"

"The big man himself."

"Doesn't he have better things to do?"

"He knows this is about to become a firestorm and he wants to get in front of it."

"Surely there are more important news stories."

"More important? Sure. But sexier? Not so much. We got a violent fiery murder allegedly committed by a canned mommy on the rampage. Throw in a cult and you've got a story that's likely to lead the news until the zombie apocalypse."

"I wish people would stop talking about the cult. It's the least important aspect of this case."

"Are you sure about that? The reporters aren't. Where have you been?"

"Down below. Recruiting help."

Sharon's eyebrows rose. "From the reclusive Ms. Emma Ortiz, Esquire?"

"I need someone who knows criminal law."

"So you and she are going to work together?" Sharon looked down, shaking her head and pursing her lips. "This is gonna be interesting."

"I'll make it work. Since I have no choice." She grabbed her messages. "Hold my calls. Cancel my appointments. I'm going to be holed up in my office all day getting a grip on this case. But I want to go to the jailhouse and check on Maya before visiting hours end. So no distractions until—"

Sharon pushed out her hand in the traditional Stop position. "I'm afraid you don't have the luxury of hibernation."

That sounded ominous. "What do you mean?"

"You've been summoned. Daddie Dearest calls."

THE MAIN THOUGHT IN KENZI'S HEAD AS SHE MADE HER WAY down the corridor was: Why aren't I being summoned by Gabriel? Isn't he supposed to be the managing partner now? Was his appointment purely ceremonial? Her father still appeared to be running the shop. Gabe probably got the donkey work, but Alejandro Rivera still held the reins.

She didn't bother to knock. She had been summoned, after all. "Look, if you're going to hassle me because—"

She stopped short. Though her father sat behind his desk, both of the chairs on the other side were occupied. On the far end, Lou Crozier sat with a Cheshire Cat grin on his face. And unless she was mistaken, the man in the other chair was…

"Shel Harrington. Our distinguished district attorney," her father explained.

Harrington rose and extended his hand. He was tall. Seriously tall. She guessed about six foot four, which meant he was almost a foot taller than she was. The height probably helped him stay thin and the salt-and-pepper curly hair helped him look younger than she suspected he was. Judging from his powerhouse grip, he worked out regularly, too.

"Good to finally meet the daughter of my longtime comrade. Congratulations on all your success."

"Thanks…"

"Please don't take anything I said in that press statement personally. We have to take a strong stance against violent crime. I'm sure you understand."

She didn't understand at all, since she hadn't read the press statement. Her brain was racing to keep up. She didn't understand why she'd been dragged into yet another ambush. Her three primary opponents in life were all gathered in one room. Wonderful.

"Kenzi," her father said. "Shel came over this morning to speak to me because we're old friends. I've had the pleasure of contributing to his campaigns on more than one occasion."

"And I haven't forgotten that," Shel said, retaking his seat. Since there were no more chairs, Kenzi was forced to stand. "Which is why I came to speak to you personally. I'm hoping we can resolve this matter without damaging anyone's professional reputation."

"I very much appreciate that," her father said.

Now she was beginning to see which way the wind was blowing. The Good Ol' Boys Network Rides Again. Or in this case, maybe it was the Over the Hill Gang.

"And you?" she asked Crozier.

He chuckled. "I'm a little surprised to be sitting here myself, given the rivalry between our firms over the years. But that's business. Professional rivalries have nothing to do with friendship. And I consider your father my friend."

"I return that sentiment," her father replied. "The reason Shel came to see me this morning, Kenzi, is that he's worried about you."

Please. None of these men were here to help anyone other than themselves. When did any closed-room gathering of men ever do anything but help themselves?

"This business with the Breville woman has gotten out of hand. This is a case we should never have taken in the first place, and just for the record, you were instructed to get rid of it"—her father glanced at Harrington to make sure he understood this—"but that's water under the bridge. We're going to get rid of it now."

"We're going to abandon a woman who's been locked up on a bogus murder charge?"

Her father drew in his breath. "We're going to resolve the situation."

"My client believes the arson was engineered by her husband so he can retain custody."

Her father's expression was not quite an eye roll…but he definitely exchanged a meaningful glance with Crozier. "That's an interesting story. But the police have her dead to rights."

"They've barely begun to investigate."

"We've almost finished our investigation, actually," Harrington said. "And I can tell you we have not the slightest doubt about your client's guilt. If we did, we wouldn't press charges."

"Sure. No one innocent ever gets wrongfully accused in this country."

"Not this time. The evidence is overwhelming."

"I'd like to see that evidence."

"And you will. In time. But the point of this visit is to see if we can save everyone a lot of heartache. And…embarrassment."

"If you have a plea offer, you should have come to me."

"Now hold on, Kenzi," her father said. "Maya is a client of this firm, not just you."

"I'm handling her case."

"The firm is representing her. And I'm the head of the firm."

"I thought Gabriel was the head of the firm."

This time, he really did roll his eyes. "Stop being difficult. Can't you see that Shel is trying to help you?"

"No," she said. "I don't see that at all."

The men exchanged exasperated expressions.

"And before you proceed," she added, "I object to opposing counsel in the divorce case being present for this. He has nothing to do with the criminal charges."

"At this point," Harrington said, "they are inextricably bound. So I'm proposing a universal solution."

"Which only makes sense," Crozier added, using that voice that always set her teeth on edge. "At this point, the custody battle is effectively over. Your client has been charged with murder."

Kenzi's lips tightened. "Using threats of criminal charges to gain an advantage in a civil case violates the Code of Professional Conduct."

"That is not what I'm doing. How about you just listen for a moment?"

"I don't think you're saying anything I want to hear."

Crozier shook his head, shifting his gaze to her father. "I have a daughter much like this myself."

Her father nodded sympathetically. "Boys are easier."

"Amen to that."

The only thing she hated more than a bunch of men deciding what was best for women was a bunch of men talking about her as if she weren't in the room. "Could we possibly get back to the case?"

"Look," Harrington said. "Lou and I put our heads together and came up with a deal that I think works best for everyone."

"Meaning it saves you a lot of work and gives you everything you want."

"The public wants your client convicted. I'm sure I would get more political capital from sending her away for life. But I'm willing to make an offer that is not in my best interests."

"Out of the kindness of your heart?"

"Out of friendship. Now would you be quiet for one moment and listen?"

They were treating her like a sassy five-year old girl who needed to be scolded by one of the Catholic school nuns. And she deeply resented it.

Crozier spoke. "Here's the deal. In the divorce, my client gets custody. That's a foregone conclusion. Your client is going to prison and the only question is how long. There's no way a woman in prison can win a custody battle. As to the marital estate, if we go to trial, given that your client is going to prison and will have no financial needs, we could claim a right to everything she possesses. But we won't. We'll ask for sixty percent. A little extra, given that Michael will be raising their child alone. But we'll leave your client something so she can rebuild her life when she's released. We'll put it in a blind trust. Might be worth quite a bit when she's released."

"Is that all?"

"On the criminal matter," Harrington said, "I'm offering to reduce the charge to negligent homicide. We'll pretend the fire was set accidentally. Your client will get eight years."

"Eight years in prison for a crime she didn't commit?"

"She could be out in six with good behavior—and me pulling a few strings. Which I'm willing to do."

"Not going to happen."

Her father slammed his hand on his desk. "Kenzi, for God's sake, listen. Your client could get life."

"With no chance of parole," Harrington added. "Seattle takes a dim view of murderers. We like our city to be attractive to tourists and entrepreneurs. Lurid crimes stories are an unwelcome aberration."

"I will not agree to this."

Harrington turned his eyes to the other side of the desk.

Her father cleared his throat. "The thing is, Kenzi...I already have."

"On what authority?"

"As the head of this firm. And your brother is in full agreement, so don't bother raising that canard. You work for me and under me. I don't like to interfere in other people's cases, but I do have the right and sadly, you've forced me to exercise it. I told you to ditch this case and you ignored me—at your own peril. So I'm taking matters into my own hands."

"Don't you have to run this by the client? Does she get any say in whether you accept this appalling offer?"

"You know full well that we're ethically obligated to take all settlement offers to the client."

"She won't accept it."

He looked at her with eyes that could cut steel. "I was hoping you would make her see the light."

"You were hoping I'd recommend a bad deal? So you could avoid some negative publicity? Or stroke a political ally? That's not going to happen."

Harrington spoke in a low-pitched whisper. "Ms. Rivera, you might find political allies are a good thing to have. Especially if you intend to continue dabbling in criminal matters."

"Maya will never accept any deal that leaves her with no hope of seeing her daughter for years. If ever."

Harrington shook his head. "Then she's making a big mistake."

Possibly. But Kenzi was not going to be intimidated by this all-male death squad. "My client says she didn't do it and I believe her. And since she didn't do it, I doubt your case is as ironclad as you're acting. I think you're bluffing, Mr. Harrington. I think your case has evidentiary holes, which is the real reason you're offering this deal. You've attracted a lot of publicity and you're going to look like a fool if you lose. So you're trying to buy us out."

"Kenzi," her father said, "I am still in charge of this firm, and I will—"

"Not do a damn thing. You can't force Maya to take the offer, and you can't force me to drop the case. You're all bluff and bluster. But listen up." She whipped her head around. "All three of you. I will not let this smoke-filled room screw over my client. The women of this world have been pushed around by men like you long enough. Time's up, assholes."

She gave Harrington her flintiest expression. "Bring it on, Mr. District Attorney." She leaned in as close as she could without kissing him. "Let's do this. And let the chips fall where they may."

CHAPTER TWENTY-EIGHT

EMMA WAS ALREADY SORRY SHE'D AGREED TO HELP WITH THIS case. But the more she went over Kenzi's notes, the more she saw how badly she was needed. Kenzi had done a decent job of investigating Maya, Hexitel, Candy Trussell, and the now-incinerated LORE. But she hadn't investigated the threatening letter from the Christians for the Sanctity of Human Life, and she certainly didn't have time now, with her first-ever criminal trial breathing down her throat.

So here Emma was, dressed in black, ready for action.

"He can see you now. Please follow me."

The name in the signature block on the letter turned out to be false. She could find no trace of anyone by that name anywhere in the organization. She knew using pseudonyms in mass-mailed solicitations was commonplace, but this letter was hardly a solicitation. For that matter, the Sanctity of Human Life was equally bogus, but Emma had uncovered a stream of posts on an online bulletin board linking it to this group, the National Unity Center.

Her research also revealed that, although LORE might have been active in stem-cell research, they were hardly the only lab in the nation doing so. They weren't even the only lab in Seattle doing so. Why did LORE get the hate mail?

She didn't know but she was determined to find out. For the occasion, she went full-out Goth, which to these people, she hoped, would scream Girl in Trouble. Girl Who Needed To Be Saved. She even wore dark eye makeup and a fake teardrop tattoo on her right cheekbone.

She called for an appointment, casually mentioning her need to donate a half-million dollars for tax purposes before the end of the fiscal year. A few carefully worded questions revealed that the executive in charge of Mail Outreach was Hannibal Holt. She was here to meet Holt face-to-face, saying that his work had inspired her, so she wanted to meet him before she wrote the big check.

Emma knew there were many sincere Christians in the world doing good work and helping others, but this outfit didn't scream love. It screamed money. In the parking lot outside, she found a reserved spot for Hannibal Holt—with a shiny new Jaguar parked in it. On Facebook, she found photos of his home, which appeared to be at least 4000 square feet, with a cobblestone patio, outdoor pizza oven, and pool.

In the Seattle area? Two million bucks at least. So she knew who she was dealing with.

The receptionist guided her to a spacious office. The walls were paneled oak and the décor smelled of interior decorator.

But the most important item she spotted was the computer on Holt's desk. Dell Precision, screen dark. The hard drive would be in the CPU tucked under his desk.

This might be easier than she'd imagined.

A man Emma judged to be in his early sixties entered the room. He had slicked-back hair that looked like it had been treated with mousse, pomade, and Grecian Formula all at once.

"Why hello there," he said, bending down to her height. "I'm Hannibal Holt. Are you Ms. Kazantzakis?"

"I am." Emma was obviously Hispanic but gave herself a Greek pseudonym. Confusion might work in her favor. Maybe he would hope she was an Onassis heir.

She clutched her bag as if she felt nervous. Which was not a complete façade. There was a reason she didn't normally circulate. She didn't feel comfortable around strangers or in social settings. "Thank you for seeing me."

"The pleasure is all mine. Please take a seat. Can I get you anything? Coffee? Diet Coke? Maybe one of those energy drinks?"

He was being all too accommodating. Good. "I'm fine. I just wanted to meet you in person before I…you know."

"And let me say how appreciative we are for your generosity. Many souls will be saved."

"I never expected to inherit all this money and I don't understand the business, but I'm glad it allows me to donate to worthy causes."

"This happens…periodically?"

"Almost every year. I feel like a character in a movie. I've got all this money to give away and don't know who to give it to."

"I can certainly help with that." He guided her toward a seat. "Sadly, we always have people in need. This is a troubled world we live in."

"I know. I—I've seen some of those troubles. I grew up in a series of foster homes."

He reached out and clasped her wrist. His hands were cold. "I am so sorry to hear that."

"It's okay. I finally found a family that loved me. And left me a business to oversee. But that was my fifth home. The earlier ones—" She let her voice choke a bit. *Good grief, girl, you are a fine actress.* "Some things are best forgotten."

"There, there. I know. Let it remain in the past." He patted her head like she was a dog. Or a goose about to lay a golden egg. "God has a plan for all of us, you know."

"Sometimes it's hard to see the purpose."

"Because we're not meant to see it, my dear. That is for the Almighty alone."

"I guess so. I've had some problems. Personal problems. Took up with men. You know how that is."

"Men can be beasts," he said, shaking his head. "Despicable. Taking advantage of a sweet young thing like you."

"I made a lot of bad choices. One of those men got me started on drugs. First it was just occasional cannabis, but—"

"It's a gateway drug. One thing leads to another."

"I know that now. Pretty soon I lived from one heroin hit to the next." Heroin? LSD? What were people doing these days? She should have researched this part more. But she had a hunch Holt was even less of an expert on narcotics than she was.

"Honey." Holt leaned in close enough that she could smell his peppermint breath. "Have you accepted Jesus Christ as your Lord and Savior?"

"I—I think so."

"There's no thinking about it. You either have or you haven't. If you have, you've got nothing to worry about. Jesus wipes the slate clean. You've made mistakes. We all have. But when you accept Jesus, he washes away your sins with the power of his blessed blood. You can start building a bright new future."

"That's what I want. More than anything."

"Will you pray with me?"

"If...you like."

He put his other hand on top of the first and squeezed. "Blessed Father, shine down your holy light on this generous woman. She has a good soul. I can feel that. Give her the strength to spread that goodness throughout the world, to all the troubled souls in need of the courage and support she can offer. Give her your holy solace and bless what she is about to do. In the name of the Father, the Son, and the Holy Spirit."

"Amen," Emma whispered.

"Amen indeed." He opened his eyes. "Now what can I tell you?"

"Can you give me more information about your organization? I read things online—"

He waved a hand in the air. "Ignore all that. The lamestream media is out to get real Americans. Christians founded this nation and have always been its greatest strength. It's not just a War Against Christmas anymore—it's a War Against Christians."

"But—you're part of the religious right?"

"The New Religious Right. We're trying to create a fresh face. To separate ourselves from some of the high-profile figures of the past who brought our ministry into disrepute."

"But you're involved in politics?"

"Our primary crusade is about education. Getting the word out. Telling it like it is." He smiled, obviously pleased with himself for using a "hip" expression. "But there are obstacles to education in this country. Young people can't pray at school. Many laws discourage parents from homeschooling their children. We've tried to organize families into a coherent and cohesive bloc."

"Haven't you also been involved in science?"

"Is that important to you?"

"Of course. I believe my birth mother wanted to abort me. If not for people like you, I wouldn't exist."

"That makes me happy." He smiled from ear-to-ear. Tears actually welled up in his eyes. "That alone is enough to prove my life's work has been worthwhile. If I can give the world one beautiful spirit like yours—everything I've suffered is worthwhile."

"So you oppose abortion?"

"It's a crime against God. It's murder. We also oppose teaching evolution. It's been proven to be mathematically impossible, you know."

"I didn't."

"Fact. We've also taken strong positions on school prayer, homosexuality, gender fluidity, euthanasia, contraception, sex education, and pornography."

"And embryonic stem-cell research?"

"If it's a sin to commit abortion, how could taking cells from aborted embryos be acceptable? Did those embryos agree to donate their cells? I don't think so."

"Do you oppose all stem-cell research?"

"We have no objection to research involving adult stem cells, amniotic stem cells, or induced pluripotent stem cells. But not embryos." Okay, he knew more about it than she thought. "Or cloning. That's a sin against our Creator. Only He has the right to create life. There are some things man was not meant to know."

"I don't want any more little girl embryos being aborted for their cells."

"That's because you have a divine spirit. I felt that the moment I walked into the room. Now how can I help you do what the Holy Spirit is calling you to do?"

"I've heard everything I need to hear. I'd like to get this taken care of today."

"I can help you with that. God's will be done. Did you want to write a check?"

"Actually, I'd like to have the money wired. It's quicker and my accountants prefer it. Don't ask me why. I don't understand all that money mumbo-jumbo."

"Don't worry your pretty little head about it. I'll take care of everything. What do you need from me?"

"I need a bank account number, routing number, and a SWIFT code."

"A...SWIFT code?"

"Right. So the funds can be wired."

"Sure. I've got the rest but…huh. SWIFT code. That's a new one."

"Do you have an accountant?"

"Honey, we have a floor of accountants. Let me write a memo and I'll get back to you when—"

"Could we take care of this now? I can have the money sent with a phone call once I have that information. It would be such a load off my mind."

He relented. "Fine. I'll call—no, I'll just run upstairs. That'll be quicker than playing telephone tag. Do you mind waiting here a moment or two?"

"Of course not." She pulled out her phone. "That will give me a chance to read my daily Bible verse."

"I'll be right back." He skittered out the door.

She knew Accounting was four floors above them. Given his size, she didn't think he'd take the stairs. So she had maybe five or six minutes…

She pushed the door mostly closed so she wouldn't be seen by any passing personnel. An instant later she was under the desk, laying the CPU on its side, preparing to open it.

Screws, not hinges. Damn. This would take longer. But she came prepared.

She pulled the battery-powered wrench out of her oversized purse and went to work. While she unfastened the screws, she shut down the computer so no record of her actions would be left anywhere. She didn't expect Holt to have the savvy to track her, but there might be someone else here who could.

A minute later, she had the lid off. She was working in record time, but her palms were sweating. She couldn't be sure Holt wouldn't pop back unexpectedly. It would be hard to explain why she was under his desk. "I'm sorry, I'm so clumsy, I tripped over your computer…"

A minute later she had her hands on the hard drive. She gently eased it out of its socket, then plugged it into the external hard drive in her purse and started copying the contents. She didn't have time to pick and choose, so she took everything, even though she knew that would take several minutes.

She could monitor the speed of the transfer through a screen on the external hard drive. All things considered, it was amazingly fast...but still too slow for her comfort.

Thirty percent. Thirty-five. Forty...

She heard a commotion just outside the door.

It was Holt's voice. "Penny, do you know anything about a SWIFT code?"

"Oh yes," a woman replied. "I have that right here."

Los cojones! She didn't have much time.

Sixty-five percent, seventy, seventy-five...

"I'll never remember that, Penny. Write it down for me."

"Way ahead of you, Mr. Holt. Here it is."

"Is that all we need?"

"That's it."

Emma felt sweat dripping from her temples. Eighty-five, ninety...

"Thanks, Penny. This meeting will probably—"

"Oh wait. That should go to the charitable account. Silly me." A brief pause. "Use this number."

"I will. Thanks again."

One hundred percent. Emma threw the external drive into her purse and shoved the original hard drive back into the motherboard. She didn't have time to mess with the screws. She closed the hatch and stood the CPU upright as it had been before.

The door opened. "Ms. Kazantzakis, I have the SWIFT code."

She didn't have time to sit so she acted as if she had been praying. "That's wonderful!"

He handed her a piece of paper. She promised to make the donation today. And hoped she would be out of the building before he realized her phone number was fake. And his computer had been shut off. And the CPU hatch was missing its screws...

As she slipped into the elevator, her heart pounded out of control. That had been a near thing. She could so easily have been caught, and she couldn't possibly bluff her way out of it. She'd have spent the night in jail. And she couldn't count on Rivera & Perez to bail her out, either.

Kenzi, what have you gotten me into?

But then again—it was kinda fun.

A small smile crept across her face as the elevator descended. Maybe she should get out of the office more often.

CHAPTER TWENTY-NINE

KENZI HAD NEVER BEEN THIS FRIGHTENED IN HER ENTIRE LIFE. Not when she sat for the Bar Exam. Not when she went to the Amazon Haunted House. Not even when she had to tell her father she was getting divorced. Never.

And judging by what she saw sitting beside her at the defendant's table, Maya was every bit as scared.

She had prepared for the trial exhaustively, or tried. Mostly she spun around in circles, telling herself this was no different from what she did all the time. She'd be persuading a jury rather than a judge, and the charges were graver, but bottom line, it was about evidence and witnesses and putting on a show and outthinking the other guy.

Except this time her opponent was the district attorney himself. He hadn't farmed this out to an assistant, which was a sign of how important Harrington considered this case. She was good in court—but was she district-attorney good? He sat at his table flanked by three associate lawyers. She had one attorney from the basement who refused to speak aloud. What's wrong with this picture?

Hell, she'd spent an hour this morning dithering about what

to wear. The first time she saw the jurors she wanted to make a good impression, right? She knew Emma would wear black, so at first she thought she should wear brighter colors. Then she thought, no, she didn't want the jury to think she was a lightweight. But what would she wear instead?

This was so unfair. Men didn't have to think twice about what to wear to court. They alternated between their blue and gray suits. She'd spent fifteen minutes choosing her undies.

The sports bra was best, she decided. Probably. Surely. She favored a sports bra even when she wasn't running and particularly for court dates. She didn't want to look busty, even though she kinda was, and she certainly didn't want to jiggle. She liked SheFit, a nylon-spandex blend. Inner mesh for extra support. Hook-and-eye closures with compression and encapsulation to better support and separate the beauties. High-end materials with antimicrobial and moisture-wicking properties—or so the package claimed. It set her back seventy bucks, but it was worth it.

She might lose the case. Maya might spend the rest of her life in jail. But at least Kenzi was wearing the right bra.

Maya leaned in. "How much longer?"

"Dunno. The judge is already ten minutes late."

"Can't someone…go get him?"

"No. Harassing the judge is not advisable. They're basically feudal warlords and this is their little kingdom. They can do whatever they want."

"Sitting here is making me crazy."

Kenzi felt the same way but, for her client's sake, she played the part of the old hand who's troubled by nothing. "Take deep breaths. Slowly exhale. Think happy thoughts." She paused. "Chatted with Brittany any?"

"Of course not. Did you think Michael would bring her to the jail?"

"Not even on the phone?"

"I called the number Michael gave me and got to talk to her for less than a minute before he took the phone away."

"He really is a bastard."

"Brittany was crying. Begging him to let her talk to me. But he refused."

"I've handled a lot of divorces. And I've had to deal with some bad spouses. But this may be the all-time worst. Is there… some reason he's being such an ass?"

Maya took another breath, counted to three, then exhaled. "I think it's Candy. If Hexitel called her my buddy, he could probably live with it. But because they call her my wife, his masculinity is wounded."

"I can see that."

"It's not like he isn't religious himself."

Kenzi nodded. "I met Adrien Messie—that guru he brought to the settlement hearing. I was not impressed."

"If he lets Michael into his flock, he's not much of a shepherd." She stared at her hands. "What if I lose this murder trial? Will I ever see Brittany again?"

She didn't have to respond. They both already knew the answer.

Emma must've been listening, even though she acted as if she were completely focused on her doodles. She cleared her throat. "Maya, have you noticed that some of your Hexitel buddies are in the gallery?"

Maya did not have to turn around. "Patricia Clare sent me a message. Said they wanted to show their support."

"Please don't be offended," Emma replied. "But that's the kind of support you do not need or want. Keep Hexitel on the down low."

"Hexitel has nothing to do with the arson. Or the death."

"Perhaps. But the cult association gives people one more reason to suspect you're guilty. Confirmation bias loses more trials than evidence. Jurors see what they expect to see, or what they want to see. Please tell those people to stay home in the future."

Kenzi didn't mind Emma delivering this message. Maybe in time they could develop a good cop/bad cop routine.

Kenzi had brought Maya clothes and makeup and grooming products so she could look respectable in court—and also, without explanation, some skin-toned coverup. When Maya emerged—looking terrific for someone who had been behind bars—she'd covered up her Hexitel wrist tattoo.

Candy had initially seated herself directly behind the defendant's table, but Kenzi politely asked her to move, saying she didn't want Maya distracted. What she really didn't want, of course, was the jury guessing what the relationship between them was. Or suspecting it of being something it wasn't.

Zelda Blake was also in the courtroom. That was not surprising either, since she'd worked with Maya and Maggie Price and was currently out of work due to the fire. But Kenzi hadn't forgotten that the woman seemed to have some kind of grudge against Maya. Or that she might blame Maya for what happened to LORE.

Kenzi waved. Zelda nodded slightly. She seemed edgy. Was she planning to testify? The prosecution had a better chance of selling the murder charge if they could explain why the murderer did it, and Zelda might be the only person who knew and disliked Maya enough to provide that.

Candy walked to the front, leaned over the dividing rail, and tapped Maya on the shoulder. When Maya turned, they clasped hands.

Kenzi sucked in her breath. She knew potential jurors were being held in a separate room, but there were reporters here and she doubted the jury would be sequestered. *The Seattle Times* and other papers had run stories about Hexitel for the past week featuring headlines about BRANDING or CULT SPOUSES or SATANIC SPANKINGS. These were supposedly more enlightened times, but sometimes she had a hard time believing it.

"Honey, how are you holding up?"

Maya seemed deeply touched by Candy's concern. "Best I'm able. Thanks again for visiting me."

"I wanted to come more often." She glanced at Kenzi. "But your lawyer thought it was best that I didn't."

Kenzi explained. "All jailhouse conversations are monitored and probably recorded. Logs are kept of who came to see whom and those could be subpoenaed by the prosecution."

"I'm not ashamed of our relationship," Maya said.

"But you do hope to see your daughter again. So please follow my instructions." She reached out and, without attracting attention, separated their hands. She felt like a prom monitor forcing the students to maintain an appropriate distance. Thank goodness Hailee wasn't dating yet. She couldn't handle it. "Candy, please say what you have to say and sit down."

Candy gazed at Maya, eyes wide and earnest. "You know I'm here for you."

"You can't imagine how much that means to me."

"All of Hexitel is behind you. We don't believe the lies the district attorney is spreading. We don't care what they say in the papers. We believe in you."

Kenzi cut in. "Candy, I'm sorry, but—"

"I'll return to my seat. Rooting for you, Maya."

As soon as Candy was out of sight, DA Harrington approached.

Smiling. He'd watched the whole interaction.

If she'd had doubts before, she had none now. He was going to dive deep into the Hexitel connection, relevant or not. And now he had a little more mud to sling.

Harrington was still pissed because she turned down his settlement offer. He seemed to take it personally, as if—how could she, a mere female divorce attorney, deny such a generous offer from Mr. Wonderful? Seemed every which way she turned she had to deal with rampaging male ego. Was there some lost Amazonian race she could join? *Please?*

At long last, the judge entered the room. The bailiff called court into session and everyone rose.

"Please be seated." Judge Foreman settled into the bench and thumbed through his papers. Given the gravity of the charges, she assumed the judge had familiarized himself with the matter before he emerged. But he seemed determined to act as if this case was just one of many, nothing out of the ordinary.

"Very well," the judge said. "Let's begin."

CHAPTER THIRTY

KENZI HAD MET JUDGE FOREMAN AT BAR FUNCTIONS BUT, SINCE he worked the criminal side, she had never appeared before him in court. He was a thin white former professor at Gonzaga. He'd been appointed to the bench a few years before during the Trump administration. His hair was immaculately trimmed, as was his full beard and moustache. He was considered conservative and a bit of an odd duck. He wasn't married, had few friends, and was believed to have his eye on a Fifth Circuit judicial seat. Emma called him a 'bellwether,' meaning he would see which way the wind was blowing and make sure he was blowing with it.

Bad news since, at the moment, the wind was definitely not blowing in Maya's direction.

Foreman called the case and rattled perfunctorily through the preliminary rigmarole. Everyone expected the jury selection to be time-consuming, so he appeared determined to get to it. Foreman had made it clear at the pretrial that he did not want anyone wasting the court's time.

"Are the parties ready to proceed?"

Harrington beat her to the punch, rising in his immaculately tailored three-piece pinstriped suit. Maybe men spent more time choosing their wardrobe than she realized. "The People are, your honor."

Kenzi followed suit. "We are ready as well, your honor."

The judge peered at her for a long moment. His forehead creased. "Have you submitted a trial brief?"

"Yes, sir. We had submitted that before the pretrial."

He scowled. "You're using pluperfect tense when I think you mean to be using perfect tense."

Damn this ex-professor anyway. "Pardon me. We wrote a trial brief."

"And submitted it?" He searched his desk. "Yes, here it is." He picked it up and, rather than reading it, rifled the pages to see how thick it was. "This is it?"

"If...there's another issue the court would like us to research..."

"Do you have co-counsel, Ms. Rivera?"

She tilted her head. "Yes, I'm here with my colleague, Emma Or—"

"No, I mean, someone..."

Male? What was he trying to say?

The judge glanced at his clerk, who subtly shook his head. "Forgive me, counsel, but it's best we address this before the jury is called. You're a divorce lawyer, correct?"

"I have mostly practiced in family courts, yes."

"And you understand that this is a murder trial? Arson and murder, actually."

What kind of idiot did he think she was? "Of course."

"I would be more comfortable if your client was represented by someone with criminal law experience."

What business was it of his? "Your honor, my colleague has handled many criminal matters."

He squinted. "I don't recall seeing her in court before."

Yeah… "She has an admirable record of settling cases before trial."

He still frowned. "I don't want your client claiming ineffective assistance of counsel on appeal. Don't you think she'd be better off with…well, to be blunt…someone else?"

She could feel her face reddening. "Your honor, I don't want to say anything that might violate attorney-client privilege. But I have…suggested alternative approaches, and my client has insisted that she wants me to handle this."

He spoke to Maya directly. "Is that true? Because the court would be happy to appoint an attorney with more criminal law experience."

Maya looked stricken. "I'm…fine, sir. I like the lawyers I have."

Judge Foreman shook his head. "Very well then. Let the record reflect that the defendant was given an opportunity to obtain more experienced counsel and turned it down. She will not be heard to complain later if…things don't go the way she hoped." He looked up and smiled. "Let the chips fall where they may."

JURY SELECTION WAS SO STRESSFUL THAT ULTIMATELY KENZI LET Emma make all the decisions. The irony was not lost on her. Let the woman who doesn't like people and prefers to stay cloistered in her office make the critical jury decisions. Sure, that made sense. But Emma had done the research and knew what she wanted. Kenzi assumed they wanted to pick as many women as possible and to avoid men, especially the ones who looked like judgmental jerks. But Emma thought men were not as hard on women as other women—especially older women—could be, especially if they disapproved of Maya's lifestyle choices.

Predictably, Harrington was the one who mentioned Hexitel first, ostensibly suggesting that he wanted to root out any prejudice against the organization, while determinedly mentioning it as often as possible and telling the jury as much about it as he could. While Harrington avoided an obvious objection by abstaining from the word "cult," Kenzi could see the way the jurors' faces scrunched up just at the mention of "Hexitel." She would have to work hard to overcome that prejudice.

She was not surprised that Harrington repeatedly mentioned Maya was an expert in chemistry and knew her way around incendiary devices, but she was surprised when he mentioned her involvement with stem-cell research. She thought of Seattle as being, overall, a progressive community. Apparently Harrington was willing to say anything that might turn a juror against the defendant.

By early afternoon, both sides had exhausted their peremptory challenges and appeared to have settled on the Final Twelve. Five women, seven men. Four of the women were younger than Maya. All of the men were older. Three jurors were retired. Two worked in the tech industry, one for Amazon. Three in retail. The rest unemployed.

So far as she knew, this was a fair jury for Maya. But she couldn't shake the feeling that they'd stumbled into a dream jury for Harrington. Maybe it was just the obnoxious smile plastered on his face. She wished she could forcibly wipe that smile away. Like with a hammer.

After a late lunch break, it was time for opening statements. Emma had advised Kenzi that although she had the option of reserving her opening until she began the defense case, she shouldn't. Don't let the prosecution's opening remarks go unrebutted for days.

Kenzi knew Harrington was a fine orator. Lousy speakers did not get elected district attorney. But she was unprepared to find out first-hand how good he really was.

"Ladies and gentlemen," Harrington began, "first and foremost, I want to thank you for your service. I know you're giving up your valuable time and I very much appreciate it. I can see that you take your role seriously and will do your best to ensure that justice is done. The jury system is the tenuous glue that holds our fragile legal system together. The police protect us in the street, but here in the courtroom, you're the thin blue line. We count on you to make sure we all remain safe."

Pretty close to argument, Kenzi thought, but she couldn't see jumping up to object this early in the game. The jury would resent it. She'd wait till he got to something seriously offensive. As she had no doubt he would.

"This case is a tragic tale of a wife, mother, and chemist who snapped. At times, you may sympathize with her. She has been the primary financial support for her family. She has worked long hours in an advanced scientific field. And her marriage had its rocky moments—as they all do. But what I hope you will not sympathize with is the way she dealt with these stressors. She sought solace in an organization—some would call it a cult—known for taking coercive control of its members.

"Though they call their programs executive training intensives, what they actually offer, the evidence will show, is something far more insidious. They took control of Maya Breville, and you will be horrified to learn what that entailed. Huge financial contributions. Mind control. Physical battering. Branding. Master-and-slave relationships. They even assigned her a wife. Yes, you heard me correctly. A wife. How is that going to help a marriage, or a job? It's not, of course. And that's when everything started to go wrong."

Though he was an excellent speaker, if anything, Kenzi thought he was downplaying his oratorical flair, trying to make it seem more off-the-cuff than it was. That made sense. The jury didn't want to feel they were getting a performance. They wanted to feel he was speaking from the heart.

"The evidence will show that a few weeks before the fiery death of her boss, Maya's husband reached the breaking point. He'd had enough of this cult and his wife's new wife and their bizarre rituals. He filed for divorce. Left the marital home and for his daughter's safety, took her with him—an arrangement that twice has been affirmed by the courts. Maya did not handle the breakup well. She spent more time with Hexitel and less time at work, which led to the loss of her job. With no job, no daughter, and dim prospects in divorce court, the stress became too much. She sought revenge against the boss who fired her, who she now blamed for all her problems. Using her advanced knowledge of chemical reactions, she torched her place of business—while Maggie Price was trapped inside. This did not happen by accident. The defendant chose the time and the place, knowing her boss tended to work late. Maggie Price was not an unfortunate victim of the fire. She was a deliberate target."

He stepped closer to the rail, leaning in. "Let me say it even more plainly. This was murder. A cold, calculated, deliberate murder. Irrational perhaps, but don't think for a minute that the defendant was insane or incapable of controlling her actions. She intentionally did what she did. As a direct result, Maggie Price died in a hellish cauldron of flames, suffering unimaginable pain as her flesh and bones slowly burned. And the defendant was arrested at the scene of the crime."

He wiped his face with his hand, shaking his head with sorrowful eyes. "Could there be a worse way to die? If so, I don't know what it would be. This is a crime that cannot go unpunished. Justice requires you to find Maya Breville guilty of first-degree murder."

He looked at each juror as if to make sure they got his message. Then he swiveled around and quietly took his seat.

Kenzi knew she couldn't equal that performance. She was several inches shorter, didn't have his deep voice, and wouldn't

talk about justice. The only way she could better his opening—
or at least not pale by comparison—was to not compete with it.
She would have to blaze her own trail and speak to them in her
own way.

"Here's what you need to know about me," Kenzi said, arms
spread wide. She noticed her hands were shaking. She swung
them behind her back to hide it. "I'm a straight shooter. I don't
go in for theatrics. There will be no dramatic surprises or courtroom tricks. I let the facts speak for themselves and let you
make the decisions. But that doesn't work unless you get the
facts—ALL the facts—and so far, you haven't. During the prosecution's case, you won't. So you will see me fighting, objecting,
going toe-to-toe with Mr. Harrington. To make sure you have
the whole story. So you can make an informed decision."

Now she noticed her knees were shaking. *Dios mio!* It's not as
if she'd never spoken aloud before. Why was it so much harder
to talk to a jury? She pivoted, moving slowly as she spoke.
Maybe the trembling would be less detectible. "Let me review
what the esteemed district attorney just said. I agree that my
client is going through a painful divorce. I agree that she has an
extensive background in several scientific fields. I agree that
there was a fire and at some point my client was at the scene."

She felt like a total amateur, trying to pass herself off as a
real-life criminal attorney when she was anything but. "And
that's about it. Everything else is contested. So don't believe
anything unless the prosecutor proves it. And he can't prove it
by saying it over and over again. You must have evidence. Since
the prosecution has the burden of proof, if you don't get that
compelling evidence on each and every claim they make, you
must find my client not guilty.

"Maya was upset by the divorce, but the suggestion that she
snapped and it drove her to murder is absurd. I know you've
heard horrible things about Hexitel, but my client considers it
her religion, and here in America we guarantee religious free-

dom, even for beliefs that differ from our own. As the evidence will show, at no time did anyone at Hexitel, or anywhere else, suggest that Maya should do something violent. And she wouldn't have listened if they had. She was upset about the loss of her job at the worst possible time, but she was not stupid enough to plan some crazed revenge that would sink her chances of obtaining custody of her daughter. She didn't want LORE burned down. She still hoped to get her job back. She was present when the fire broke out for a good reason—but she did not set the fire and she did not plan to kill her boss. The prosecution's case is a wild amalgamation of suppositions and lies."

Kenzi stopped moving and focused. "I would not say any of this if I didn't know it to be true. And I will prove what I say. But remember, I don't have to prove anything. The burden of proof is entirely upon the prosecution. They can give speeches all night long, but if they don't prove their claims, you should not believe them. And frankly, even if you secretly suspect they might be right—that's not enough. Guilt must be proven beyond a reasonable doubt. And since the prosecution cannot do that—because what they claim did not happen—you must find my client not guilty."

CHAPTER THIRTY-ONE

KENZI WASN'T SURE IF HER OPENING WAS GOOD, BAD, OR indifferent, but at least it was over. Now if she could just get through the rest of the day without completely embarrassing herself, she would treat herself to a long soak in the tub with candles, soothing classical music, bath oil…

Or just go to bed early. But the opening, praise God, was finished.

"That was the most embarrassing thing I've done in my entire life," she muttered.

Emma sat beside her at the defendant's table. "Far from it."

"It was. It so was."

"How about that time in high school, senior year, when you and your cool buddies went to the lake on Senior Ditch Day? You got drunk and fell out of a tree. Broke a toe and started laughing hysterically. Fought them when they tried to take you to the emergency room."

"That is not what—" She stopped short. "Were you there?"

"Of course not. It was a school day."

"Then how—"

"The whole world was talking about it the next morning. They said you threw up on the attending physician."

"That's...grossly exaggerated."

"Uh huh."

"The whole incident was a...bizarre abnormality that didn't recur."

"Until the next time you drank tequila. What about that time you made out with Marjorie Evans' boyfriend at her eighteenth birthday party?"

"That is so not accurate. And he was planning to break up with her anyway."

"At least you didn't break another toe."

"I didn't realize you followed my exploits so closely."

"I kept thinking that in time you might glow up."

"You mean, *grow* up?"

"No. Glow up. Transform. Mentally and emotionally. That's why I subscribe to your KenziKlan livestreams."

"Shut up. Really?"

"How else would I find out what's going on in the firm?"

THE FIRST PROSECUTION WITNESS WAS DR. MADISON CHANG, THE county medical examiner. Kenzi offered to stipulate that a death had occurred, but Harrington insisted on putting Chang on the stand.

Harrington spent about ten minutes discussing Chang's impressive credentials, including the more-than-a-decade of service that led to her appointment as medical examiner. Then they turned to her examination of Maggie Price.

"The remains evidenced everything I would expect from death by immolation. The upper airways revealed damage due to smoke inhalation. I saw both soot soiling of the nares and oropharynx plus soot-stained mucus lining the trachea and the bronchi. She would eventually have lost consciousness but may not have died immediately thereafter. I did detect burns to the tongue, glottis, larynx, and pulmonary edema, which would suggest that she inhaled a great deal of hot air."

"Would this have occurred before or after the body was in contact with the fire?"

"Difficult to be certain, but based upon my examination, I would say before. When the building collapsed, the integrity of her airways may have been compromised. But I believe she was already dead. She may have passed out from smoke inhalation, which of course would explain why she didn't leave. Many parts of her body show the cherry-pink discoloration we associate with carbon monoxide poisoning."

"Did you have any trouble identifying the body?"

"No. She was found at her desk. The body was deeply charred, but it had not been reduced to carbonized bones and ashes. Fingerprint identification was impossible due to skin slippage. Most of the soft tissues and fluids were destroyed. But her teeth survived intact. I used a variety of specialized glues and fixatives to protect the dental material before it was moved. By matching that with her dental records, we were able to make a conclusive identification."

"Just to be clear, Dr. Chang, is there any doubt that the fire caused this death?"

"I know there have been cases in which murderers killed someone then set the house on fire to disguise a homicide. But this victim was still breathing when the fire broke out."

"So whoever set the fire killed Maggie Price."

"That's correct."

"Thank you. No more questions."

Kenzi rose. "I'd like to ask a few questions, your honor."

Judge Foreman looked at her as if she were crazy, or worse, wasting his time. "Does the defense dispute the fact that a woman died?"

"No, your honor. But Dr. Chang is a state employee that tends to give testimony—"

"Who."

She blinked. "Excuse me?"

"Dr. Chang is a state employee *who* tends to give testimony. I'm sure the jury would prefer that you speak proper English, counsel. As would I."

She spotted a few grins in the jury box. Was he encouraging them to laugh at her? Was this his subtle way of undermining the defense?

She strode within a few feet of the witness stand.

"You've stated that the victim was still alive when the fire broke out."

The medical examiner looked her straight in the eye, as if to make it clear she was not going to be intimidated. "Correct."

"And you attribute her failure to leave the building to unconsciousness due to smoke inhalation."

"Also correct."

"In his opening, the prosecutor suggested that she suffered when she burned. But if she was unconscious, or dead from smoke inhalation, she would not have suffered pain when her body burned, correct?"

Chang's eyes darted toward the DA. "That is…correct."

"And it seems to me there's another possibility. Couldn't Ms. Price have been alive but already unconscious for some other reason, when the fire broke out?"

"I don't think—"

"Can you exclude the possibility?"

"My expert opinion is based on many extremely technical medical and anatomic matters that might be…difficult for a layperson to comprehend."

"I feel certain I can handle it. And the jury can too." Never hurt to stroke the jurors, right?

"Very well. When I examined the body, I found extensive

fracturing of the bones and epidural heat hematomas. That occurs when a great amount of heated blood accumulates between the dura and the skull."

"What would cause that?"

"Antemortem fractures theoretically could, but I saw no evidence of that."

"Which doesn't prove it didn't happen."

"It makes it highly unlikely."

"So you say. But you're a witness for the district attorney. Your job is to give him what he wants."

She seemed deeply offended. "I would never give false testimony."

"But you have to make choices. And unsurprisingly, you've made all the choices that favor the prosecution." She took a file folder from Emma. "I notice in your report that the collection of heated blood you mentioned has a"—she took a deep breath —"carboxyhemoglobin level similar to the peripheral blood."

The doctor raised an eyebrow. "I'm impressed."

"Am I right?"

"You are."

"But that's what you would expect if unconsciousness preceded the fire, isn't it?"

"We don't know the exact timeline involved here."

"I also note that there was quite a bit of splitting. Am I using that term right? To describe skin when it contracts and tears."

"You've done your homework."

"Always." But she didn't mind getting an attaboy from the witness. The judge and jury were bound to notice. "Splitting is associated with antemortem wounds. Not burns. Am I correct about that?"

Chang's smile was more than a bit patronizing. "You have to understand how traumatic incineration is to the human body. You can't expect everything to happen in a textbook fashion. The victim may have fallen as she lost consciousness, and the

minute differences regarding when wounds occurred are difficult to establish after the fact with complete certainty."

"But would you be willing to acknowledge that it is at least
possible that the body was wounded—perhaps mortally—before
the fire broke out?"

"I don't think—"

"Is it possible?"

Dr. Chang sighed heavily. "I suppose it is…remotely
possible."

"Consistent with the medical evidence?"

Her shoulders heaved. "Yes."

"Thank you. Nothing more."

A small victory. She suggested that someone might've
attacked Price before the fire—but that didn't prove it wasn't
Maya, at least not until they established the time she arrived on
the scene. It did mean the death was not an unintended result of
the arson. The prosecution couldn't fall back to a felony murder
or accidental homicide theory. They had to prove intent.

A small victory. But in this case, she would take whatever
she could get.

CHAPTER THIRTY-TWO

KENZI DIDN'T GET MUCH TIME TO CONGRATULATE HERSELF. Before she had a chance to blink, Harrington had called his next witness.

"The People call Dr. Anson Kirk to the stand."

Kirk was the arson investigator the police used to determine what happened at LORE. Kenzi offered to stipulate that a fire had been set, but once again, Harrington refused the offer. Some of that was undoubtedly because he wanted to horrify the jury with the details—a human being burned to death, another evil human being deliberately setting the fire. But she had to think there was more to it than that.

After establishing that Kirk was one of the top men in his field, frequently used by police departments all across Washington, Harrington lunged into the case at hand.

"How does an arson investigator go about determining the cause of a fire?"

Kirk was a short, squat man, but full of energy. Clearly he loved fire and loved talking about fire. "Arson investigators typically start with the Big Three: location, fuel, and ignition."

"Can you explain what that means?"

"Certainly." He turned slightly so he could address the jury, though he still kept an eye on Harrington. "Location is important because some parts of a building are more likely to catch fire and spread fire. If the goal is to take down the entire structure—and it usually is—then location is critical. Typically an arsonist will plant the incendiary device in the attic or basement. Those are out of normal view, giving the arsonist a free hand, and a fire starting there will quickly spread to the entire structure. In this case, there were three labs, plus the front office building, and the arsonist clearly wanted all of them to go up in smoke."

"So where was the fire set? The attic?"

"There is no attic. No basement, either. The fire was set in the third lab building—which of course is also where the defendant worked prior to being terminated."

Kenzi thought about making a relevance objection, but decided against it. Surely that connection was too tentative to impress a juror.

"Why would the arsonist choose that lab?"

"Because it's full of chemicals. Not all of them would catch or spread fires—but many would. It was basically a Molotov cocktail the size of a hotel lobby. Once the fire started, it quickly grew to such a size that it could not be easily stopped. The entire complex had ceiling sprinklers, but by the time they kicked in, the fire was too large to be doused."

"Who was working in the lab at this time?"

"No one but Maggie Price. At least, we've yet to speak to anyone who confesses to being in the lab at the time. Most people had gone home. Which of course left the arsonist a free hand."

"You also mentioned fuel. Would the chemicals be the fuel?"

"Yes." Kirk scooted forward, almost bubbling with enthusiasm. "This was a perfect storm for an arsonist. Most of the needed ingredients were already on site. It's possible the arsonist brought an accelerant or something to ignite the fire, but given the amount of destruction, that would be impossible to detect."

"Why would an accelerant be needed?"

"To get the fire going quickly, before anyone could do anything about it."

"Can you give the jury an example of a possible fuel?"

"Some of the most common fuels are good at starting fires, but spread slowly. Gasoline, kerosene, lacquer thinner, alcohols —all these evaporate at high temperatures, which can interfere with both the ignition and the spread of the flames. Wood alcohol and grain alcohol are more volatile but have the same drawbacks. There are dozens of ways to start a fire, and actually, taking account of the fact that the defendant was a trained chemist—"

Emma jabbed Kenzi in the side. She formulated her thoughts as she rose. "Objection. That statement...assumes my client committed the arson."

"That's true," the judge said, nodding. "I'll ask the witness to stick to his scientific observations, unless he's specifically asked to speculate. Sustained."

But now Emma was kicking her under the table. "And...I ask that the jury be instructed to disregard those remarks."

"The jury is so instructed. Just the last statement. You may of course consider the rest of the witness' testimony."

Damn it all, Emma was still kicking her. What did television lawyers say? "And I ask that the remark be stricken from the record."

The judge almost smiled. Did he realize she was making this up as she went along? "The remark will be so stricken. May we proceed?"

"Yes, your honor. Thank you." She sat down, relieved once again that she hadn't made a complete fool of herself. So far as she knew.

Harrington addressed the witness. "Could you provide examples of common accelerants?"

"Paint. Brush cleaner. Glue. Rubber cement. They are literally all over every home in this country. And every laboratory."

"You also mentioned ignition."

"That's very important here. The fire was set in the lab using a mixed bag of combustible chemicals present in their purest form. But we assume the arsonist did not want to be incinerated. How do you set the fire so it ignites quickly but still leaves you time to get away?"

"And the answer is?"

"A fuse. Some kind of time-delay device. Preferably one that will incinerate and thus leave no trace. Fuses can be divided into three categories."

She was getting tired of this man's lists. He was supposed to be giving testimony, not writing a Wiki page. But she supposed his effusive display of knowledge helped establish his expertise.

"Pyrotechnic, safety, and cords. The pyrotechnic fuse uses flammable powder tucked around a string core. The flame travels along its length and ignites the combustible substance when it reaches it. Usually takes around ten to thirty seconds per foot of fuse, so the arsonist can build the needed escape time. These are easy to find. Hobby stores call it rocket fuse. For that matter, you could use a birthday candle, but it might not be long enough to give you the time you want, and it would leave traces of wax, which I did not find. Safety fuses have black powder within layers of string and asphalt wrappings. Or a plastic water-resistant tube. You can get these from people who sell commercial blasting supplies."

"What kind of fuse do you believe was employed in this case?"

"Clearly this arsonist used an igniter cord. That will have a core of pyrotechnic powder wrapped in wire. The advantages are quick burning times and high temperatures."

"How can you be certain that fuse was used in this case?"

"Because I discovered a spiral of wire left behind. That's also how I know where the fire began."

"How long was the fuse?"

"In terms of time? About three minutes. Plenty long enough for the arsonist to escape. Or to get to the convenience store across the street." Where Maya had been observed on a security camera.

"Where would the arsonist find such a fuse?"

"You would need a professional chemical supplier. Someone who sells to hospitals and demolition services and...research scientists."

Two jurors nodded appreciatively. They got what he was saying.

"So a person who worked in this lab would know how to get it?"

"Yes. And according to the police reports, chemicals were found in the defendant's automobile that match what likely started the fire."

Kenzi detected an audible sucking of air in the courtroom. Maybe they were gasps. Kirk's little bombshell was having its desired effect.

"Thank you," Harrington said. "Pass the witness."

"Should I cross?" Kenzi muttered to Emma. She hadn't planned to. But now she thought maybe she needed to do something.

"Yes," Emma muttered back.

"What should I ask him?"

"No idea. But don't let it end on that damning note. If nothing else—distract them."

Thanks. Very helpful.

"Ms. Rivera?" Judge Foreman asked. "Cross?"

"Yes. Of course." She pushed herself to her feet. "Dr. Kirk, you say the chemicals found in my client's car are the same kind of chemicals that started the fire."

"Beyond question."

"Are you the one who found the chemicals in the car?"

"No."

"So you have no first-hand knowledge of what was found?"

"I read the police report."

"Which is not first-hand knowledge. It's hearsay. Were the police who searched the car chemical experts?" Lame. But she had to sow doubt wherever she could.

"I understand they brought in experts to analyze everything that was found."

"So you're relying on the police here, not your personal investigation."

"True. But it's quite a coincidence, don't you think?"

"Not at all. My client took her ongoing experiments from that very same lab. So it stands to reason that the same chemicals would be present both places."

"Why would she be using incendiary chemicals? I thought her work was in stem-cell research."

Which Kenzi did not want to get into. "In the future, sir, please wait for my questions and answer them. Without speculation or other irrelevancies. You've said that these chemicals were abundant in the lab where the fire started, right?"

"That's correct."

"Couldn't any of the scientists working in that lab remove chemicals? Or use them to start a fire?"

"I'm not aware that anyone else had chemicals in their car."

"No one else had been fired. But they all had access. Did the police search any other cars?"

"I don't know."

"Did they question any other scientists?"

"I don't know."

"So anyone could've wandered into that lab after hours."

"My understanding is that it was locked and only employees had keys."

"Did they question other employees? Or did they just arrest my client because they found her nearby?"

"Finding her at the scene of the crime seems…indicative."

"Of guilt or innocence? If I'd just set a fire, I wouldn't be anywhere near the place."

"Objection," Harrington said. "Counsel is arguing."

"Sustained."

"You might behave more rationally," Kirk said. "But your client had been fired, was obviously angry, and is a member of that crazy cult."

And then the courtroom descended into chaos, so quickly Kenzi suspected the spectators in the gallery had been waiting for something like this all day.

The judge slammed his gavel. "Order. I will have order in this courtroom." He leaned forward, still banging away. "We are not required to admit spectators. And if we have another outburst like this one—we won't."

"Your honor," Kenzi said, "I move—"

"Yes, I know. The last remark will be stricken. The jury is instructed to disregard. The witness is admonished. Is there anything else?" He was clearly irritated and she felt he was blaming her. Was she going to be at fault for everything that happened because she had poor grammar? Or because she was a mere divorce lawyer?

"No, your honor. Nothing more." She'd made the point that any of the scientists—and for that matter, anyone else—could get access to the chemicals in the lab. It wasn't going to get any better.

"I think that's enough for the first day," Judge Foreman said. "Let's break and start again tomorrow morning at nine. I will remind the jurors that, although you are not sequestered, you should not discuss this case with anyone, not even the other members of your family. And you should not read or listen to any news reports relating to this case."

He banged his gavel. "Court is adjourned."

The marshals started toward the defendant's table. Kenzi frowned. "I wish you didn't have to go back to that horrible place tonight."

"You and me both. Are we…losing?"

"No," she replied, perhaps too quickly. "The prosecution is presenting its case. But don't worry. We'll get our chance."

Maya's eyes widened. "I didn't kill Maggie. I didn't burn that building. I would never deliberately hurt anyone."

Kenzi squeezed her shoulder. "I know. Now we just have to convince everyone else."

CHAPTER THIRTY-THREE

BY THE TIME KENZI STUMBLED HOME, IT WAS AFTER TEN AND SHE was not at all sure Hailee would still be awake.

She should have known better.

Hailee sat at the kitchen table surrounded by a mound of documents. She looked up from her work, wide-eyed and bright as the sun. "Ready for a Day One recap?"

Kenzi plopped her briefcases onto a chair. Hadn't she just finished that? After court ended, she and Emma retreated to the office and analyzed and re-analyzed and over-analyzed everything that had happened, then tried to create a vague plan for responding to the next wave of prosecution witnesses. "What is all this?"

"I've been scrutinizing the first witnesses and the prosecution strategy. I've got charts, files, witness background info, and a Kanban board."

Kenzi's eyes scanned the table. "How do you know what happened in court today? There were no cameras in the courtroom."

"Emma texted me updates periodically."

"She didn't mention that to me."

"She didn't want to distract you. You were busy."

"I thought she was too." But Kenzi was impressed. Hailee had put a lot of effort into this. "You know, you've never seemed terribly interested in my work in the past."

"Mom, before you were handling divorce cases. Helping silicon princesses fleece their spouses. This is a murder case."

"You're in it for the drama?"

"I think you need help. Which I can provide."

"Is the KenziKlan is still trending downward?"

"Actually, you got a small uptick today. Not enough to compensate for the fall, but still. Better up than down."

"And what does my social media manager think caused the uptick?"

"Pity. People think you're in over your head, but they're impressed that you're hanging in there. No one likes a quitter. And you got high marks for your opening."

"I did not livestream my opening."

"Someone in the gallery with excellent shorthand skills took it down and posted it."

"Is that even legal?"

"Who cares? You gave a great speech. I thought your content was much better than that blowhard DA's."

"His delivery was slicker."

"This isn't a game show. Content is king."

Or should be. "At least I didn't make a complete fool of myself. If pity brings my numbers up, I can live with that. The jury, however, will require more."

"Which is why I've appointed myself to your defense team."

"Don't you have homework?"

"Long done. This is way more interesting. Everyone online is quizzing me about the trial, so I might as well know something about it."

She couldn't argue with that logic. And truth to tell, she

could use all the help she could get. "Before we plunge in, I need to whip up some dinner."

"It's waiting for you in the oven."

She didn't need to be told twice. All at once, she realized she was starving.

She opened the oven door. *Yes!* Pizza. God must love her after all.

She carefully slipped a slice onto a plate. "Is this from Dino's?"

"Best pizza in Seattle."

Maybe for someone who can walk long distances. "How did you…?"

"Mom. Don't make me OK Boomer you. I can get anything delivered these days."

She wasn't going to argue. "Mr. Pink!"

"Best pizza from the best pizza place. I figure after the day you've had, you deserve it."

Mr. Pink was legendary in Seattle. A square pizza topped with fresh mozzarella, ricotta, basil, and best of all, sweet vodka sauce. The crunchy crust was black on the bottom just enough to make it perfect. "Garlic knots?"

"No. I don't want you gaining weight during the trial." Hailee looked up and laughed. "JK. They're in the fridge."

"Best daughter ever. Let me pay you back."

"You can add it to your tab."

"I'm running a tab?"

"You don't think I'm doing all this legal work for nothing, do you? If I'm going to be associate counsel—and I am—then I expect to be paid."

"Except you can't be any kind of counsel, because you haven't been to law school. Last I heard, you were planning on med school."

"Maybe I'll do both. You can pay me like a legal assistant. They haven't been to law school."

But they have taken legal assistant courses, she thought, but it seemed smarter to go with the flow. "Okay, you get paid."

"Cool beans."

Kenzi picked up a stack of papers. Each sheet had a photo at the top and a bio beneath. The faces looked familiar. "Are these the jurors?"

"Every single one."

"How did you get their names? They weren't released to the media."

"Emma wrote them down. Texted them to me during a break."

"And you hired a private eye to invade their privacy?"

"Of course not. I went on social media. Ten of the twelve have Facebook pages, which makes prying into their personal lives pretty darn easy. The other two have children with pages full of info. Eight of them are on Twitter. Six on Instagram. Three have LinkedIn pages. Seriously, I don't know how PIs make a living anymore. People complain that the government pries into their personal lives, then post everything about themselves online."

Kenzi thumbed through the profiles. The amount of information Hailee had compiled was astounding. "This is kinda crazy."

"But useful. I can't be for sure but, based upon my review of their posts and likes, I think you have seven Democrats on your jury and five Republicans, three of whom are women."

"That may not help Maya."

"You can overcome whatever law-and-order bias they might have. Emphasize how hard Maya worked to support her family. Emphasize what a good mother she is. Don't criticize law enforcement officers. Even when they're on the stand."

"Of course, being conservative doesn't guarantee a juror will convict."

"True. But that's not all you know. Seven of your jurors have dogs. Three have multiple dogs. Four have cats. One has a horse."

"So…?"

"It's a well-known fact that cat owners are soft-hearted but independent, while dog owners crave affection. Why else would they get a big animal that jumps up and down and slobbers all over them?"

"I fear we may be veering from science toward supposition."

"Here's the bottom line. You need to become their newest dog."

"Excuse me?"

"You need to show that you like them and respect them—so they will like you. And you should play up the idea of duty. Do your duty. Don't disappoint America. Play by the rules. If the prosecution doesn't provide enough evidence, you must acquit."

"That's kind of what I said in my opening."

"Keep saying it. Every chance you get."

"Anything else?"

"Only three of your jurors are religious enough to mention it online, so I'm hoping Maya's stem-cell research won't hurt you much. But the cult is another matter. Eleven of the twelve have children. Everyone loves their children and wants them to be safe. If it starts to look like Maya put her daughter in danger…"

"It will be a lot easier to convict her." Kenzi pushed the papers into her satchel. "Okay, I want to spend more time with these. But…thanks. You did good work." She combed through some photos of the ashy remains of LORE. "Where did you get these?"

"I snapped them with my phone. Sent them to the printer."

"You—How did you get out there?"

"Carrie took me."

"Carrie." Okay, she didn't want to admit she didn't know her daughter's friends but…

"It's okay, Mom. We don't hang that much. Carrie's in my homeschool group, but she's also a track star."

"I feel I'm missing something."

"Carrie is able to do the one thing I can't. Run."

Kenzi bit down on her lower lip.

"I asked Carrie to walk, then run from the lab to the convenience store. Then back to the lab. No one can run faster than Carrie. Certainly not some scientist in street shoes."

Hailee handed her mother an Excel spreadsheet. "I think you'll find these numbers interesting."

She found them more than interesting. She found them amazing. "Hailee...this is—this is wonderful."

Hailee beamed. "Can I get the coroner's reports? All the medical stuff?"

She was surprised Hailee didn't have them already. "I'll scan them tomorrow morning and email them to you."

"Thanks, Mom."

"What are you looking for?"

"I don't know exactly. But Emma said the DA's expert left a door open, a slim possibility that Maggie Price was unconscious or dead before Maya arrived. If we can prove that, the murder charge goes away. The convenience store security cam footage establishes when Maya was there, right?"

"Yes. But it's possible she was sneaking around LORE long before she went to the store. Or set the fire." Kenzi took another bite of the pizza. She knew the alcohol content in the vodka sauce burned off during cooking, but she liked to at least imagine it was having a calming influence on her nerves. "I can't tell you how stressful this is. Maya could spend the rest of her life behind bars. And never see Brittany again. Leaving the child in the hands of the hot-tempered bastard who fathered her."

"The jury has the ultimate decision-making power. Not you."

"I'm the one who has to make sure Maya gets a fair shake." She looked up abruptly. "I'm afraid I'm going to blow it."

"You won't."

"Harrington thinks I will. Even my own father thinks I will. They both tried to buy me off."

"But you persisted."

"But did I do the right thing?"

Hailee wheeled in closer and laid her head on her mother's shoulder. "None of us can predict the future. But I know this. I'm very proud of my mother."

CHAPTER THIRTY-FOUR

KENZI ENTERED THE COURTROOM FEELING SLIGHTLY STRONGER than she had the day before. The difference was minor and it was certainly not based on her previous day's performance. But she was starting to feel less like a complete poseur and more like someone who belonged here.

She spotted most of the same faces in the courtroom, but one new one—Patricia Clare. The woman who ran Hexitel. Candy had mentioned that Hexitel supported Maya, but Emma had asked them to stay away. What brought Clare to the courtroom?

Kenzi greeted her. "Information gathering? Or recruiting?"

"In a courtroom? Rather unlikely, don't you think?" Maybe it was just Kenzi, but Clare's upper-crust accent made her sound snotty even when she wasn't trying. "I need to stay on top of this situation."

"Why?"

"I'm worried about Maya. And of course, the impact all this press coverage will have on Hexitel."

"Damage control?" Kenzi narrowed her eyes. "Are you testifying for the DA?"

"Actually, I thought you might want to call me as a character witness."

To emphasize Maya's connection to Hexitel? "Hard pass."

"Perhaps I should hold a press conference. Or issue a statement. This may be a critical juncture in the life of our organization."

"Translation. You see this as a recruiting opportunity. Or a fundraiser. You're going to harness the publicity arising from Maya's tragic situation and use it to your own benefit."

"I find your cynicism predictable and banal. As Maya has told you, Hexitel is her church. Is it wrong to defend our church? We used to make saints of our defenders of the faith."

"Faith didn't used to be so expensive." This conversation wasn't productive, and she probably shouldn't alienate one of the few people who might actually say something positive about Maya to the press. So she moved on.

Maya was already in the courtroom, dressed in a modest but professional pantsuit. Probably best she didn't look too attractive. She didn't want to threaten all those dog lovers on the jury. "How are you holding up?"

"Better than yesterday. You?"

"'Bout the same. I've got some new—"

"Have you heard anything from Brittany?"

"No. Sorry. Michael is keeping her tightly wrapped up. I don't think either of them will come anywhere near the courtroom."

"Can't you arrange some kind of meeting?"

"I tried. It's too complicated, what with the jail and the marshals and all."

"Michael is taking advantage of the situation."

True enough. "This will be over in a few days. And then… we'll see what develops."

"If I lose, I'll never see Brittany again."

Kenzi clenched her teeth. "Prisons have visiting hours…."

"He won't let her come."

"And she won't be a minor forever."

"By that time, it will be too late."

What did Maya mean by that? She was almost afraid to ask.

Emma sat on the other side of their client. Shaking her head. Translation: leave her alone. Get your head in the game.

Because what Maya said was true. If she lost this trial, Brittany would never see a loving parent again.

———

THE FIRST WITNESS OF THE DAY WAS A FINGERPRINT EXPERT, A tech from the CSI division named Harold Lauter. Because the fire eradicated most of the possible evidence, there would be little of the usual forensic testimony. But Lauter testified that Maya's fingerprints were all over the lab and especially in the area where the fire ignited. Kenzi thought this was somewhat less than earth-shattering since Maya worked there. It was only toward the final moments of Lauter's testimony that it became interesting.

"Where else did you find the defendant's fingerprints?"

"On tabletops, equipment shards, doorknobs. As you might expect. But I also found her prints on something that shouldn't have been there at all. A twisted spiral of wire."

DA Harrington nodded. "Earlier, we heard Dr. Kirk testify that the igniter cord used as a fuse could contain a wire spiral."

"The actual fuse would have been subjected to such extreme heat that you couldn't expect to find prints on it. What I found was another spiral not used as the fuse. But on the premises nonetheless."

"Why would that be?"

Lauter shrugged. "Perhaps the arsonist goofed up the first one. Threw it away. Started over. Or perhaps it was a spare that was dropped accidentally. Or—"

"Objection," Kenzi said. "This is speculation."

"It's within the witness' field of expertise," Harrington replied. "An expert can speculate, as all experienced criminal attorneys know."

Kenzi clenched her teeth. "He's not speculating about fingerprints. He's speculating on why someone he doesn't know might've brought wire into a lab. That's way outside his expertise."

The judge almost smiled. "I will have to agree with that assessment. Sustained."

Harrington looked completely unruffled. If the jurors didn't follow the legal terminology, they might think he won. "Did you find a fingerprint on that strip of wire?"

"Yes. And the print matched the defendant."

"Thank you. No more questions."

Kenzi could see that this revelation troubled the jurors—but what else was new? She was starting to realize what a massive disadvantage the defense had in any criminal trial. They had to sit quietly for days while the prosecution piled insinuation and suppositions sky high, then after the prosecution show was over, try to overcome what the jurors had firmly entrenched in their brains.

She positioned herself squarely in front of the witness. He seemed competent but not particularly strong. She thought she could lead him where she wanted to go. "I noticed you didn't precisely say the fingerprint *belonged* to the defendant. You said it matched. Why?"

"That's the preferred terminology in my field."

Emma had given her a lengthy lecture on dactylograms the night before. "To translate your testimony into layman's terms, you're saying the fingerprint *might* have come from my client, but you can't be certain that it did."

"I wouldn't put it exactly—"

"You keep saying you found a print, but you didn't find a complete print, did you?"

"No. It was a partial. That's common. You rarely find a perfect complete print in the field."

"Especially on a small unsmooth surface like a twist of wire."

"Exactly so."

"Isn't it true that the print you used to reach your conclusion was actually less than thirty percent complete?"

"Again, this is common—"

"Please answer the question."

Lauder sighed. "Yes, that is correct. But—"

"So it is entirely possible that the rest of the print did not match."

"In my opinion, that is—"

"Sir, I didn't ask whether you, a prosecution witness, think it's likely. I asked whether it's possible."

Another sigh. "Yes. It is…possible. But—"

"You mentioned extreme heat. Could that possibly have damaged the partial print you recovered?"

"I saw no evidence of distortion."

"Again, sir, I will have to ask you to answer the question. Is it possible?"

"It could happen, sure. But—"

"Did you run the partial print through any databases to see if it matched anyone else?"

"I saw no need. It matched the person who had already been arrested."

"Was it a perfect match?"

Lauter craned his neck. "It fell well within the standards and guidelines used in my profession to establish identity."

She took a step closer. "You're using gobbledygook to avoid my question. Was it a perfect match?"

He squirmed a bit. "There's no such thing. All fingerprint analysis requires a degree of…interpretation."

"Meaning guesswork? Supposition?"

"Meaning expert analysis."

"You're admitting that the fingerprint you found did not perfectly match the exemplar taken from my client."

"Because in my field, there's no such thing as perfect."

She glanced back at the defendant's table. Emma was pointing at her hand.

Got it.

"Speaking of the many fallacies in your field that prevent it from being as certain as you lead people to believe, isn't it also true that fingerprints can be planted?"

Lauter chuckled. "Now *you're* speculating. Wading into the realm of science fiction. You've seen too many Mission Impossible movies."

"Can't prints be copied? Placed on adhesive materials and transferred to another surface? Placed on gloves to give the false impression of hands?"

He grinned. "There are technologies that enable the reproduction of prints, but they are far beyond the capabilities of most people. I think we can rule that out. Unless the fire was set by James Bond."

"Would it be James Bond? Or Q?"

Lauter twitched. "Now…what?"

"Q was the armorer. The quartermaster. If someone was going to come up with a fingerprint gimmick, it would be Q."

"I…suppose."

"Because Q was a scientist." She paused. "Like every single person who worked in that lab."

"Including your client."

"And about fifty other people."

Harrington rose. "Objection. Your honor—who's speculating now? The wire bears the defendant's print."

Judge Foreman pursed his lips. "I will allow this conversation to proceed. It is cross-examination, after all. She's permitted to explore alternate possibilities. However remote."

Thanks for nothing, your honor. "One last question. Wouldn't an arsonist wear gloves?"

"Apparently not."

"Isn't it standard practice in that lab to wear gloves when performing experiments or handling chemicals? Both for safety and to maintain the integrity of the work?"

"That…may…"

"If you were going to handle wire, which cuts, or combustible chemicals, which burn, wouldn't you wear gloves?"

"Would I? Yes. But I would never do this. Criminals aren't always the brightest bulbs. That's why we catch them."

"If you were talking about a mugger, I might agree with you. But it's clear that whoever committed this crime was smart. Educated. Wouldn't you agree?"

The witness did not reply.

"The arsonist gained access to the lab and knew which chemicals to use, then constructed an igniter cord fuse perfect for the situation. And left few clues behind. Doesn't that suggest an above-average intelligence?"

"I hate to speculate…"

"Are you seriously suggesting that the arsonist was smart enough to set this fire—but not smart enough to wear gloves?"

Lauter opened his lips—but no words came out.

"Thank you," Kenzi said. "That's all I have for this witness."

CHAPTER THIRTY-FIVE

Okay, Kenzi, she told herself. Not too shabby. Maybe you can get the hang of this criminal stuff yet.

Maybe.

But she couldn't allow herself to get a swelled head. The next witness would be a thousand times more challenging.

Steve Atherton was the eyewitness who claimed he saw Maya running away from the fire only a few seconds after the initial explosion. As far as Kenzi was concerned, running from a huge chemical fire was the smartest thing anyone could possibly do. But now the prosecution was using it against her, suggesting that she was fleeing a fire she started and a murder she committed.

Atherton was a thin man, perhaps seventy, retired, widowed. He looked like a TV sitcom grandpa. Kenzi knew she would never convince any juror he was lying. She didn't think he was lying herself. If she was going to undermine his testimony, she would have to come at if from a different direction.

"How did you happen to be in the vicinity of the fire on the night in question?" Harrington asked.

"I went to the convenience store on the other side of that

huge front lawn. Across the street. SpeedyMart, I think it's called. Needed to get gas and some of that jalapeno dip they sell. I inhale that stuff. Can eat an entire tub in one sitting."

"Yes," Harrington said, gently nudging him back to the topic, "but did anything unusual happen while you were there?"

"I heard this huge explosion. Like the loudest thing you've ever heard in your life. And I wasn't even that close to it. The clerk wondered if a plane had crashed. I ran outside and that's when I saw the fire. Actually, I felt it before I saw it. Even from that distance, the heat was impressive. Felt like I'd walked into a fireplace."

"What did you do then?"

"Crossed the street and tried to get a closer look. I knew they had some kind of scientific setup over there. Might be dangerous, all those chemicals in the air. I wondered if I needed a gas mask."

And yet, Kenzi thought, he kept moving closer.

"I saw someone running. They started near the burning buildings, then crossed the entire lawn. It was dark, but there was a lot of light coming off that fire. I could see the long hair. Slender figure."

"What happened next?"

"I watched the fire for a while. Checked my phone to see what was going on, but nothing was posted. Eventually I went back into the convenience store."

"What did you see there?"

"The defendant. Maya Breville." He pointed.

"You're sure about that?"

"Saw her clear as day. For a minute. Then she went back outside. Guess after that the cops got her."

He was right. The SpeedyMart security camera footage showed Maya was in the store. When the police arrived at the scene, a minute or so after the fire department, they found Maya as close to the fire as it was safe to be. After talking with her a few moments, they detained her for questioning and later arrested her.

"You saw the defendant fleeing from the scene of the crime. Did you see anyone else running around?"

"Nope."

"Driving away?"

"Nope."

"Anyone else at all?"

"Just the defendant."

Harrington turned toward the jury. "And that is a telling fact. Pass the witness."

Telling fact, yes, but what did it tell? That the actual arsonist was too smart to be spotted? Or had set a long enough fuse to disappear before the fire broke out? Unfortunately, Emma said juries gave eyewitness testimony enormous weight, despite how fallible memories are.

Kenzi addressed the witness. "You've acknowledged that it was nighttime when you first spotted the person you claim was my client. How close were you?"

Atherton pondered a moment. "Maybe a couple hundred feet or so."

"That's quite a bit. Especially in the dark. How can you be certain it was Maya?"

"Like I said, I saw the long hair. Slim figure."

"And that proves it was Maya?"

"It looked like her."

"Was any light shining on her?"

"Only from the back. The fire."

"You didn't see her face?"

"I didn't need to see her face. I'm telling you, it was her. I wouldn't lie about that."

No, he wouldn't lie. But he might be...overly certain. "Basically, you saw her silhouette."

"I saw her in bright fluorescent lighting inside the store!"

"Yes, but that was later, right?"

"Maybe a minute or so."

"Did you see Maya enter the store?"

"How else would she get in there?"

"Please answer the question."

He folded his arms across his chest. "No, I did not actually see her enter the store."

"So the person you saw running across the lawn, and the person you saw in the store, might be two different people."

"I'm telling you, I saw her. Outside. Then in the store. Then I saw her leave."

"Do you have any idea how far the lab is from the convenience store?"

"I dunno. Maybe five hundred feet?"

"Just over three thousand. Three thousand one hundred and twelve. I measured. You said the lawn was long, but it's even longer than you realized."

Kenzi saw Judge Foreman look up from his notes, eyebrow raised. Was it possible he was impressed?

"Do you know when the explosion occurred?"

"Not precisely…"

"As confirmed by satellite, it was 10:24 pm. Do you know when the police arrived?"

"Noooo…."

"According to their time-stamped car cam, it was 10:29. They were on the scene fewer than five minutes after the explosion occurred."

"Impressive."

"And the first thing they did was arrest Maya. Who was already there when they drove up. How long do you think it would take to run from LORE to the convenience store and then back again?"

"I have no idea. She was moving pretty darn fast, I can tell you that."

Kenzi took a folder from Emma. "According to your testimony, Maya crossed the front lawn to the convenience store, stayed in the store for a few minutes, bought nothing, then returned across the street before the police arrived...about five minutes after the explosion."

"Like I said, she was a fast runner."

"She's over thirty and she was wearing work shoes."

"That don't mean nothing. Some people can move fast. Back in the day, I used to—"

"Yes, some people are fast. Athletes. Track stars. The only sport my client has ever played is chess. But just for giggles, we contacted a middle school track champion and asked her to run this distance. I have the reports here, and if opposing counsel wishes, I have the champion I mentioned ready to testify. She ran the distance three times. From the lab to the convenience store, one minute pause, then back to the middle of the front lawn."

Kenzi paused and looked up from the report. "Her best time was seven minutes and three seconds. And let me tell you, she's fast." Pause. "But not fast enough. Because what you're claiming, sir, is impossible. A track star couldn't do it. The Flash couldn't do it. And a scientist in street shoes definitely couldn't do it. I don't know who you saw out there—but it wasn't Maya."

CHAPTER THIRTY-SIX

THE SENTINEL SAT IN THE BACK OF THE COURTROOM PONDERING the deepening and darkening situation. The lawyer was getting too close. Closer than she realized, he suspected. It was like watching a Perry Mason episode play out before your eyes. If someone had the sense to put all the pieces together…

There was a vague chance, however remote, that Maya might dodge the murder charge but still go down for arson. Or vice versa. Either way, her time in prison could be less than anticipated.

That was a disturbing thought.

The Sentinel had been following Maya, watching her, watching everyone associated with her, for a reason. She was a threat to all those future plans. And that was unacceptable. This was a decisive moment, not just for the Sentinel, but for everyone.

A new beast, slouching towards Bethlehem…

This minor disturbance could not be permitted to impede the plan.

The Sentinel had broken the shackles of convention before, in the most dramatic way possible, and would not hesitate to do so again. Fate could not be slowed by plebian morality or commonplace tropes. They had moved far beyond all that, never to return. A higher plane of existence awaited, for those who had the courage to walk the path. This could be the next step in human evolution.

This could be the time when everything changed. Because the Sentinel kept watch. Protected the populace. Guided the masses toward the beckoning horizon.

Assuming everything went the way it should in this court-room. If it didn't...

Steps would have to be taken.

The Sentinel watched like a fly on the wall, the invisible observer, seeing all. Michael sneaking into the courthouse conference room. Brittany looking more like a kidnap victim than a daughter. The woman from the lab. The so-called wife. And so much more...

That was how the title "Sentinel" came to be. It belonged to the one who saw all, who had insight and foresight and profound powers of perception.

But you could never be certain who'd taken their thirty pieces of silver.

The Sentinel must be watching. Always watching.

And when appropriate, nudging the pieces into place. With a sledgehammer, if necessary. With the purifying flames of perdi-tion, if that was what the situation demanded.

If the Sentinel had to kill again, so be it. Amen. *Requiescat in pace.*

CHAPTER THIRTY-SEVEN

KENZI PEERED INTO MAYA'S EYES. "REMEMBER, NO REACTION. None. Whatsoever. I don't care what he does. I don't care what he says. I told you this before the settlement conference but you didn't listen—and look what happened."

Stress was apparent on every inch of Maya's face. "What if he tells lies about me?"

"We both know he will tell lies about you. We expect that. Even the judge expects that. Rise above it."

"Those jurors don't know me. They have no way of realizing who's telling the truth."

Kenzi picked up the file that contained Hailee's juror profiles. "Don't they, though? According to our background checks, seven of the twelve have been divorced themselves. Every one of those seven people has heard their ex tell lies about them. They will not expect Michael to take the stand and sing your praises."

"How will we rebut his testimony?"

"Leave that to me. I'm not too shabby on cross-examination."

"You won't trick him. And he'll never admit he's lying." A weariness seemed to consume her. "I'm going to have to take the

stand, aren't I? And even then, it will just be he-said/she-said.
Leaving the jury with no way to perceive the truth."

Kenzi laid her hand on Maya's shoulder. "One step at a time.
Let's get through today. Then we'll figure out what to do
tomorrow."

Michael Breville took the stand. Harrington did not spend
much time on the preliminaries, though he made sure everyone
understood that Michael and Maya were in the middle of a
divorce and Michael currently had custody of their daughter—
by court order. He established that, although the two were
technically still married, Michael had waived all spousal privilege. He wasn't being forced to testify against Maya. He
wanted to.

"What do you do for a living?" Harrington asked.

"At present, I'm a househusband. About to be an ex-house-
husband, I guess. I have a science background too, but I was let
go. I've focused on raising our daughter...who has needed a lot
of assistance."

"So you're financially dependent upon your wife."

"For the time being." He seemed uncomfortable, crossing
and re-crossing his legs. "I do hope to get back to work, once
things settle down and Brittany is in a secure place." He paused.
"Away from her mother."

"Are you suggesting that her mother is a dangerous
influence?"

"Objection," Kenzi said, springing up. "This is a murder trial.
Not family court. And that's a leading question."

"I have no intention of trying the divorce," Harrington said.
"But there is some...overlap. The same factors that explain why
the court awarded this witness custody of their child help
explain why the defendant committed the murder."

"Allegedly," Kenzi insisted. "I urge the court to exclude—"

Judge Foreman cut her off with a wave of the hand. "I will
allow questions that are relevant." He gave Harrington a

warning look. "Don't descend into irrelevant mudslinging. And that last question was leading, so the objection is sustained."

Harrington turned back to the witness. "Please tell the jury why you felt it was important to distance your daughter from her mother, the defendant now on trial for murder."

Michael nodded. "As I think you already know, Maya has joined the cult known as Hexitel—"

Kenzi jumped up again. "Objection to the use of the word 'cult.' That's judgmental and prejudicial. My client considers Hexitel her religion."

The judge didn't quite curl his lips…but almost. "Overruled. I'm not going to choose the witness' words for him."

She didn't expect to win that one. But she did want to make the point in front of the jury. 'Cult' was in the eye of the beholder, right?

Not according to Michael. "Hexitel is nothing like a religion, except maybe Scientology. But it's even more money-grubbing and potentially dangerous. Everything is about dollars and power. Rise through the ranks so you can be the master instead of the slave. Recruit more people so you can share in the wealth. Get involved in more orgies."

"Objection!" Kenzi said loudly. She couldn't actually think of a reason, but there had to be one. That was offensive and obviously meant to turn the jury away from Maya. "Lack…of personal knowledge."

"Overruled," the judge said without missing a beat. "The man lived with the defendant. I think we can assume he knows what he's talking about. Please continue."

Michael did. "They do in fact engage in sexual rituals involving large numbers of people. For instance, Maya told me about a mass spanking. Obviously, some people are into that."

Kenzi tucked in her chin. Couldn't deny that one…

"And they assign same-sex partners. As I think you already know, they assigned Maya a wife." He looked directly at the jurors. "And what's worse—Maya brought the wife home to meet my daughter."

Kenzi felt Maya leaning forward. She pushed her back and glared. No reactions, remember?

"What happened?" Harrington asked.

"I don't know what happened before I got home and met this...woman. But when I arrived, she was telling Brittany all about their cult, how it trained women to be executives and helped women find the power within themselves and all that claptrap. She even said something about sexual energy, which I took to be a coded message. It's all a false front for what they're really doing."

"And what would that be?"

"These people are witches. I mean, that's what they call themselves. I guess you could say that's female empowerment, in a black magic sort of way. But we're not talking about cute Samantha Stevens-type witches. We're talking about sick people committing foul deeds to advance their own agendas. And this woman was trying to drag my daughter into her club of sex-fiend witches."

Harrington bore a grim expression. "What did you do?"

"Threw the woman out. Not physically, not violently, but I told her I did not want my daughter exposed to anyone calling themselves her mother's wife. And she left."

"What was the impact on your daughter?"

"Devastating. She was so confused. She thought Mommy and Daddy loved each other. And then Mommy comes home with a wife."

"Did you ask Maya why she brought this woman to meet your daughter?"

"Yes. And with no shame or embarrassment she told me they were trying to educate Brittany about the cult. She said it was only natural for her to want her daughter to join her church.

She said that to survive, every religion needs to indoctrinate new members."

Maya clenched her fists. "Not true," she whispered. "I would never use the word 'indoctrinate.'"

"If you don't shut up," Kenzi whispered back, "I'm telling the marshals to take you away."

"Hexitel had so warped my wife's thinking," Michael continued, "that she was willing to expose our daughter to these sickos. That's when I had to intervene. I filed for divorce and asked for an emergency custody order. Which was granted."

Maya scribbled on a legal pad. FREEDOM OF RELIGION?

Kenzi ignored it and tried to pay attention to what was happening on the witness stand.

"Have things been more peaceful since then? Without your wife trying to influence the child?"

"Much more. And Brittany's talking to me, telling me about things that happened before. Things I didn't know about."

She could feel Maya clench. Here it came...

"What kinds of things?"

"Things her mother said and did. She loves her mother and didn't want to tattle. At first. Now, with a little more distance, she's opened up more."

"And what have you learned?"

"Apparently, Hexitel gives its members...quests."

"Like crusading knights?"

"Except these won't get you the scarf of a fair maiden. These will get you into the upper hierarchy of Hexitel."

Harrington paused, bracing himself against the podium. "Did Brittany tell you what the defendant's quest was?"

"Yes." He paused, drawing in his breath. "Apparently she was given a mission to strike out against her employer. Against the lab where she worked. The one that burned."

Kenzi could see the jurors looking at one another. You didn't have to be clairvoyant to know what they were thinking.

"Why would Hexitel want that?"

"I'm not sure. It might be a loyalty test. Like making a random hit so you can become a made man in the mob. But I think Hexitel was trying to get something from that lab. Trying to gain access to its research. Or to stop its research. And the lab wasn't cooperating."

"So the defendant went after them?"

"Eventually. Maya tried to steal something and got caught. I don't know what she was after. But I know she was held by the lab security officer for hours. I think this is the real reason Maya was fired. Not because she was in a cult. Because she tried to steal proprietary research."

Maya scribbled furiously. HE'S LYING.

"At that point," Michael said, "the quest changed to something else."

"Burn the place down?"

Michael nodded solemnly. "And take out the woman who fired her."

"Objection," Kenzi said. This is pure hearsay. I'm sure the prosecution loves it, since they don't have any evidence of motive. But the witness' claim that he got this information from an extremely young child who is not in the courtroom makes it inadmissible. If he—"

"Actually," Michael said, "I also talked to Maya about this after she was fired."

Kenzi fell silent.

Michael continued. "We were separated, but she'd asked to see Brittany. I told her I couldn't allow that unless I knew what happened at LORE. And her reply was, 'A spy was sent into Canaan.'"

"What does that mean?"

"Not sure. But it confirms what Brittany said about her mother's quest. She was fired for a good and valid reason."

"Did you ask the defendant to explain?"

"Of course. But all she said was, 'The sinners will be purged with fire. And the fallen angel will be punished.'"

Harrington paused to let the jury absorb that message. "What do you think that meant?"

"At the time, I had no idea. But after the lab burned and the woman who fired Maya was murdered…."

"Yes. Exactly. Thank you, sir. No more questions."

CHAPTER THIRTY-EIGHT

MUCH AS KENZI HATED TO LET MICHAEL'S TESTIMONY END ON such a dramatic note, she couldn't think of a good reason to keep him any longer. He wasn't going to admit he was lying and she wasn't likely to get a sudden confession. Best to get that man off the stand as quickly as possible.

"Your honor," Harrington announced, "we need to make a change to the schedule we submitted earlier. We want to call someone different for our final witness."

Kenzi stood, already concerned. "I haven't heard anything about this."

"This witness is on our list and the defense has had full access to her and all our documents concerning her. We were not planning to call her. But now, due to recent developments... we've changed our plan."

Her? Who was he talking about?

"As long as she's on the witness list, I see no problem," Judge Foreman replied. "Please proceed."

Harrington nodded. "The State calls Candy Trussell."

Maya looked shellshocked. Her lips parted but no sounds emerged.

Kenzi and Emma exchanged a worried look. They had both heard Candy pledge her undying support to Maya. And now the prosecution was calling her to the witness stand?

This could not be good news...

Despite the circumstances, Candy looked good. She sported a new straight-locks hairstyle. Her outfit looked new. And rather expensive, for a yoga instructor.

"Ms. Trussell, the jury has already heard about the defendant's membership in the organization called Hexitel. Have you been a member of that group?"

"Yes."

"Are you still?"

"No."

Maya's eyes bulged. Kenzi nudged her. No reaction, remember?

"We've heard talk about Hexitel assigning the defendant a wife. Do you know anything about that?"

"Of course. I was her wife."

That got the jury's attention. As Hailee would say, this thing just got real.

"What is entailed in...being another member's wife?"

"Let me make one thing clear up front. It's not about sex. I'm not a lesbian, and so far as I know, neither is Maya. But we could all use a good friend, right?"

"Hexitel didn't call you her friend. They called you her wife."

"Right. Not the word I would've chosen. But they want to make the point that this isn't just another come-and-go friendship. This is supposed to be permanent. Something that endures."

Okay, Kenzi thought, so far I can live with this. She's being reasonable. Not trashing Maya. We'll survive this, if it doesn't get any worse.

But of course, it did.

"What did you do in your capacity as the defendant's wife?"

"We went out for coffee. Got dinner. Maya was busy with her work, so there wasn't all that much time for socializing."

"Her husband said you came by the home to see the defendant and their daughter."

"That's true. But I wasn't proselytizing. Brittany was the one who initiated the conversation. She'd heard her father denouncing Mommy's religion so she understandably wanted to know more about it. At no time did Maya or I suggest that Brittany should join the group. She's much too young to make decisions of that nature. Michael barged in and created a scene, but his description of what happened was wildly exaggerated."

"At the time that you met the child, were you a fully-fledged member of Hexitel?"

"Yes. Hexitel was providing what I needed. A support group. A faith worth believing in. And genuine executive training. Under Patricia Clare's guidance, they're building the next generation of leaders, a generation dominated by women. You know, they have over 6,000 members nationwide. They dramatically improved my business and communication skills. I'm planning to build my own business, and believe me, before Hexitel that would have been completely impossible."

"Were you concerned about the financial aspects of membership?"

"Frankly, yes. I couldn't afford the fees. I thought it should get less expensive with time, but instead, it gets worse and worse until you transition from servant to master—if you do."

"That must have raised some concerns."

"I was grateful to be included. I think they recruit the best and the brightest for a good reason. They needed people able to pay the fees. But it's an investment. You need to have some skin in the game before you start taking it seriously."

"Were you able to pay the fees?"

"Not at first. It's kind of a pyramid scheme, I suppose. Like Amway on steroids. I told them I had money issues and they made accommodations. That's how I got the wife assignment, actually. I took on additional duties instead of paying additional money. But I started to feel pressure. What I've heard people call coercive control. When I couldn't keep up with the payments, they expected me to do more to compensate."

"Sexual favors?"

"Never."

"Witchcraft?"

Candy sighed. "I suspected you'd want to hear about that. Yes, there is talk in Hexitel about witchcraft. Sexual magic. But that too is another form of female empowerment."

"So you weren't…" Harrington waved his hands in the air. "Casting spells. Raising demons from hell."

"No, of course not." She giggled a little.

"We've heard a witness talk about orgies. Spanking."

"I never saw any orgies, and given that the organization's membership is all female, I think that rather unlikely. The NXIVM cult went down because of sex trafficking charges. I think Hexitel has made a point of staying away from any activitites that could be considered sexual in nature."

"And the spanking?"

"The spanking is real. I've participated in that."

The discomfort in the jury box was evident.

"Yes, we took a few on the bottom, but it wasn't because it was a turn-on. It's about submission. Accepting that you're an entry-level servant. You submit to your mentor. That's how you learn. And that's how you gain the knowledge and strength that, one day, will allow you to rise in the ranks. The servant becomes the master."

"Wouldn't it be better if we had neither servants nor masters?"

Candy shrugged. "The Christian Bible uses the same kind of language. The ancient Jews were slaves in Egypt, and then after they took Canaan, they kept slaves. Jesus is the King of Kings. And we are His subjects."

Harrington gave the jury some side-eye. "You're suggesting that Christianity is just like Hexitel?"

"Religion is about faith. Nothing can be proved, so religious beliefs are easy to ridicule. The world would be a better place if we stopped fighting and let everyone else be who they want to be. Stop expecting everyone in the world to be a mirror of ourselves."

Harrington paused a moment. "Ms. Trussell, I must compliment you. You're doing a fine job of defending Hexitel, something I would've thought impossible. But didn't you say you recently quit the organization?"

"Yes."

"Why?"

Kenzi braced herself. Here it came.

"I visited Maya once. I mean, since she's been incarcerated."

Kenzi felt the short hairs rise on the back of her neck.

"I just wanted to check on her," Candy continued. "Make sure she was okay. I wasn't trying to get information. I had no reason to do that. But after I heard what she said...I had to contact the district attorney." She reached out toward Maya. "I don't want to hurt you, honey. I still—" She stopped short. "But I couldn't keep this secret. It isn't right."

Kenzi divided her attention between the witness, the jury, and her client. She didn't like what she saw in any of those faces.

"We thank you for your honesty," Harrington said, "and your sense of duty. What is it the defendant said to you?"

"At first we just chatted. She seemed glad to see me. She asked if I had any news about Brittany, which unfortunately, I did not."

"And then?"

"Eventually I got around to the charges that landed her in jail. I wasn't trying to pry a confession out of her. But I was curious, of course. I mean, we were supposed to be bonded for life. I needed to know whether she'd done anything I should be worried about. And that's when she told me about the quest."

Harrington arched an eyebrow. "Like her husband Michael testified. Hexitel gave her an...assignment."

"She had an assignment but it wasn't from Hexitel. Hexitel preaches a message of love and empowerment. It would never do anything like this."

"Then why quit?"

She seemed to struggle for an answer. "I just decided I needed a break from religion for a while. But somebody else got to Maya. Maybe another religious group. She didn't give me their name, but they pushed her to steal some kind of research. She didn't specify what it was and I probably wouldn't have understood it if she did. Maya tried to steal it and she got caught. Then fired. According to her, it was a holy battle. She said, 'I could not let my sisters down.'"

"Did she say anything else?"

"Yes. She said the sinners would be purged by fire. And the offenses they committed would be avenged."

"Anything else?"

"Yes. I looked her in the eye and said, 'Maya. This is your wife talking. Your eternity partner. I want to know the truth. Did you kill your boss?'"

"And what was her reply?"

"She stared at me, and this creepy thin smile spread across her face. She said, 'It was a holy deed. It was an act of right-eousness.' So I kept pushing. 'Maya, what does that mean?'"

"And her answer?"

Candy shuddered. "She whispered, 'I have loosed the fateful lightning of His terrible swift sword.' I pleaded with her. 'Maya, did you murder Maggie Price?'"

"And Maya replied, 'It wasn't a murder. It was a ritual sacrifice.'"

FAITH IN A BOTTLE

CHAPTER THIRTY-NINE

KENZI FELT AS IF SHE'D BEEN SLEEPWALKING SINCE SHE LEFT THE courtroom. At one point she remembered Emma taking her by the elbow and steering her in the right direction. She recalled Maya being hauled away by the marshals, a stricken expression on her face, as if she knew she would never see her child again.

Because Kenzi blew it. Because in her arrogance and over-confidence, she bungled a case that was way out of her league. And the prosecution buried her. Maya told Kenzi everything Candy said about her jailhouse confession was untrue, but the jury had heard it. And she had no way to refute it.

Emma came back to the apartment with her and chatted with Hailee. Kenzi didn't absorb much of what was being said. She kept hearing her father's voice. *I told you to dump that case. I gave you a chance to plead it out. But you wouldn't listen. And now your stupidity has ruined people's lives.* He would never let it rest. Soon it would be an indictment of her entire life. *There's more to practicing law than smiling and streaming. Small wonder I made Gabriel the managing partner. He's got more sense in—*

"Did you hear me, Kenzi?"

She tried to shake herself out of her stupor. "Uh…what?"

Emma frowned. "Hailee has done something truly impressive here."

What were they...? "Of course. That's right."

Hailee peered at her mother with squinted eyes. "Do you even know what we're talking about?"

She quickly considered whether she had enough information to bluff. They were in Hailee's room. They were staring at a wall. The wall had...yarn thumbtacked to it. And photos and news clippings and...

She took a step closer. "Is all this about Maya's case?"

Hailee shot Emma some side-eye. "She does not know what we're talking about."

Emma nodded. "I don't think she's heard a word since we left the courthouse. Actually, I don't think she's heard a word since Candy uttered the phrase 'ritual sacrifice.'"

"I can see where that might induce some trauma." Hailee turned her iPhone around so Emma could see the screen. "That tidbit has gone viral. It's all over the internet. Including the KenziKlan. Expect it to be in every headline tomorrow. Probably alrady a meme."

Emma nodded. "It did not sound good."

"You think the jury bought it?"

She nodded. "Candy provided the essential plot details for a story that finally made sense. And was sexy. Why believe in a rando arsonist when you could believe a hotblooded tale involving religious cults and mind control and...ritual sacrifice. Kenzi, have you rejoined the real world yet?"

She tried to grasp the thread of the conversation. "This is about Maya's case. Hailee has created a...diorama about the case."

"It's not a diorama." Hailee sounded miffed. "It's a murder board."

"Okay, you lost me there."

"Like on television. Don't you ever watch cop shows? They

post photos and articles on the wall with yarn showing the connections between them."

"And what exactly is the point?"

"Frankly, I never understood that. Seems like a good loose-leaf notebook would accomplish the same thing. And these days you could put all this in a digital file and arrange it any way you want. But it does look cool."

She had to smile. Her daughter was one of a kind. "Very cool." She took a step closer. "I get the yarn connecting Candy to Maya and Patricia Clare. But why Hannibal Holt?"

"Candy said Maya got her quest from some religious group. And for that matter, someone is calling Candy's shots. I don't believe she had a sudden rush of conscience that caused her to turn on Maya. Someone is pulling her strings. Or yarn, in this case."

Kenzi stepped closer. "You've got yarn connecting Michael to…the woods?"

"He's living in a settlement with that guy. Adrien Messie. The Jesus wannabe. Maybe they're the relisious group Candy was talking about."

"Maya said Candy's story was a complete lie. There is no quest."

"Still. We have a lot of churches running through this story." Hailee smiled a little. "And the wall looks cooler with more yarn."

"True." Kenzi spotted a corner of the board that held, not a photo, but a sketch. "Is this the medical examiner?"

"Yeah. Dr. Chang."

Of course. Hailee used a courtroom sketch from a newspaer. "Why is she on the board? Surely you don't think she did it."

"I'm not ruling anything out."

"In those Golden Age murder mysteries," Emma noted, "the butler did it. Or the least likely suspect. The suspect you didn't know was a suspect."

"I'm not saying Chang committed the murder. But I didn't buy her testimony. I thought she looked kinda...sketch."

"Ha ha. But seriously..."

"She was way too helpful to the DA. She assumed murder based upon insufficient evidence."

"May I remind you that you're fourteen and, unlike Doogie Howser, haven't been admitted to medical school yet?"

"I read medical books and articles all the time. I don't think her testimony holds up."

"Maybe you should focus more on—"

Emma intervened. "If Hailee wants to poke holes in the medical examiner's testimony, let her. If we could undercut her testimony, it would help in a big way."

Kenzi shrugged. "Fine, fine. Keep working on it."

Hailee beamed. "So I have an assignment? An official, honest-to-God assignment?"

"I guess."

"What's my consulting fee?"

"I'll continue to feed you." The doorbell rang. "Excuse me." She skittered around the corner and opened the front door. "Sharon?"

Her assistant strode in. "Thought you were returning to the office."

"Did we not go back to the office?"

"No. I have about a thousand phone messages for you and almost as many suggestions. So I dropped by." She followed Kenzi back to Hailee's bedroom. "Is this some kind of sad postmortem?"

"The trial isn't over yet," Kenzi insisted.

"Everyone on the internet thinks it is."

"They're wrong."

"Did you know Candy had another wife? Before Maya was her wife. In the cult, I mean."

"No. Is that relevant?"

Hailee wheeled herself forward. "Of course it is, Mom. Get with the program. Sharon, how did you find out about this?"

"Buzzfeed."

"Do you know anything about the other wife?"

"Not yet. But give the trolls another half hour or so and I will. Someone needs to keep an eye on Candy. And dig into her background."

"Why bother?" Kenzi asked. "She's done testifying."

"Can't you call her back during the defense case?"

"I suppose I could. If I asked questions that weren't redundant."

"What if you have newly discovered evidence?"

"That would work."

"Then that's what I'll bring you." All four migrated to the kitchen and took seats around the table. Sharon continued. "You won't be in the office much for the next few days anyway. I can do more than fielding phone calls."

"What do you expect to learn?"

"I have no idea. But if you don't do something to bury that ritual sacrifice testimony, Maya isn't going to see the light of day till she's old and wrinkly. And her daughter won't remember who she is."

Emma cut in. "I think Maya has to testify."

"That would be a disaster."

"Michael was lying!"

"But he did a good job of it. Maya will be a poor witness. Defensive. She'll start thinking about Brittany and she'll fall apart. Even if she holds it together—cross-examination will be endless questions about the cult and the spanking and the wives and the orgies. Harrington will tear her apart."

"But someone has to—"

"We can revisit this later. But I'm hoping we'll think of another approach." Kenzi felt she should be giving some sort of guidance. Like a team leader or something. But at the moment, her spirit was crushed and she didn't think she could muster the energy.

Emma filled the void. "I'll prep outlines for the defense testimony. Sharon will investigate Candy. Hailee will scrutinize the medical evidence. And Kenzi will focus on the courtroom and continue being brilliant."

"Ish," Kenzi mumbled. And that was generous.

Hailee grinned. "This is fun. All us girls working together."

"Which is why we'll prevail," Sharon said. "Nothin' in the world more powerful than four ladies with bees in their bonnets."

"But it's late," Emma added. "So let's relax a little."

"Cocktail hour!" Sharon shouted.

"Yes!" Hailee echoed.

Her mother pointed a finger. "You are much too young."

"I've tasted wine before."

"And you will again. In seven years."

Sharon laughed. "Your mama's right, dear." And then she winked. Which either meant Mama was wrong or Sharon would slip her some booze when Mama wasn't looking. Or both.

Emma raised her hands. "I'm not much of a drinker. Or a… joiner. This is more social interaction than I've had in the last ten years. Combined."

"Has it been unpleasant?" Sharon asked.

"Not…entirely."

"I say it's time you got out of that basement they got you holed up in. Time to break out of your shell, girl."

"But I like my shell."

"You're cheating the world out of your effervescent personality."

Hailee spread her arms across the table. "I know what we can do! 7 Wonders!"

Sharon looked puzzled. "Is that a drink or—"

"It's a board game. Well, card game. Well, both. It's super fun. Very strategic."

The sound of crickets.

"I'm more of a Scrabble girl," Emma said.

"Because you're old-fashioned," Kenzi replied.

"Because you can play it online. You don't have to interact with anyone. And I'm very good at anagramming letters. Which reminds me of something I've been wanting to tell you, Kenzi. I've stayed up late every night going through that hard drive I copied. And last night, I struck paydirt. I found the threatening letter LORE received—on Hannibal Holt's hard drive."

"That's incriminating. But he won't admit he wrote it."

"Have you looked at the signature? Does that sound like a real name to you?"

"Probably not. But what does that tell you?"

Emma looked at her and smiled. "It tells me who you're going to call as your first witness."

CHAPTER FORTY

"That's it for today, KenziKlan," she said to her phone. She'd reached the courthouse, so it was time to wrap up the livestream. "But remember—keep the faith. I haven't given up on you, so don't you give up on me. I'm trying to prevent a horrible misjustice, to prevent a loving mother from being separated from her child. So don't be judgy and don't make up your mind until we get to the last page of the story."

She didn't know how much good that little speech would do, but she had to try, if only for Hailee's sake. That beautiful girl had put too much work into her social media presence to let it all go down in flames.

Inside the courtroom, Harrington seemed particularly relaxed and confident, which made her want to talk to him even less than usual. He clearly thought he had this in the bag.

Patricia Clare was still in the audience. "Candy said you weren't behind Maya's so-called quest," Kenzi said. "I'm glad to hear it."

"We only want what's best for that troubled woman. We still consider Maya one of ours."

"Tell me if I'm mistaken but..." Kenzi tilted her head in a tiny

way, as if pointing while hoping to not attract any attention. "…
that man in the back row. With the long beard. Isn't he the one
Michael has been hanging out with? Has a church out in the
woods?"

Clare glanced, then nodded. "Adrien Messie. It's a cult."

This seemed like the pot calling the kettle black. "Why do
you say that?"

"Hexitel may have a radical theology. But no one is
pretending to be the Second Coming. I'd rather deal with
witches than a would-be messiah."

"Are you saying…"

"Look at how he dresses."

Same look as before. Long robe. A sash. Long hair and beard.
And the crowning stroke—sandals. On a cold day in rainy
Seattle.

"He thinks he's Jesus?"

"He wants people to think he's Jesus."

"He's not exactly the first."

"And he won't be the last. It's all a power scheme. He craves
attention. He's like a politician, only worse. There's no better
way to get attention—not to mention financial support—than
by convincing people you're their savior."

"Surely no one believes that."

"Last I heard, he had about fifty sheep in that little broken-
down settlement of his. And they are true believers. Like the
Magi, they're just waiting for a sign."

She decided to chat the man up. After all, she'd been raised
to be a good Catholic. She should get on well with the Son
of God.

Messie didn't exactly scoot away, but he didn't look like he
wanted to strike up a big gabfest either.

"Adrien Messie, right? I'm Kenzi Rivera. We met before."

He did not take her hand but nodded politely. "I am
honored by your presence. And you don't need to use my

government name. My friends and followers call me the Architect."

"Ah. Where did you get your degree?"

"It's an honorary title. I don't design buildings."

"What do you design?"

"Souls."

"If you're not an actual architect, maybe you should discourage people from calling you that."

He continued smiling. It was like trying to converse with a kewpie doll. "I have read of a noted teacher whose followers called him "Rabbi," though he had not undergone formal religious training."

"May I ask what brings you to the courtroom today?"

She saw the tiniest crack in his smile. "This case concerns Hexitel. Many members of my flock came from Hexitel. And some of the others, like Michael, were touched by Hexitel. Negatively."

"Gotta keep an eye on the competition?"

"That is not correct. Patricia Clare wants an organization focused not on theology, but on paganism and witchcraft and feminist politics. She wants a female-only group. I have always been a feminist and a strong proponent of women's rights, but excluding one gender to promote the other is wrong. We must learn to live together in harmony or we are doomed to perish."

"Patricia has built Hexitel into a popular and prosperous outfit."

"Certainly she's made a lot of money, which exemplifies how wrong the direction she's taken truly is. Render under Caesar what belongs to Caesar. Our focus should be on the soul."

"That sounds good, but as a practical matter—"

"We live in a time of crisis. Not an energy crisis or a climate crisis. A crisis of the soul. So many lonely people. So many souls in anguish. If we could stop fighting and start loving, this world would be a much better place."

HANNIBAL HOLT HAD NOT WANTED TO TESTIFY, HAD RESISTED testifying, and ultimately had to be subpoenaed. Even now, as he sat on the stand, he was visibly unhappy and pointedly uncommunicative—far from the amiable senior Emma had described meeting at the National Unity offices. Did he know she'd duplicated his hard drive? Or was he just offended to be forced to sully himself in this heathen courtroom?

"The National Unity Center's mission is to restore the values that made this country great," Holt explained. "Family values, like hard work, honesty, and brotherhood. We've had enough emphasis on our differences. It's time to focus on what we have in common. We were once a united nation of individuals. It's time to get back to the principles of our founding fathers."

Fathers, she noted. "Would those principles include freedom of religion?"

"Of course. I recognize the right of every individual to worship as they choose."

"Including Hexitel?"

He practically snorted. "That's not a religion."

"What is it then?"

"I prefer not to use labels. There are many established religions in this world. That is not one of them."

"I noticed you mentioned founding fathers. What about women?"

"Sadly, through no fault of their own, women did not play as large a role in the founding of this nation."

"So women aren't important?"

"I didn't say that. But I won't rewrite history or be part of the cancel culture. We are making changes these days. And I am all in favor of them."

"So you support women's rights?"

"Absolutely."

"Aren't you on record telling women to stay home and take care of their children?"

"I believe women should have a choice. If they choose to enter the workplace, they should be given the same respect as anyone else. If they choose to have children, then for heaven's sake, they should honor their commitment and take care of the children. Raise them to be wholesome productive members of society. So many of the problems we face today can be traced back to poor mothering."

Not poor parenting. Poor mothering. She hoped the women on the jury picked up on his pervasively sexist language. She only needed one stubborn woman to get a hung jury.

"You're aware that Hexitel is an all-female organization, right?"

"I am."

"Does that bother you?"

He took a deep breath before answering. His face suggested that he knew he was being baited so he chose his words carefully. "I believe God created both man and woman to live together and help one another. Complete one another. Any suggestion that one sex should function to the exclusion of the other strikes me as contrary to God's wishes."

"So you oppose women's book clubs? Garden clubs? Junior Service Leagues?"

"There's a difference between clubs, something a woman might attend once a month, and an organization that presumes to take control of your life. And income."

Harrington rose to his feet, a weary expression on his face. "I'm sure we're all fascinated to hear the witness' theological opinions, your honor, but I'm having a hard time seeing how it relates to the murder case."

Pompous ass. As if he couldn't connect the dots. "I will make that clear right now, your honor."

Judge Foreman nodded. "Please do so."

Kenzi took a few steps closer to the witness. "How do you feel about stem-cell research? Or women who work in that field?"

He pressed his hands against his chest. "I'm opposed to abortion, of course. And any use of cells that should never have become available."

"Not all stem cells are embryonic."

"But we believe the ones LORE used were. It's an abomination against God. An intrusion into His holy work."

"Is that why you sent LORE a threatening letter?"

The abrupt change of topic clearly jarred the witness. "I— don't know what you're talking about."

At Kenzi's direction, the bailiff passed an exhibit to Holt, who stared at it as if it were written in hieroglyphics. "This appears to come from...Christians for the Sanctity of Human Life."

"And that's you, right?"

"I don't know what you mean."

"I mean you wrote that letter and others like it." She passed the bailiff all the similar letters Emma found on his hard drive. "You composed all of these, didn't you?"

They all used the fake Sanctity of Human Life letterhead and bore the same signature. "Let me make this easier for you, sir. The signature on all these letters. Bonita H.N. Hall. That's an anagram of Hannibal Holt, isn't it?"

"I'm...not..."

She was uncovering the truth, thanks to Emma's undercover work—plus her Scrabble skills. "That was your way of disguising your identity, while also being able to prove you wrote the letter whenever you wanted select members of your conservative clan to know. Probably a good way of fundraising to a certain element."

Holt remained silent.

"Are you denying it?"

No response. He looked as if he might speak, but didn't.

"The jury is waiting for your response."

Harrington rose slowly. "Your honor, I wonder if… perhaps…the witness should receive an instruction about the availability of Fifth Amendment protection."

Before the judge could answer, Holt spoke. "No. She's right. I'll admit it. I wrote those letters."

Kenzi took several steps back, suppressing her smile, glancing at the jury to make sure they were following. "Why?"

"It wasn't my idea. Christians for the Sanctity of Human Life was basically an unofficial dba we used when we took a position we didn't want traced back to the National Unity Center."

"Like violent threats?"

"We needed a way to put forth our ideas without incurring the wrath of the politically biased media."

"Like misogynistic views? Anti-science views?"

"I'm not against science, except when it's used in defiance of God's will. When God creates life, no one has the right to terminate it except God himself."

*Him*self. "So you oppose a woman's right to choose?"

"If she's choosing murder, yes."

"And you sent letters under a false name and false letterhead to threaten LORE. Because they used stem cells in some of their research."

He straightened himself. "Fruit of the poisonous tree."

"What impact did you expect your threatening letters to have?"

"They weren't threats. Jesus charged us to go out into the world and spread his word. That's the Great Commission."

"The jury will have a chance to read these letters themselves when they deliberate, but let's put some of them up on the screen now so they can take a preliminary look."

Emma turned on the overhead screen. A few moments later, the letter in question appeared. Key phrases were highlighted in yellow as soon as Kenzi mentioned them. "'Sinners will burn in eternal torment.'"

"That is what the New Testament says," Holt replied.

Actually, it doesn't, Kenzi thought, at least not in the original Greek. Gehenna was an actual desert location, a garbage dump outside Jerusalem, and the word "Hel" came from Norse mythology. But she didn't want to get sidetracked. "You consider scientists who used stem cells in their research to be sinners."

"God considers them to be so. I make no judgments myself."

She read more from the letter. "'We will purge sin with the fires of righteousness.'"

"Also from the Bible."

"But this letter isn't talking about an afterlife. Your letter says, and I quote: 'Those who traffic in murder will face judgment. *We will* purge sin with the fires of righteousness.'"

"This is no different from the angel Michael pro—"

"With a flaming sword?" She turned off the screen. "That's exactly what happened, isn't it? Exactly what you promised. LORE was purged with fire."

"What—What are you trying—?"

"Sir, where were you the night LORE burned?"

"I—I was at home. Minding my own business."

"Any witnesses?"

"Why would I have witnesses? I live alone. I would never do anything like that. I'm a man of God and a man of peace."

"A man of peace who sends threatening letters under an assumed name. Threats which came true. And coincidentally, framed a scientist who practices exactly what you preached against. Who you promised torment. Which has most assuredly been delivered."

CHAPTER FORTY-ONE

AFTER SIX HOURS ON THE STAKEOUT, SHARON WISHED SHE'D stayed in the office taking phone calls. Trailing a suspect, it turned out, was much harder. And ironically, more boring. And irritating. And a reminder that she wasn't rich and stood out like a sore thumb any time she got near rich people.

She'd been tailing Candy Trussell since the last confab at Kenzi's apartment. Today was clearly Candy's Me Day. She was out on the town and everything she did screamed money. Far more money than anyone would expect a former exotic dancer and current yoga instructor to have. But according to Kenzi, Candy had looked sharp when she showed up in the courtroom to turn traitor. And Kenzi knew expensive clothes when she saw them.

Sharon rarely drove to Bellevue, a city of around 150,000 just across the lake from Seattle. For good reason. This was one of the most expensive residential areas in the United States. This was where Steve Jobs had lived. Where Bill Gates still lived. And a bunch of other tech billionaires who sent real estate prices skyrocketing. Candy sped through the town in her little two-seat sports car like she owned the joint—or at the very least, soon hoped to own a piece of it.

Just after noon, Candy zoomed to the Bravern, Bellevue's upper-crust shopping mall, a playpen for the exorbitantly rich. Sharon had never been here before. Why bother? She couldn't afford anything they had to offer. To be fair, she didn't want anything here. She suspected the combination of her clothes, her skin color, and her attitude made her more likely to be picked up for shoplifting than treated as an honored guest.

She pulled up to the parking area. Correction! There was one thing here she could afford—the $9 valet parking. Seemed like a ridiculous waste of money, but Candy was doing it, and if Sharon didn't follow suit, she might lose her quarry.

She spent the next hour trailing Candy from a discreet distance. Fortunately there was enough traffic at the mall to make it relatively easy to stay out of sight. That did not, however, relieve the tedium. The only thing worse than browsing at a mall you couldn't afford was watching someone else browse at a mall you couldn't afford.

Where was Candy getting the kind of dough she was throwing around? Seven-dollar cupcakes from Trophy. I mean, seriously? Maybe if you were a tastemaker it would be a decent Instagram post, but who else needed that in their life? Candy might find no one wanting to be her next wife if she kept packing these sugary confections away. Was she one of those irritating white girls who could eat all night long and never gain a pound? If Sharon tried that, it would all go to her butt, and she'd be able to see every pound when she looked in the mirror the next morning.

Hermes. Neiman Marcus. Louis Vuitton. Who needed this crap? Fifteen-hundred dollars for a plastic purse, just so you could have someone's logo swinging from your shoulder. Were people that insecure? Then Candy doubled down on Le Mer face cream. Once Candy moved on, Sharon checked the price tag. Roughly equivalent to her bi-monthly paycheck.

Never mind. She had great skin and she didn't need it. The moisturizer she bought at Walmart probably worked just as well. Or so she told herself.

She was never more relieved than when Candy ducked into some restaurant called John Howie Steak. The place looked expensive but she was starving, so Kenzi would just have to write this meal off as a business expense. She managed to persuade the hostess to seat her on the opposite side of a divider from Candy.

She settled into the booth and scrunched down, just in case. You couldn't see through the divider, but you might look over it if you rose. Sharon hadn't been in the courtroom yet so she didn't think Candy would recognize her. But better safe than sorry.

After she ordered she started wondering if this surveillance was a complete waste of time…and then Patricia Clare walked into the restaurant. And joined Candy at her table.

Now there was a woman who belonged in this mall. Her outfit looked like it cost more than Sharon's car.

Above the divider, she saw Candy and Clare exchange air kisses. She felt disappointed. She thought for sure there would be a secret Hexitel handshake. Or a password. Live Long and Prosper. Or something like that.

They settled into the booth and ordered drinks. Sharon noticed how cozy the two seemed. The upper-crust leader of Hexitel rubbed shoulders with a former exotic dancer who, so far as Sharon knew, had only been in the lower ranks of the organization and now had quit.

The waiter took their drink orders. Candy asked for a diet soda, but Clare's choice was predictably more complicated. Something about a double decaf half-caf with oat milk. And a twist of lemon, of course.

"Thanks for meeting me," Clare said.

"Least I can do for our fearless leader."

"I'm not the leader. I'm the steward."

"That sounds better than the Architect." Sharon could hear the smart-aleck in her voice.

"I want to thank you for...what you did in the courtroom. That was immensely helpful."

"It was nothing."

"I disagree. It was everything."

Candy's voice took a more somber tone. "Just to be clear, Patricia—my loyalty to Hexitel is one hundred percent. This organization gave me my life back. Helped me find my inner magic."

"I don't know where Hexitel would be without you. You deserve to be rewarded."

"I never expected any reward."

"Nonetheless, you've earned one."

"That's not why—"

"I know. But since time immemorial, people of faith have honored saints and martyrs. You are a modern saint."

Saint Candy? Seriously?

"You're overstating the case."

"I'm not." Clare paused. Sounded like she was reaching or stretching. "I want you to have this."

A sudden intake of breath. Maybe even a gasp. "Patricia! You're not— I don't—"

"Stop. You must've known this was coming."

"Not in my wildest dreams."

"Hexitel knows how to take care of its own."

Sharon grabbed her phone and started making notes. She wanted to remember everything so she could give Kenzi a full report. Then she realized she could be recording the conversation. Might not be admissible in court. But it would help her convince Kenzi.

She started the recorder, set the phone on the table, and ordered the avocado toast appetizer.

And smiled.

CHAPTER FORTY-TWO

Kenzi felt buoyant, better than she had in days. Good intel made her feel less incompetent. But she knew she couldn't rest. One alternate suspect would not be enough to defeat the prosecution case. She still had work to do.

She didn't think she was winning yet, but she was surviving —because she had a great posse. Sharon. Emma. Hailee. They were propping her up.

She'd bitten off more than she could chew. But she could chew a lot more with a great group of girlfriends.

She took her chair beside Maya. "How're you holding up?"

"Better than when Harrington was running the show."

"It's going to improve."

Maya's gaze softened. "Anything from Brittany?"

"No. Michael won't let me anywhere near her. But I have a guardian ad litem checking on her regularly. And I've talked to her teachers. I'm confident she's not being mistreated."

"Not while the eyes of the world are on us. Michael isn't completely stupid. But once the fanfare has died down…"

"I know. But…one thing at a time."

Maya's eyelids closed. "I miss my beautiful baby girl."

"I will do everything in my power to make sure you see her again. Soon."

Emma appeared on the other side of Maya. "That goes for both of us." To Kenzi's surprise, Emma laid her hand atop Maya's.

This might be the most open display of affection she'd seen from Emma in...well, possibly ever.

This case was changing all of them.

Emma passed her a note written on bright yellow legal pad paper. She unfolded it surreptitiously.

LOOK BEHIND YOU. STAY CHILL.

As if she didn't already know everyone and their dog was watching this trial? It was like trying to obtain justice in a carnival. Nothing could possibly happen at this point that could make it any—

She swiveled around.

Her father was in the gallery. He was on the second row—and sitting on the prosecution side. Not behind her. And not low key.

This wasn't a wedding. People could come for the bride but sit on the groom's side. Still...

He was closer to Harrington than he was to her.

And why was he here anyway? Spying? Looking for something to criticize? Gathering evidence to sling at her? When disowned her? Cut her out of the will?

This was why Emma told her to stay chill.

She took a deep breath and tried to calm her pounding heartbeat.

Her father turned his head. They made brief eye contact. Neither revealed the slightest facial expression, much less attempted to speak.

At last she turned away. She wasn't sure why he was here. But she was absolutely certain it wasn't to support her. She'd had the audacity to act contrary to his wishes.

She reminded herself that she was leaving the firm as soon as she had a chance, so she shouldn't let this bother her. Took time to set up a new firm, hire support staff and do all the administrative garbage, but as soon as she was past this trial, that would be Priority One.

JUDGE FOREMAN RETURNED TO THE COURTROOM. "MS. RIVERA. Would you like to call your next witness?"

She rose. "Yes, your honor, I will. We—"

The judge cut her off. "I asked if you *would*, not if you *will*. Grammar is the key to advocacy, counsel."

And here she thought evidence was key. Stupid her. "We call Candy Trussell back to the witness stand."

Harrington rose. "Your honor, this witness has already—"

"We will be questioning her about different matters. Outside the scope of the direct."

Harrington arched an eyebrow. "This should be interesting."

You have no idea.

Candy was obviously displeased to be back on the witness stand. She volunteered the first time, but never expected to give a repeat performance. Apparently she'd thrown a tantrum when the subpoena was served. But Kenzi felt no sympathy.

"Just to remind the jury, you testified that you were a member of Hexitel for some time, but quit the organization recently."

"True."

"But the truth is, you're still connected to the organization, aren't you? And you met with its leader, Patricia Clare, recently."

Kanzi could almost hear the air sucked out of Candy's lungs, which was all too satisfying. Candy's eyes darted to the gallery —probably to Clare—then back to Kenzi.

"That's…true. We had lunch. It was just casual…"

"I will also remind the jury that you were assigned to be my client's so-called wife."

"It's a lifetime commitment and I will honor it."

"Interesting. Since you sold your wife down the river the last time you offered testimony."

"I told the truth. I had no choice."

"Oh, you had a choice. And you chose to sell your wife down the river."

"Everything I said was accurate."

"Maya says you lied. Specifically about what she allegedly said when you visited her in jail."

"Objection," Harrington said. "If the defendant wants to give testimony or deny claims, she needs to take the stand."

The judge nodded. "Sustained."

Kenzi had expected that objection. But the jury heard what she said. Maya's denial would be planted in their brains, whether she took the stand or not.

"Look," Candy said, "I'm not a liar. I couldn't make up all that stuff about quests and sacrifice and purging with fire."

"Actually, that kind of talk is pretty common at Hexitel, isn't it?"

"I don't know if I'd say it was common…"

"Did Maya say, 'I'm not talking about the afterlife. I'm talking about setting fire to the lab where I worked?'"

"Not in those words…"

"But you're basically claiming Maya flat-out confessed to the murder. While in jail. To you."

"Which proves she's a murderer."

"If we believe you, not only does it prove she's a murderer, it proves she's the stupidest murderer who ever lived." Kenzi turned toward the jurors. "But my client has a Ph.D. and she's not stupid. Why would *anyone* say that, even if it were true? It makes no sense. But jailhouse snitches, fabricating incriminating conversations, are all too commonplace."

"She was gloating. She thought I'd be impressed."

"That she killed someone? Baloney. Jailhouse conversations are typically recorded. So if this happened, why hasn't the district attorney submitted an audio recording of the conversation?"

Candy and Harrington exchanged a glance. Neither spoke.

Kenzi continued. "And I noticed you were looking at Patricia Clare, the leader of Hexitel, when you dropped the line about 'ritual sacrifice.'"

"She's just as appalled by these allegations as I am."

"Do you know Ms. Clare well?"

"Of course, she's my—" Candy stopped. "She was my leader. She runs Hexitel."

"Were you about to say 'leader?' Or 'Master?'"

"Don't put words in my mouth."

Kenzi took several steps closer. "You've recently come into some money, haven't you?"

Candy's discomfort was visible. She appeared jarred by the sudden change of subject. "I—don't know what you mean."

"I'm talking about an influx of money. Enough to go shopping at Bellevue."

She saw several members of the jury raise their eyebrows. They understood the significance of that kind of shopping.

"Is there something wrong with that? Am I not allowed to go where I choose?"

"I can't stop you from going," Kenzi replied. "But people don't generally buy fifteen-hundred-dollar purses unless they have money to burn."

Candy drew up her shoulders. "A woman is allowed an occasional indulgence."

"Like designer cupcakes? Jimmy Choo shoes?"

"What are you implying?"

"Earlier, you testified that you couldn't afford Hexitel's fees, but now you've got a huge infusion of disposable cash—just after you offered unverified but damning testimony in this trial. Coincidence?"

She glanced at the jury. For the first time, they were giving Candy a skeptical look. Was she getting through to them?

"I…just…thought I deserved a little…splurge…"

"You sold out your wife and got paid handsomely for it."

"That's a lie!" Candy's eyes drew closer together. "I have not been paid one penny for my testimony."

"Well, I'm sure the check stub doesn't say BRIBE, but nonetheless, you testified, and suddenly you're throwing money around like a trust-fund baby."

"I earned that money!" And no sooner than she said it, Kenzi could see she regretted it.

"Earned it by doing what exactly? You can't make that kind of loot teaching yoga classes."

"I've…started earning a small stipend from Hexitel."

And then the penny dropped. "You haven't quit. You said that to help sell your story. You've been promoted, haven't you? You've moved up the ranks. You've become a master. Maybe a lesser master, beneath Patricia Clare. But still a master. So you're receiving a percentage of the funds taken from your underlings. Your slaves."

"There's nothing wrong with that." Red splotches appeared on Candy's cheeks. "I've worked hard. I've brought many people into Hexitel. We share the wealth. That's how we spread our good news—"

"By bribing people? Suborning perjury?"

"There was no perjury. Everything I said—"

"Did you discuss your testimony with Patricia Clare before you gave it?"

Candy hesitated. Her eyes darted to the gallery.

"Don't look at her. Answer my question. I'll subpoena her too if that's what it takes to get to the truth. Did you discuss your testimony with Patricia Clare before you offered it to the DA?"

Candy still hesitated.

The judge intervened. "You're under oath, Ms. Trussell. Answer the question."

"We...had a brief discussion..."

"She told you what to say. Or perhaps, informed you what would best help Hexitel. You echoed parts of Michael's false testimony to lend your story credibility. You worked hard to rehabitate Hexitel. And then you buried the member who had become a liability to the organization."

"That's not what happened."

"Clare probably fed the story to you so many times you began to believe it yourself. Memory is extremely malleable and subject to outside influence."

"I'm telling you, I only said what I remembered—"

"And then you reeled in a huge commission."

"That isn't—isn't how it—"

"Yadda, yadda, yadda. So after testifying you were given a promotion that's raked in major-league loot."

"You weren't there. Maya said—"

"Did you record the conversation with your phone?"

"I would never do that."

"Accusing your wife of murder is ok, but recording a conversation would be gauche?"

"I didn't say—"

"Did anyone else hear the conversation?"

"She wouldn't have said it if anyone else was present."

"But she thought she could trust you?"

"Well...yes."

"And coincidentally, the conversation that made you rich accomplished everything Patricia Clare and Hexitel needed. You invented another religious group and made up all that garbage about ritual sacrifice."

"It's the truth!"

"Your testimony had nothing to do with truth. The only thing your testimony had anything to do with is…Jimmy Choo shoes."

"That's not—"

"Of course, if Patricia Clare could get you to tell lies, what wouldn't you do? Maybe you swiped your wife's keys, broke into LORE, and set the fire yourself. That would allow Hexitel to deep-six Maya once and for all."

"That's not—It's not—"

"I think we've heard enough of your traitorous testimony." She turned her back on the witness. "No more questions."

CHAPTER FORTY-THREE

Kenzi stood with Emma in the hallway outside, waiting for the judge to call court back into session. "Did the jurors buy it?"

Emma thought a moment before answering. "You gave them something to think about."

"You're not answering my question."

"I'm not a mind reader."

"I wish you were."

"You gave them serious reason for doubt. You've given them two alternate suspects and good cause to question the prosecution case. Remember—the jurors don't have to buy your version of the facts. They just have to recognize that there's room for doubt. Doubt equals acquittal. At least in theory."

"This isn't law school. If I'm going to win, I need a slam dunk. Was that a slam dunk?"

Emma drew in her breath, then slowly released it. "Probably not. But I will say this. You're doing a fine job out there."

Just when she was certain Emma was a stone-cold lawyer machine, she did something that suggested she might have human feelings. "Thanks."

From the opposite end of the corridor, they heard a loud voice. Almost a scream. "Hoooooold up! *Wait!*"

Kenzi's brow creased. That sounded like— But it couldn't possibly be—

A few moments later, Hailee wheeled herself around the corner.

Kenzi's eyes widened. She didn't know where to begin. "What are you doing here? Why aren't you in class? How did you get downtown?"

"I'm very resourceful. And today is a school holiday."

"Says who?"

"Me. Look I don't have time to explain." She seemed breathless. Kenzi couldn't even begin to guess how hard it must've been for her to find a ride downtown.

She glanced at her phone. Yup. Lots of texts from Hailee. None of which she'd read, because she'd been busy in court.

"I think I've found something, Mom. Something that could turn this case around."

Emma was quicker on the uptake. Probably because she didn't care whether the kid was playing hooky. "What've you got?"

"A lot. Problem is, we don't have time to get a medical witness of our own. Can you buy us some time?"

Emma shook her head. "The judge will never give us a continuance. He wants this over yesterday."

"Figured as much. A woman in the clerk's office told me Dr. Chang is in Courtroom Three on another case."

"Meaning…"

"She can be our medical expert."

"She's a prosecution witness."

"You can ask her nicely."

"Not gonna happen. She works—"

"Okay, subpoena her. Write one out and get it stamped and signed before she escapes."

"She's not gonna like this. And neither will Harrington."

"All the more reason to do it."

Kenzi gave her daughter a stern eye. "Hailee, are you sure about this?"

"Absolutely. Get the subpoena going. Then I'll explain."

She noticed Emma was already filling out the form. "We're going to take this on faith? Put our careers on the line and potentially alienate the judge? Because my teenage daughter thinks she has something?"

Emma shrugged—and continued writing. "Girls got to stick together."

DR. MADISON CHANG WAS CLEARLY NOT DELIGHTED TO BE dragged back into this trial. Although Kenzi did not for a minute think her prior cross did that much damage, it had perhaps put a chink in Chang's armor. Harrington complained that the medical examiner had already been on the stand, but Kenzi insisted they were going to discuss new issues and evidence not considered on direct. Given that the woman was on Harrington's witness list, he could hardly claim undue surprise.

Even though Kenzi was about to surprise the heck out of him.

"Dr. Chang, thank you for returning to the witness stand."

Chang grunted her reply.

"You'll recall that before, I suggested that it was possible the victim was dead before the fire broke out. And you agreed."

"I did not agree. I said it was vaguely possible."

"In fact, this possibility is entirely consistent with the medical evidence as laid out in your report, correct?"

"As I said, it's vaguely possible. Not probable."

"How can you say that if it doesn't conflict with the medical evidence?"

"I find it all too coincidental and—"

"Wait a minute. Are you testifying as a doctor now? Or are you weighing the evidence? With a prosecution bias."

"I think I can—"

"Because weighing the evidence is the jury's job, Dr. Chang. I'll ask you to stick to offering expert opinions based upon your examination of the corpse."

Her expression lay somewhere between miled irritation and extreme anger.

"Dr. Chang—why does your report make no mention of the hyoid?"

Chang hesitated. "I…what…I mean, why would it?"

"Hyoid evidence can be relevant when determining cause of death, can't it?"

"Only if there's been some kind of neck injury."

"And had there been a neck injury in this case?"

Kenzi could see the wheels turning inside her head. "This is the problem with calling me to the stand without prior notice. I've had no chance to review my notes."

"I have copies." Emma handed her the relevant documents. "May I approach?" The judge nodded. "These are your notes, your reports, and everything else you've generated relating to this case." She gave Chang a moment to review the documents. "I can see why you might've ignored the hyoid—if you went into the examination assuming the victim burned to death or died of smoke inhalation. But if you open your mind to other possibilities, it can be quite informative."

Chang was staring intently at a particular X-ray.

She'd spotted it. Good. That might make the rest of this easier. She hoped she wouldn't have to go toe-to-toe with the doctor. Hailee was the would-be physician, not her.

"I see you're staring at Exhibit 47. Before we discuss that, doctor, would you explain to the jury what the hyoid is? I'd never heard of it before this trial, and I may not be the only one."

Chang cleared her throat. "The hyoid is a minute horseshoe-shaped bone in the neck. It's key to tongue movement, chewing, swallowing, and other similar movements. Keeps the airway open during respiration."

"What's the significance for a criminal investigator?"

"It can be damaged when there's significant injury to the neck."

"Like when people hang themselves?"

"No. Hanging rarely damages the hyoid. Only occasionally, mostly when the victim is older."

"What about strangulation?"

"Yes, the hyoid is often damaged in strangulation cases. I mean, deliberate strangulation. Manual strangulation. The killer's hand gets up high, beneath the victim's chin, and crushes the hyoid while cutting off the air supply."

Kenzi paused, building the jury's anticipation. "Doctor, was the victim's hyoid shattered in this case?"

Chang looked down at the X-ray, then up again. "Yes. Decisively."

"Which means the victim was strangled."

"It means it's possible. It is far—"

"So we first established that the victim could've died before the fire broke out, then we established that the victim could have been strangled. Before the eyewitness saw a long-haired figure racing across the lawn. How long before the fire did the victim die?"

"We've covered this. I can't say with certainty. It's possible the neck was injured some other way. She could've fallen."

"Please. What fall would be sufficient to break the hyoid? Tumbling from the top of the Space Needle?"

"It...would have to be significant."

"An accidental fall wouldn't do the trick."

"Probably not."

"So when Maya arrived at the lab to get her things, Maggie Price might have already been dead. Or unconsciousness, which would explain some of the internal damage you described earlier."

Chang glanced at Harrington. "We can't say for certain—"

"But it's possible?"

Chang drew in her breath. "It's…not inconsistent with the medical evidence."

"Given the damage to the hyoid, it's even probable, wouldn't you say?"

"I…need more time…"

"But you can't rule out the possibility?"

She frowned, paused, but eventually answered. "No."

"Thank you, Doctor. I have nothing more."

Kenzi pivoted around—and saw Hailee sitting in the gallery with a triumphant fist in the air.

Sharon sat beside Hailee, patting her on the back. Emma and Maya were both smiling. For the first time since this trial began.

Yes, it seemed she had assembled quite a team here…

CHAPTER FORTY-FOUR

KENZI WAS PLEASED WITH CHANG'S TESTIMONY, BUT SHE STILL had a lingering feeling that she hadn't clinched it. She needed to give the jury more than possibilities. She needed to tell them who committed this crime and how it was done.

Emma thought they should put Maya on the stand to defend herself. But Harrington would go scorched earth on her, talking about spankings and wives and cults. She'd come out of that cross looking like Jack the Ripper.

Kenzi huddled in the courtroom hallway with Maya and her three cohorts. The judge had given them a ten-minute break, but after that, he expected Kenzi to call her next witness.

"You can put me on the stand," Maya said. "I'm tough. I'll survive."

"I know you will. But Harrington won't play fair. He's losing ground and he knows it. He'll go to EF4 before you've finished stating your name."

"If I get my little girl back, it will be worth it."

Maya assumed testifying would help her. But Kenzi was not so sure. "Forgive me, but I have to be the lawyer. You can be the mother."

"That's all I ever wanted." Maya's eyes suddenly widened. Kenzi was afraid she would cry—because she knew that if Maya started, she would soon join her. "From the moment my little Brittany was born, I wanted to be the best mother ever. I wanted to take good care of my little girl."

Emma laid a hand on Maya's shoulder. "I admire your devotion to your child."

"I've always felt that way. I was adopted, and because of that I've always felt unworthy. Like I needed to earn parental love but never quite measured up. I wanted my girl to know she was loved every day of her life. I wanted her to know that no matter what happened, her mother would always have her back." She covered her face with her hands. "And now I can't even see her."

"We're going to fix that," Emma said. "One way or the other."

"Absolutely," Sharon chimed in. "I love that little girl. Totally tots adorbs. I'll kidnap her myself if that's what it takes to get her back."

Emma raised a hand. "Please don't do that."

"I was just saying—"

"Don't. Do. That."

Sharon looked sidewise. "Some people around here need to grow a sense of humor."

"Michael is in the courtroom," Emma observed. "I assume he has someone watching Brittany."

Sharon smiled. "If Daddy's away, this might be the perfect time—"

Emma looked at her sternly. "Don't. Do. That."

"Fine, fine."

Kenzi was listening and absorbing, trying to plan her next move. But something new was rattling around in her brain. She couldn't quite put her finger on it yet...but something...

Why did she have a feeling the solution to the whole mystery was floating right before her eyes—but just outside her reach?

She crouched beside Hailee and whispered in her ear.

Hailee bubbled with excitement. "Seriously? You're giving me an official assignment? Again?"

"Do you think you can do it?"

"Easy peasy. There's a computer in the library." She swerved her chair around and rolled down the hallway at breathtaking speed.

Emma tapped Kenzi on the shoulder. "Bailiff has returned. We need to return. And you need to call your next witness."

Kenzi nodded. "Think I've got that figured out. And no, Maya. It isn't you."

"THE DEFENSE CALLS MICHAEL BREVILLE."

Michael looked as if he'd received a spear through the heart. His lips parted, but he didn't move.

Harrington rose. "Your honor. Please. This is a criminal trial, not divorce court. There's no need to call the defendant's soon-to-be ex-husband."

"Didn't stop you from doing it," Kenzi snapped back.

The judge gave Kenzi a stern look. "This relates to the criminal matter?"

"One hundred percent. That's all we're wanting to talk about."

"All we want to talk about. The present participle is unnecessary."

Kenzi clenched her teeth. Class, she told herself. Show class. Fake it.

She bowed slightly. "As you say, your honor."

"You may call the witness."

Michael slowly ambled up the aisle and settled into his seat, treating it more like the electric chair than the witness chair.

"Mr. Breville, are you married at this time?"

"Obviously. To the defendant, Maya Breville."

"And as the district attorney mentioned, you are currently in the process of divorcing her."

"True. This murder trial has delayed the divorce proceedings."

"And you currently have custody of your six-year-old daughter Brittany, correct?"

"I was awarded—"

"Just answer the question."

He cleared his throat. "Yes."

"You currently reside in a rural settlement near Seattle, correct?"

"Yes."

"Led by a religious leader named Adrien Messie?"

"He's more of a…shepherd than a leader."

"Is this group a cult?"

"Of course not. There's no…weirdness. He doesn't try to force anyone to do anything they don't want to do."

"Are you currently employed?"

"No. I'm busy looking after our daughter and dealing with these legal matters."

"In fact, you haven't been employed for years. You've been supported by your wife. Who you are now divorcing."

"I don't see how that's relevant."

She could see Harrington was antsy and ready to object. Time to go for it. "Shortly before the murder took place, you asked to borrow your wife's keys, correct?"

Michael's head jerked around. "I—I don't—"

"Maya mentioned it to me shortly after we met. I just didn't grasp the significance then."

He hesitated.

"You're under oath. So tell the truth. You borrowed your wife's keys."

"Y—Yes. I remember that now. I misplaced mine and locked myself out of the house."

"Did she give you just the housekey you needed? Or her entire keychain? As most normal people would do in that circumstance."

"She gave me the entire keychain."

"So you had access to all her keys."

"I…suppose."

"Including her key to LORE. Her workplace."

A murmur rose from the gallery. Finally people seeing the significance.

"I don't know what you're implying."

"Just answer the question."

Harrington jumped up. "Your honor. I object on—"

The judge waved him away. "Overruled. The witness will reply."

Michael stuttered. "I suppose those keys might've been on the ring. But—"

"You had access to the LORE keys. You had an opportunity to make copies."

"I did no such thing."

"My question was whether you had the opportunity. And you did, right?"

"I…suppose. But why would I ever—"

"If your wife is convicted of murder, you'll retain custody of your daughter."

"I would hope so."

"For that matter, you'll gain access to all Maya's bank accounts. You'll be awarded everything Maya has, since you'll be caring for the child."

"I'm…not an expert on…legal…"

"You'll have your final revenge, won't you? Steal the child, steal the money, and watch her rot away behind bars for a crime she didn't commit."

"Objection," Harrington said, looking thoroughly exasperated. "This is pure speculation."

"Speculation that an ex might want revenge?" Kenzi replied. "More like fact. Are we surprised that a lame-o unemployed loser resents the woman who supports him and outshines him in every possible respect?"

Harrington shook his head. "You can't turn an innocent man into a suspect just because a clever lawyer invents a motive."

"No," Kenzi shot back. "But motive plus opportunity creates an alternate explanation. Doubt. With those keys, Michael had opportunity. Who's more likely to commit a strangling? A gentle mother? Or a man who outweighs Maggie Price by fifty pounds and has a history of anger and violence."

Michael started to look scared. "I did not kill that woman."

"Prove it."

"How can I prove something that didn't happen?"

"You were the only one who had access to those keys."

"But I—I didn't—"

Her voice boomed. "No one else could've done it. You were the only one!"

"I'm not!" he shouted back. "I gave them—" All at once, he stopped, frozen, his face a mask of horror.

Kenzi stepped forward, her voice a notch softer. "You gave them to whom?"

Michael was shifting back and forth. "I'm not saying another word. I'm...what did the other man call it? I'm pleading the Fifth."

"Because saying more would incriminate you?"

Michael didn't respond.

Kenzi gave the jurors a raised eyebrow.

The judge intervened. "If the witness is asserting Fifth Amendment privileges, I'll have to terminate this line of questioning. I will advise the witness to seek legal advice as soon as possible, as charges may well follow. Counsel, do you have anything more?"

"Not from this witness. But..."

She swiveled around. In the back of the gallery, the man with the beard scooted down the bench, then crossed in front of people.

"Don't let that man leave the courtroom!" Kenzi shouted. The bailiff blocked the door. "He's my next witness. Whether he likes it or not."

CHAPTER FORTY-FIVE

KENZI REMAINED SILENT THE ENTIRE TIME HARRINGTON ARGUED. She knew this was a foregone conclusion. Yes, neither he nor the proposaed witness had advance warning, but the defense didn't have to tell the prosecution anything about their plans, the witness was in the courtroom, and Michael's testimony had made everyone curious about who he gave those keys. It wasn't so much the law as human curiosity that guaranteed she'd be able to call her next witness, who the bailiffs were currently restraining.

During the extended break, Hailee delivered her report—which gave Kenzi not only what she expected but much more. More than she'd dreamed possible.

The pieces were falling into place. Could she assemble the jigsaw puzzle, bizarre though it was, in a way that made sense to the jury?

Barely an hour later, her final witness took the stand, rubbing his beard pensively. He was still wearing the robe.

"Please state your name."

His demeanor was calm and placid, projecting a beatific facade. Or to use a different word—saintly. "Adrien Messie."

"Is that your real name?"

He looked at her contemplatively. "What is real? What is unreal?"

She refrained from making a gagging expression. "Is that the name on your driver's license?"

"I don't have one."

"Is that the name on your tax return?"

"Haven't filed in years."

"You're evading my questions. I want to know if that's your legal name or one you've adopted."

"All names are adopted. There is no organic connection between a person and the amalgamation of sounds and letters we call names."

She pressed her hand against her forehead. "Is that the name you were born with?"

"No. I changed my name after I had a religious conversion experience. Like Saul on the road to Damascus. I suddenly realized I was wasting my life. I was being called to do more."

"And what exactly is it you do?"

"I lead an organization camped outside the city limits."

"Where exactly?"

"I would prefer not to say."

She could press him for an answer. But the actual location was just a blip on Google Maps. His evasion would irritate jurors. And make them suspicious. "I gather this is some sort of…compound? For you and your followers?"

He tilted his head slightly. "I call it a settlement."

"Where you're holed up with a bunch of other religious fanatics."

"We are not fanatics."

"Hermits, then."

"We maintain our purity by living apart from the world. So much as possible, we remain separate. Building our strength."

"Like white supremacists? Militia groups?"

"Far from it. My message is one of love, not hate. My message is one of peace, not strife. We don't allow weapons of any kind."

His message, he said. Not ours. "What kind of group is this?"

He spread his arms wide. "It's a church."

"Your church."

"Indeed."

Harrington rose. "Your honor, while this is vaguely intriguing, I see no connection to the murder or the fire. Counsel has presented a long series of distractions, but nothing that—"

"We'll get there as soon as possible," Kenzi replied. "Some matters can't be rushed. I want the jury to completely and fully understand what's been happening. This man's testimony impacts every other person involved in this case."

Judge Foreman pondered a moment, then nodded. "I'll admit I'm intrigued. I will allow this—but if the relevance isn't obvious soon, I will hold you accountable."

"Understood." She turned her attention back to the witness. "Does your church have a name?"

"Again with the names. Names are just labels. They have no connection to the human beings in my flock. Or their beliefs. They say nothing of the spirit."

"But you must call yourself something."

He exhaled heavily. "We call ourselves the New Dawn."

Nothing pretentious there. "And your settlement is where Michael Breville has been living, correct? Since he took his daughter from her school and disappeared?"

Harrington sprang. "Objection. These questions relate to the divorce, not the murder."

"Are you sure about that?" Kenzi asked. "Maybe you'd better hear the ending before you judge the play."

"I'm willing to give counsel some latitude," Judge Foreman said. "If counsel wastes our time, I'll consider a motion for sanctions. But I don't want to shut down testimony that might turn out to be important."

Thank you, judge. About time you did me a solid. "Please answer the question."

Messie looked into the gallery. "I'm sorry, Michael, but I'm under oath and, even if I weren't, I would have to tell the truth. The truth will set you free."

Actually, this truth might put him in prison, but whatever.

"Michael and Brittany have been living with us, yes."

"And that's why you didn't want to reveal your location. So he could continue hiding."

"It's not just that. I prefer…seclusion. Secular influences tend to impair faith. Some distance from this wicked world is always desirable."

"You admit both men and women to your settlement?"

"Of course. I believe women are beautiful. Sacred."

Time to spring the trap. "And that's why Hexitel has a policy of assigning so-called wives, right?"

"I…don't know what you mean."

"I think you do. Today Hexitel is run by Patricia Clare, but it was founded by a man named Randie Salvador, who left to start a different organization." She took a step closer. "That was you, wasn't it?"

Messie paused. He did not answer.

"Please answer the question."

Harrington intervened, looking as if he'd been pushed to the end of his rope. "Objection. Your honor, I've tried to be patient. But this doesn't even make sense. This man's name is not Randie Salvador."

"Ah," Kenzi replied. "But names aren't real. They have no connection to the human being. And therefore some people feel they can change them any time they want to. Or need to."

They judge appeared to be getting the drift. "I will allow this. Overruled. Continue."

Kenzi got right back in the witness' face. "Sir, you're Randie Salvador, aren't you? Or I should say, that was the name you used at the time that you founded Hexitel. It may not be any more real than your other names."

He pursed his lips for a moment, then shrugged. "You're right. I was Randie Salvador."

"And you founded Hexitel."

"True. My vision was to create an organization to help women. A sisterhood of strength. All this business with witch-craft and spanking was added later by others. Not me. I wanted executive training. I wanted to give women the tools they need to find their place in the cosmos."

"Why did you leave Hexitel?"

"As I said, I heard a calling. Other work I needed to do."

"Were you thrown out?"

"Absolutely not. I didn't like the negative direction Hexitel was taking. You've exposed some of that yourself. Greed. Coercive control. I decided to take a sabbatical."

"To form your commune in the forest. The New Dawn."

"Which has been a wonderful experience. The New Dawn is an upgraded and improved Hexitel. Correcting my initial errors. I'm proud to say I'm their shepherd."

"But you're more than just their shepherd, right?" She paused for maximum effect. "You're their savior."

Messie opened his mouth, then stopped, as if he thought better of it. He fell silent for several more seconds before finally answering. "I told you I had a religious experience. An awakening."

"But that happened long before the New Dawn, right?" The jury seemed mesmerized, so she kept plugging away. "In fact, that happened long before you started Hexitel, right?"

"Once upon a time, I was a stockbroker, believe it or not. A very successful one. I also inherited some money from my father. We never got along well, but he left me the stake I used to make my initial investments. In just a few years, I made enough money to live well for the rest of my life."

She believed it. "And where did you live when you were a stockbroker?"

"A small town near Portland."

Bingo. Hailee was right. She felt sure of it. But she had to keep the excitement out of her voice. Don't give him any indication where she was going. "And remind me, when did you have your spiritual awakening?"

"About thirty-two years ago."

She turned slightly to catch Hailee's eye. Her daughter was nodding.

"And then you stopped working as a stockbroker?"

"God had other plans for me. In a vision, he told me that my old life had come to an end. I would be reborn."

"As the Architect?"

He paused. "As the Sentinel."

"I had a good Catholic school education, sir, but I have no idea what that means. Can you explain?"

"It means that it is my job to keep watch. Until the New Dawn rises."

"And then?"

"And then I will be the leader for the next millennium. The teacher."

"Jesus 2.0?"

He bowed his head slightly. "If you wish."

Rustling. Shuffling. Sounds of disquiet. No one could believe what they were hearing—what this man was volunteering. They might not grasp how it related to the murder. But they were spellbound. "You're the Second Coming."

"My commission is to create a paradise on earth, a place where true believers can live in peace. That includes all people —but I was given a special mission regarding women."

"Which would explain why you created Hexitel, a group only for women. What was this special mission?"

"Women feel lost in the modern age. Disconnected. They feel scorned if they are only housewives, mothers. But they have a hard time breaking into the business world. Even with all this talk of #MeToo and breaking glass ceilings, we are not even close to workplace equality. So I created executive training for women who wanted to work, who felt compelled to enter the world of commerce. And I created a system of…wives…to reinforce the domestic life. And unions between the two so all could attain their highest level of fulfillment."

"Is this the lifestyle you promote in the New Dawn?"

"Yes. We include both genders and we give all people options. Training for women who want to work. Support for men who prefer to remain at home. No sexism. Everyone can be wahtever they wish to be."

"And that's working?"

"When you preach the truth, people will find you. Our membership tripled during the coronavirus lockdown. Some saw that as God's plague sent to root out the wicked. But my flock felt safe living outside the mainstream with me."

"I'd like to know more about this conversion experience you had. What were your instructions?"

"I was told to leave everything I had behind. To sever all connections to my past life and build a new one."

"And would that include…severing yourself from your family?"

"Sadly, yes."

"Your wife?"

"Yes."

"Children?"

"If necessary."

"And it was, wasn't it?"

He stared at her and, all at once, his eyes seemed to burn brighter, as if lit from behind.

But he did not answer.

"Your honor, I will ask the court to take judicial notice of three published news accounts relating to a tragedy that occurred over thirty-two years ago. Involving a man named Darien Christos. For reasons no one was able to discern at the time, the father of a large prosperous family—a stockbroker—in a small town near Portland, in a single night killed first his wife then his children. With a shovel. He buried the bodies, poured concrete over the grave, and disappeared. Despite years of effort, the police have never been able to track him down."

The jurors looked at one another, horrified.

"Only one child escaped. A girl, barely a toddler. Somehow she found her way to another house in a nearby neighborhood. She survived and was later adopted. But she was too young to help the police much."

The judge raised an eyebrow. "And the significance?"

"I don't blame you for being confused, your honor. I was at first too. But my ace investigator put it all together. Maya was adopted in Portland many years ago, something she only recently mentioned to me. After I heard that, I asked my crack research team to investigate the adoption and major news events occurring at that time in that area. And this is what we found."

Kenzi turned toward the jury. "That little girl who survived was my client. After adoption, her name became Maya Hanover. After she married, Maya Breville." She turned back to the witness. "And that man who killed his family was you, Mr. Messie. Jesus 2.0. You murdered your wife and kids. Then disappeared."

All eyes were on the witness stand. "I don't know what you're talking about."

"Why did you do it? Family life too hard for you? Or was this demanded by your divine calling?"

Messie turned toward the judge. "Do I have to sit here and listen to someone accuse me of murder? I know she's desperate to help her client, but—"

Kenzi cut him off. "After the murders, you disappeared, understandably, till you could rise again with a new name and a new look. Following your messianic quest, you started Hexitel. You were successfully building it into a profitable outfit. And then Maya showed up. Even though she was young when you tried to kill her, a few photos of her father existed and you worried that it was remotely possible she might recognize you. So you left Hexitel and started yet another group. Deep in the forest. Far from Maya or anyone else. Grew a beard and let your hair grow long to change your appearance. And you reached out to Michael, who you probably knew from your constant surveillance needed a place to stay. Even though you couldn't get near Maya, that would allow you to see your granddaughter. That's why you disappeared the day of the settlement conference as soon as Maya arrived. You didn't want her to see you."

"That's...that's not what happened."

Kenzi continued. "You come to this courtroom, but always sit in the far back, out of Maya's sight."

"I have no reason to hide—"

"Hexitel has thrived under Patricia Clare's leadership. To use her own words, she built an army. When you realized how large and successful Hexitel was now, you wanted back in. Combining the two groups you founded could jumpstart your ministry in a big way. But reemerging wouldn't be safe for you —unless Maya was eliminated."

"You're...just...inventing..."

"I don't think you were worried about law enforcement. They gave up on your case years ago. I don't think you had many friends or co-workers in your stockbroker days. And after the murders, no family. The only threat to your freedom was Maya."

"This—This is exactly why we left the city. Opportunists like you will stop at nothing to crush people of faith be—"

She ignored him. "You murdered your family. But as always seems to happen with people like you, since you got away with it once, the irresistible urge returned. You used the keys Michael gave you to break into LORE, strangle Maggie Price, and set the fire. You got the chemicals and wire from Maya's car, which explains the fingerprint. You were the skinny long-haired figure Atherton saw running across the lawn. You induced Michael to make up those lies about Maya's so-called quest and the workplace theft to cover your plans. Michael told you Maggie Price had fired Maya, so you knew the fire and murder would be blamed on her. You wanted Maya out of the way so you could safely continue building your ministry." She paused. "With your granddaughter."

The buzz in the gallery was loud and growing. The judge slammed his gavel several times, trying to maintain order.

Kenzi ignored the tumult. "Admit it. Everything I've said is true. You executed your wife and children."

"I don't know this…Darien…"

"Because he had a different name? Names are just labels."

"I did not commit this crime. I—"

"Here's what I think is interesting." Kenzi took a cheat sheet from Emma. "We have three names here. Adrien Messie. That's you. Randie Salvador, the Hexitel co-founder. And Darien Christos, the mass murderer. Am I the only one seeing the pattern?" She walked to the chalkboard and scribbled the names. "Here I have to thank my partner, who is a Scrabble ace and great with anagrams. Guess what? All three of those first names are anagrams of one another. Adrien. Randie. Darien. All the same letters, rearranged. You probably thought you were being really clever, didn't you?"

The witness did not answer. And the DA didn't interrupt.

She continued. "I bet none of them is your birth name. Christos is Greek for *Christ*, meaning *savior*. Salvador is Spanish for *savior*. And Messie, in many Eastern European languages, means *messiah*."

The stir in the gallery rose. Maya looked stunned, her lips parted in disbelief.

"You're all three of these men, aren't you? They're all reinventions of your murderous messianic persona." She stepped closer, leaning over him, refusing to let his eyes escape hers. "Admit it. You killed your own family. And Maggie Price. You're a murderer of the worst sort—the kind who hides behind God to justify his twisted arrogant actions."

He stared up at her. "I didn't...I acted on instructions from God."

"Instructions only you heard."

"People have always persecuted the prophets. The powers-that-be always want to eradicate the sentinels."

"Get over yourself. You're a murderer. You probably couldn't handle family life, so your psychologically messed-up mind fabricated holy orders. You hid your money and made travel plans before you executed your family—all signs of premeditation."

He rose slightly out of his chair. "I am a man of God!"

Kenzi's voice soared. "Who killed his own family. And tried to kill the only child who got away!"

"No, I—I—"

"Your own daughter. Your own flesh and blood."

"No..."

"What kind of monster would hurt his own daughter?"

"*No!*" He stood, reaching out his arms. "I never wanted to hurt Annalise. I—"

He froze. His eyes widened.

Kenzi's voice dropped to a near-whisper. "And how did you

know the birth name of the little girl who escaped was Annalise?" She walked to the jury box. "I never said it. And you claimed you'd never heard of this case before."

"I didn't—I mean, I wouldn't. I—I—"

"Man of God. Jesus 2.0." She made a snorting noise. "You're a wife murderer. A baby killer. The worst excuse for a human being who ever walked the face of the earth. And guilty as sin, unless you're completely insane. Which would not surprise me at all."

Messie jumped out of the witness stand and raced toward the back door, but the bailiffs apprehended him before he was halfway down the aisle. He screamed and shouted and fought them, to no avail. Everyone in the gallery skittered away, gaping in disbelief.

Kenzi calmly approached the judge's bench. "Your honor, I respectfully request that the charges against my client be dismissed. And I strongly suggest that the bailiffs prevent this man from leaving the courtroom. Mr. Harrington may wish to prefer charges."

CHAPTER FORTY-SIX

Despite the fact that she couldn't stand the man, Kenzi had to admit Harrington behaved like a pro after Messie's testimony cratered the prosecution case. He did not object to dismissal of the charges and instructed law enforcement to take Messie into custody for interrogation. She suspected the Sentinel would be arrested by nightfall.

"Not a bad job," Harrington said.

She almost blushed. "Thank you. I'll admit I had—"

"For a dilettante. You got lucky and no serious damage was done. But in the future, I hope you'll stay in family court. Criminal law is for the big boys."

"But I—"

He walked away, leaving her gaping in mid-sentence.

Just when you thought it might be remotely possible to like him...

Maya's reaction was completely different. She wrapped her arms around Kenzi and hugged her the instant the judge told her she was free to go.

"Thank you," she gasped, tears streaming down her face. "You believed me. You fought for me."

"I did my best."

"You were brave. Strong."

"You're the strong one. You survived that nightmare father. Twice."

"Will they let me see my daughter now?"

Michael had revealed Brittany's location, a smart move since he now faced possible conspiracy charges for giving Messie the keys to LORE and Maya's car. In the space of a few moments, Maya had been transformed from dangerous murder-mommy to the best parent available.

"I'll stop by Judge Benetti's office before I leave, Maya. But you know, he's going to ask—"

"I'm quitting Hexitel."

Thank God. "What brought you to this decision?"

"I should have done it long ago. I always sensed there was something...not right there. But I was so desperate for family. Support. Something I've never had."

How true that was.

"After I heard Candy tell all those lies about me on the witness stand, I realized what a fool I've been. My stupidity almost cost me my child."

"If I can tell the judge you've severed ties with Hexitel, I bet Brittany will be back in your arms before bedtime."

"Thank you so much. I can't say it enough." She hugged like she never intended to let go. "Thank you."

After a few more moments, Maya turned to Emma, arms outstretched. "And you too."

Emma held up a hand. "Sorry. Not a hugger."

"Oh. Right."

"But." Emma stepped forward and touched Maya on the shoulder. "I'm very glad about the way this turned out. So give Brittany a big hug for me."

"I will." She turned back to Kenzi. "Can I admit something? When I first met you...I didn't like you very much."

She didn't blame her. "I was having a rough day."

"I thought you were superficial. Self-absorbed. I was in the KenziKlan and that was fun and harmless, but in person, you seemed much more interested in yourself than your clients." She offered a broken wet smile. "Look how wrong I was."

"Thanks, but you weren't entirely wrong. I have some soul-searching to do."

Emma made a face of mock astonishment. "What? Kenzi Rivera admits to imperfection?"

"I know. Hard to imagine. Sign of inadequacy, I guess."

"No. A sign that you're glowing up."

"Really?"

Emma nodded. "And I think the whole KenziKlan will agree. You've come a long way since high school, kiddo. And you still have some miles left on your journey. But don't we all?"

KENZI PACKED HER BRIEFCASES AND BANKER BOXES AND HEADED out of the courtroom. She was almost through the door when she spotted someone sitting in the back of the gallery.

Her father.

She started to speak, but felt tongue-tied. Why did he always have that effect on her?

"Did—Did you see how it ended?"

"I did."

"And…"

He cleared his throat. "It occurs to me that I may have voiced some objection to you taking this case."

That was putting it mildly. But she kept her mouth shut.

"And I may have expressed some…lack of confidence in your ability to handle a criminal matter."

Wait for it…

He drew in his breath, then slowly released it. "It is just possible that I may have been mistaken."

Not exactly an apology. But as close as she was ever going to get from him.

"And now," he added, "I hear rumors that you're going to use this high-profile success to start your own firm. Where you can be managing partner. And you won't have to deal with...me."

"Nope." She wasn't even sure where that came from. She had been thinking about leaving, but now she knew exactly what she wanted to do. "I'm not going anywhere."

"You're not?"

She stepped forward and gave him a friendly jab in the chest. "I'm not starting my own firm. I'm launching a hostile takeover of your firm."

"You're...what now?"

"And then I'm going to take over Crozier's firm and merge the two to form the biggest firm in the state. With me as its queen. I'm going to own Splitsville."

"That seems...rather unlikely."

She pivoted on her heel. "You just wait and see."

As she walked to her car, Kenzi realized it had been days since she livestreamed to the KenziKlan.

Had she outgrown it?

Should she put it in her past?

No. Put it to better use.

Maybe it was time she put her entire life to better use.

She set down her boxes, pulled out her phone, and started streaming. Since this wasn't her usual airtime, she made sure copies would be stored on YouTube for later viewing.

And told the story of the case's tumultuous final day...

"So that's how it turned out, KenziKlan. Justice was done

and a flawed but loving mother will be reunited with her daughter. Which is wonderful. Because we're all flawed, but there's nothing more important than family and never will be. Here's what I've learned, and what I hope you will learn too, if you don't already know it. You want to be religious—fine. If it helps you, I'm happy. But when people start exerting coercive control, look out. No one should dominate you, and if anyone tries, run. Immediately. I don't care what they offer or what they promise. Run. And if your husband tries to turn your daughter into a weapon he can use against you—shoot him."

She paused. "Okay, I meant with a camera. Video the rant. Record the abusive phone call. Don't resort to violence, but do collect evidence. Because you are important. You matter. And you don't have to take that crap from anyone. Hashtag KenziK-lan. Hashtag RiveraLaw." She paused, then added, "Hashtag MeToo. Hashtag Time'sUp. Hashtag GirlPower. Hashtag InThisTogether. Hashtag...LoveIsAllWeNeed."

CHAPTER FORTY-SEVEN

That evening, Kenzi sat at her kitchen table and shared much too much pizza and wine with her friends.

"I propose a toast!" Sharon said. She hadn't drunk that much, but Kenzi could see she was already a bit giddy. Maybe the exuberance arising from a successful day in court. "Raise your glasses!"

Hailee pouted. "I don't have one."

"You do." Kenzi pointed. "Sparkling grape juice."

"Ick. I'm not a baby."

"You're too young to drink." And it might not mix well with her meds. "Just raise the glass."

Emma leaned toward Hailee. "Just between you and me, this wine sucks."

"That does not make me feel better."

"You know how people say alcohol is an acquired taste? That means it tastes terrible."

Hailee slowly turned. "Really?"

"Really. The grape juice is much better."

"Well…okay." Hailee raised her glass. "Who are we toasting?"

"Your mama, of course." Sharon pushed herself to her feet.

"Here's to the mighty Amazon warrior. She took on the husband, the cops, the DA, Jesus 2.0, and the worst them all, her father. And triumphed. Let's hear it for Kenzi."

They clinked their glasses together. Lots of hooting and hollering ensued.

"Thanks," Kenzi said. "But I couldn't have done it without you. All of you." She faced each colleague in turn. "Emma was my criminal law rock. I would've embarrassed myself a hundred times over if not for her. Sharon was my eyes and ears when I couldn't be three places at once. Sharon, you are seriously under-utilized as an assistant."

"Does that mean I'm getting a raise? We discussed—"

"You're getting a raise."

Her eyes bugged out. "You got Gabriel to—?"

"It's coming out of my salary."

"Kenzi, no!"

"Yes, and no arguing. I want you in my posse. I need you." She turned. "And of course, I must thank the greatest joy in my life, my daughter. Hailee, you came through just when I needed it. You gave me proof of the strangulation. You gave me the goods on Messie. In fact, your murder board predicted the relationship between Michael and Messie. You proved you can do anything you want to do. You can be anything you want to be. Nothing can hold you back. Absolutely nothing."

"Hear, hear," Emma said. Another round of clinked glasses. "But I think I should get some sort of special commendation. I broke into that religious joint and copied the hard drive. And I don't even like going outside."

"Maybe Emma needs a raise, too," Sharon suggested.

"She's a partner." Kenzi winked. "Talk to the boss, Emma."

"You mean our brother or our father? Because neither of them has listened to a word I've said since the day I was born."

"I can relate to that, sister."

Sharon blinked. "Um...sister? You mean that metaphorically, right?"

Hailee tucked in her chin. "No, she means Emma is her sister. And my aunt. You didn't know?"

Sharon looked as if she'd been smacked in the face by a bus. "She—*now what?*" She glared at Kenzi. "She's your sister and I didn't know? Even though I work at the same firm with both of you?"

"Emma likes to keep a low profile," Hailee explained. "Doesn't want people to think she got her job through nepotism."

Sharon was still gaping. "You two are *sisters?*" She took a huge gulp of wine. "Guess that explains why you've known each other since high school."

"And before that," Emma added.

"But you have a different last name."

"Marriage. Big mistake. Didn't last."

"Well, I'll be—" Sharon paused, drinking it all in. "So everyone in this room is family except me?"

Kenzi laid her hand on Sharon's. A moment later, the other two laid their hands atop hers. "We're all sisters."

SNEAK PREVIEW OF EXPOSED

William Bernhardt's next novel, *Exposed* (Splitsville Legal Thriller Series Book 2), will be released September 21, 2021. Here's a sneak preview.

Sometimes, even the fastest girl alive can't move swiftly enough to escape all the predators.

Chessie liked to think of herself as the fastest girl alive, but it probably wasn't true. She wasn't a superhero. She hadn't been doused with radioactive chemicals or struck by lightning or anything like that. But she was the fastest person in her high school, and now she was the captain of her college soccer team, in no small part due to her speed. Also her dazzling charisma, she liked to think. But mostly her speed.

Truth to tell, she'd always been a bit on the shy side, and that had only worsened since she lost her parents. Competing in sports was easier than making small talk on a date or figuring out what to do with herself at a rave. She wasn't particularly bookish either, and she would never qualify as a mathlete, so she was grateful for that speed. If not for her twinkle toes and Title 9, she might have nothing at all.

So what on earth lured her to a frat party? I mean, she should know better, right? And yet, here she was. She had resolved to try to get out more. Although she loved her teammates, occasionally she wanted to talk about something other than the Rivelino and the Cruyff Turn.

Okay, reality check. She was flattered to be asked. Not that she was homely or anything, but she didn't go in for a lot of makeup or haircare, and that plus shyness and a physique that put most Big Men on Campus to shame, left her alone on most Friday nights.

Okay, bigger reality check. She hadn't been out once since she started college. Not once. Was that her fault? Did everyone assume that since she was the captain of the team she must be a lesbian? That was so cliché and totally...wrong. She thought. She was pretty sure. She liked boys. Or would, if one gave her a chance. Which they never did.

So she was totally caught off guard when that guy who sat in front of her in nutrition class invited her to a frat party. Was it a prank? Was her making fun of her? Was this one of those things where frat boys compete to nail the ugliest girl in school?

Bottom line—he asked, and here she was.

Loud music. Loud talking, necessary to be heard over the music. Alcohol flowing from abundant portals. Herbal scents she wasn't cool enough to identify. Heavy doses of Axe cologne, which she could identify. Lots of crazy dancing, in many cases, too crazy to be called dancing. Before he died, her father tried to teach her the Batusi. That was dignified compared to most of what she saw here in the Beta house. A few people were attempting to have actual conversations, but she suspected the chat topics were not binomial equations or the work of Caravaggio.

She made a few unsuccessful attempts at conversation, but mostly she listened. Didn't take her long to realize that, although some fraternities claimed they'd cleaned up their acts, nothing had changed much. They still made racist remarks, only more quietly. A few token members of color, but still essentially a white rich boys club. And they still treated women like meat, conquests to be conquered. Notches on the belt. They acted as if they knew the way the world really worked, even though she suspected most had privileged upbringings and had never worked a day in their lives.

Did she need this? Absolutely not. Especially not in the middle of soccer season, when the online news agencies were focusing on all the women who had disappeared recently under mysterious circumstances. This was a bad idea from the get-go.

Just when she'd convinced herself to leave, the guy who'd invited her strolled up, a lopsided grin on his face. What was his name? Brian. She thought. Several inches taller, perfect hair, great smile. His red eyes and loose manner suggested he'd already had a few.

"You came!" He virtually shouted, with a bug-eyed expression and jazz hands fluttering overhead.

"You invited me."

"But you actually came."

"You thought I was too stuck up?"

"I thought you were too cool."

She relaxed a bit. "I try to be open to new experiences."

"How are you doing in class? I love nutrition. Like, nutrition is my life. Call me Mr. Nutrition."

She probably wouldn't. "It's interesting."

"I best it's easy for you. You're awesome."

"You mean…"

"On the soccer field."

"You've seen one of our games?"

"I've seen all of your games. I'm like your groupie, you know?"

She had groupies? Cute groupies? "You should've said hello sooner."

"I wanted to. I tried to sit next to you in class. But..." His voice trailed a bit. "It took me a while to work up the courage to speak. Aloud, I mean."

This was too much for her to handle. Her head was spinning, and not just from the blaring music. "I still can't believe you came to all our games."

"I love those games. I love the way you move." His voice dropped. "To be honest, when I watched run across the field...I got kinda hard."

Okay, TMI. She did not need to hear that part.

"No pressure or anything, but would you possibly like to step outside? Get some fresh air? We probably could have a deeper conversation if we got away from this electronic hook-track FM radio crap people pretend is music."

She was still fixated on his previous statement, but a chance to get out of this den of iniquity was welcome. They walked out the front door—a few guys whistled and winked as they passed—and walked into the front yard. She admired the English country house façade, white pillars, and brown oak shutters. A balcony on the upper floor.

He motioned her to the side of the house. Dark here, she noted. Darker than she expected. She doubted anyone could see them from the street. And there was no way anyone in the house could hear them.

Maybe this was a bad idea.

"Aw, man, this is so much better," he said, pressing a hand against the side of his head. "My ears were ringing."

"They do look red," she replied. "So what do you do when you're not in nutrition class?"

He shrugged. "Like everyone else in the frat. Mandatory Study Hall. Mandatory functions. Mandatory fundraisers."

"Do they let you pee by yourself?"

"Usually." He did a doubletake. "Wait, you were joking, weren't you?"

She pointed. "Nothing slips past you."

"Maybe now I'm not at my best. I'm...well, I'm a little intimidated. Being here. With you. Alone."

She tried to change the subject. "You must do something other than frat stuff."

"Yeah. I like music. Video games. A good burger."

"Hobbies?"

He hesitated a moment, as if weighing options. "I'm kinda into...strangulation games."

She cocked her head to one side. "Did I...hear you correctly.?

"It's not dangerous. Just good fun. Have you smoked weed?"

"Once." And it made her sick. She preferred not to think about it. "Didn't do much for me."

"Me neither. But you can get a high six times strong and better..."

"From strangulation games?"

"Bingo. Wanna try?"

She took a step back. "I don't think it's for me."

"You never know."

"I think I do. And you—"

"Could be perfect. You're an athlete, so you can't take drugs. You're in training, so you can't do alcohol. This high is stronger and leaves no traces in your bloodstream."

Another step backward. "Still a hard pass. Maybe we should go back—"

She thought she was fast, but he proved faster. His arm shot out like a springing cobra. He grabbed her by the neck with surprising strength, whirled her around and slammed her back against the side of the house.

Her heard reeled. Flashes of light fired before her eyes. She wasn't quite unconscious, but she wasn't offering any resistance either.

"Just go with it," he said, his voice breathy and urgent. "You're going love this."

"I…won't," she managed. "Let go."

"Trust me. I've done this before."

She tried to squirm away, but she couldn't. What was wrong with her? She knew she was stronger than this pampered preppie. She couldn't seem to get her head together.

"Don't struggle. Relax. Enjoy it."

She gritted her teeth and fought. She tried to kick him, but he was too close, leaning in, pressing against her, blocking her arms and legs.

And all at once, she remembered the news stories about all the disappearing women…

Oh my God. She was going to be the next one.

"If you want," he said, whispering, "a little arousal makes the experience even more powerful. Like an orgasm etched in rocket fuel. It's like nothing you've ever felt before in your life."

"I—don't—" She twisted from side to side, but nothing seemed to work. He counteracted her every attempt to escape, usually before she'd begun it. He had this routine down cold. Her speed wasn't going to help her. Not while she was trapped under his icy grip.

He was fumbling with the button at the front of her slacks. She was losing consciousness. Just a few more moments and she suspected she wouldn't notice anything…

"Hey! What's going on back there?"

Her eyes flew open. Someone was lurching toward them. She couldn't make out the details, but the voice was male. As he approached, she saw that he had a cast on his left arm and a slight limp. He was older—too old to be a frat boy. He was moving their way.

"Screw off, Grandpa," Brian said. "This doesn't concern you."

"Let go of the girl."

"Make me." He grinned a little. "Did you think you were going to be the knight in shining armor? Were you going to play

Superman? We're just having fun. Consenting adults and all that."

The newcomer looked straight at her. "Is this consensual?"

It was a struggle, but she managed to shake her head no.

"Let go of the girl."

"Look, loser, I'll call some of my buddies out—"

Before he could finish the phrase, the interloper kicked the man in the hip—hard. He had the leverage she couldn't get. Mr. Nutrition flew sideways and fell.

Chessie clutched her neck. He'd hurt her, bad, and her skin was tender. But she could breathe again.

The newcomer followed up, hovering over Brian as he lay on the ground. "Two choices. Disappear right now and never hurt this girl again. Or I call the cops and report that you're the Seattle Specter and I just witnessed an attempted homicide."

The frat boy released a string of swear words. But at the end, he brushed himself off and skittered away.

"I don't think he'll bother you again," the man said. "Are you okay?"

She was still clutching her neck. "I'll live." She took in a deep breath. "I thought I was toast. Thank you."

"No big deal. I live not far from here. I power-walk every night. Thought I heard someone struggling back here, though it's a miracle I could hear anything given how much noise that party is making."

"He almost was." Although the light was low, she got a clearer view of her rescuer. He was older than the college kids, but hardly old enough to justify being called Grandpa. Seemed friendly. Earnest. "Again, thanks. What happened to your arm?"

"Oh. That. Stupidest story imaginable. Fell out of a tree. How'd you get hooked up with that loser?"

"God knows. He's in one of my classes."

"And that meant he could assault you in an alley? You should probably report this. You never know. He might try it one someone else. You might be able to sue him. I have a lawyer friend who specializes in representing women. She might be willing to help."

"I'd rather just forget about it."

"What did that guy want?"

She shrugged. "He talked about strangulation games."

"What?"

"I think the idea is that you get a buzz from almost dying but not quite. Supposed to be super-powerful."

"Unless his timing is off. And then you don't get the buzz. Because you're dead."

"Right. Definitely not something I care to pursue."

"Well, I should probably finish my walk. If you're sure you're okay."

"I am. And thanks again."

"No problem. Hey, maybe next time, screen your dates. Pass on the guys who are into dangerous sex. It isn't worth it."

"No doubt."

"Plus, he was doing it completely wrong."

All at once, she felt her head slam back against the house, this time so hard she almost lost consciousness. It took her a few moments to realize he had brought his knee up between her legs. Pain radiated in two opposing directions.

He gripped her neck and slammed her head back several more times. She started to scream, but a fist collided with the side of her face before she had a chance. She felt blood dripping from her lip.

Not again! She summoned all her strength to resist—

And he knocked it out of her with a single blow. Her head drooped.

The fake cast fell from his arm. He pinned her back with both hands his knee.

"This is the proper grip," he explained. "The hand has to go way back, pressed up against the throat, thumb under the hyoid. That's how you induce strangulation. Trust me, I would know."

She could barely whisper. "You're—You're—"

"Not so much into the twisted orgasm thing though. I pursue a different endgame."

"Please." It was more air than voice. Barely audible. "Please don't—"

"Say goodnight, Gracie." She felt his hand tighten and her lungs constrict. She struggled for air but there was none to be found.

Her last thought, perversely enough, was about who would captain the soccer team for the rest of the season. Because she knew it wouldn't be her.

Kenzi had a problem. Her client, Melba Conners, the wife in the divorce, had not done well on the witness stand. Not that she lied or anything. But her nervousness translated to a cold unemotional delivery that she could see had not moved Judge Melbourne in the slightest. Her husband, David Conners, on the other hand, despite being possibly the worst excuse for a husband in the history of mankind, was warm, witty, and persuasive, scoring point after point. Though the division of marital property was supposed to be a matter of cold economics, Kenzi knew that in reality judge sympathy could make a huge difference.

She was feeling desperate. This case was slipping through her fingers. And she knew it.

ABOUT THE AUTHOR

William Bernhardt is the author of over fifty books, including *The Last Chance Lawyer* (*#1 National Bestseller*), the historical novels *Challengers of the Dust* and *Nemesis*, two books of poetry, and the Red Sneaker books on writing. In addition, Bernhardt founded the Red Sneaker Writers Center to mentor aspiring authors. The Center hosts an annual conference (WriterCon), small-group seminars, a newsletter, and a bi-weekly podcast. He is also the owner of Balkan Press, which publishes poetry and fiction as well as the literary journal *Conclave*.

Bernhardt has received the Southern Writers Guild's Gold Medal Award, the Royden B. Davis Distinguished Author Award (University of Pennsylvania) and the H. Louise Cobb Distinguished Author Award (Oklahoma State), which is given "in recognition of an outstanding body of work that has profoundly influenced the way in which we understand ourselves and American society at large." In 2019, he received the Arrell Gibson Lifetime Achievement Award from the Oklahoma Center for the Book.

In addition Bernhardt has written plays, a musical (book and score), humor, children stories, biography, and puzzles. He has edited two anthologies (*Legal Briefs* and *Natural Suspect*) as fundraisers for The Nature Conservancy and the Children's Legal Defense Fund. In his spare time, he has enjoyed surfing, digging for dinosaurs, trekking through the Himalayas, paragliding, scuba diving, caving, zip-lining over the canopy of the Costa Rican rain forest, and jumping out of an airplane at 10,000 feet.

In 2017, when Bernhardt delivered the keynote address at the San Francisco Writers Conference, chairman Michael Larsen noted that in addition to penning novels, Bernhardt can "write a sonnet, play a sonata, plant a garden, try a lawsuit, teach a class, cook a gourmet meal, beat you at Scrabble, and work the *New York Times* crossword in under five minutes."

ALSO BY WILLIAM BERNHARDT

The Daniel Pike Novels

The Last Chance Lawyer

Court of Killers

Trial by Blood

Twisted Justice

Judge and Jury

Final Verdict

The Ben Kincaid Novels

Primary Justice

Blind Justice

Deadly Justice

Perfect Justice

Cruel Justice

Naked Justice

Extreme Justice

Dark Justice

Silent Justice

Murder One

Criminal Intent

Death Row

Hate Crime

Capitol Murder

Capitol Threat

Capitol Conspiracy

Capitol Offense

Capitol Betrayal

Justice Returns

Other Novels

Challengers of the Dust

The Game Master

Nemesis: The Final Case of Eliot Ness

Dark Eye

Strip Search

Double Jeopardy

The Midnight Before Christmas

Final Round

The Code of Buddyhood

The Red Sneaker Series on Writing

Story Structure: The Key to Successful Fiction

Creating Character: Bringing Your Story to Life

Perfecting Plot: Charting the Hero's Journey

Dynamic Dialogue: Letting Your Story Speak

Sizzling Style: Every Word Matters

Powerful Premise: Writing the Irresistible

Excellent Editing: The Writing Process

Thinking Theme: The Heart of the Matter

What Writers Need to Know: Essential Topics

Dazzling Description: Painting the Perfect Picture

The Fundamentals of Fiction (video series)

Poetry

The White Bird

The Ocean's Edge

For Young Readers

Shine

Princess Alice and the Dreadful Dragon

Equal Justice: The Courage of Ada Sipuel

The Black Sentry

Edited by William Bernhardt

Legal Briefs: Short Stories by Today's Best Thriller Writers

Natural Suspect: A Collaborative Novel of Suspense

Printed in Great Britain
by Amazon

65373562R00201